TROUBLEMAKER

TROUBLEMAKER

C. R. Westbrook

PRESS

Published by Vulpine Press in the United Kingdom in 2025

Cover by Claire Wood

ISBN: 978-1-83919-673-7

www.vulpine-press.com

For Emily

Seven Years Ago
LAURA

Of all the things that could have happened today, I can't say I had 'get pushed out of a fourth-storey window' on the bingo card.

I hadn't contemplated my death all that often because it's not something you do when you've only been living for twenty-two years – but when I have done it's never been that bleak. Why would it be? You'd drive yourself bonkers if you spent your life mulling the prospect of a sudden and violent exit from this world, taking your final breaths in agony after some freak accident.

So, I've always convinced myself I would be one of those lucky people who coasted through life; untroubled by serious accidents or terminal illnesses, accumulating children and grandchildren until, aged ninety-five, I went to bed one night and didn't wake up again. Isn't that the dream for most of us?

If I hadn't caught my nemesis in the act of doing something she definitely should not have been doing, it might have come true. She knows I've seen her. I've got evidence. Now she's pleading with me, hoping I won't blab to our boss about her appalling behaviour. That she can bluff her way out of this like she has done everything else over the past few months.

Why shouldn't I report her, though? I doubt she'd stay quiet for a second if it was the other way around. Given the seriousness of her actions she'll probably be marched out with a P45 wedged where the sun doesn't shine, in the morning. That's not my problem, as I realise, listening to her bluster and excuses, and attempts to persuade me we're friends, how naïve I've been all this time. Thinking that I'd ever fit in at that so-called dream job of mine, with people who would always view me as an interloper.

She has me cornered, pushing me back on to the windowsill in a frantic bid to destroy the proof of her wrongdoing. I'm determined not to let her do it. No matter how much she screams, shouts or tries to scratch my eyes out. That's when things get messy. Because as I try to dodge her grasp, she shoves me with incredible force into the windowpane itself. The one that neither of us realised was already cracked. It gives way, sending me out into the evening sky in a powerful explosion of glass.

Well, that was unexpected!!

The trauma of being flung so abruptly into the air rips the breath from my body, my cries for help torn away by the wind. It doesn't matter. The band and their screaming fans below are making such an almighty racket that nobody would've heard me anyway. I would have stayed at home, written up my notice and started looking for another job if I had thought the day might end this way.

At least I wouldn't be about to die. Because that's what's going to happen. It's obvious.

And I'll take the knowledge of who did this to the grave. I'll be dead long before my killer is caught. If they ever find her that is. There's no time even to consider how upset my family will be about this turn of events. Or worry about everything I haven't done in my too-short time on earth.

Instead, all I can think to myself is:

Honestly, some people will go to any lengths not to get fired.

Seven Years Later
ELENA

There's an intruder in my bedroom.

I hear them before anything else. My eyes ping open at the unmistakable sound of the window creaking, the snap of the blinds pushed aside. Feet drop to the parquet floor, the squeak of the stranger's shoes sounding ominously loud in the darkness. All I can see at first is the imposing crimson numbers on my bedside clock, teasing me with the time. 2.12 a.m. Far too early to be awake for work or for my best friend Lindsey to be up and functioning.

This should not be happening. Waves of panic prickle across my abdomen. Where is Daniel when I need him? The biggest day of my career is looming, and I deliberately went to bed early tonight, alone, to be refreshed for what lies ahead. Fat chance of that now. There's no point fetching Lindsey either since she is doubtless sleeping off the effects of all those flaming Sambuca shots she had this evening, bothering my phone with countless WhatsApp messages that reminded me what a good time I was missing.

I'll have to handle this by myself, although the horror of what could be invading is leaving me unable to shift, sealing me to the mattress with dread. I can detect movement out of the corner of my eye.

That's when I see it.

A ghostly silhouette stalks around the room, rasping in that unnerving way serial killers do in slasher movies, right before they redecorate the walls with the blood of the perky blonde cheerleader character.

Me, in other words.

That thought is enough for the adrenalin to kick in. I sit bolt upright with an ear-curdling scream loud enough to take the roof off. It has the desired effect. The figure trips over the edge of my bed and crashes to the ground, taking with them the vase of rhubarb and custard tulips I acquired over the weekend. I can make out petals flying everywhere in the shadows on the wall before they float gently to the floor. With my potential assailant grounded, the bravery takes over. I spring up, grab the nearest chunky item to protect myself, and click on the light.

Only to be faced with Lindsey, splayed out on the floor, as sozzled as a wasp in an orchard full of apple trees.

The horror etched on my face is further upped when I look at my improvised defence weapon – and see I am holding one of the white platform shoes I wore for Saturday's date night. Not sure how long I would have survived with that if it had turned out to be Jason Voorhees at the window, ready to chase me through the downstairs bin room with a pickaxe.

"Forgot your key again?" is all I can say, my distorted friend giving a low groan in response.

"You know you could have just knocked."

I've calmed down now it's morning. I might be tempted to see the funny side – I admit I was terrified when that happened last night. God knows I love Lindsey to bits – but I hadn't reckoned upon the quiet night out she alleged she was having to end in a drunken stupor on my bedroom floor. Nor am I going to ask how she managed to get

4

in through the window given we live one storey up. Part of me doesn't even want to know since it would only add to last night's overall weirdness. All I do know is that she's in 6.45 a.m. tantrum mode.

"Elena!" she yells, banging on the bathroom door. "Are you going to be in there all day?" I ignore her and turn back to my mascara wand, taking my time brushing the black tendrils across my lashes in a frantic bid to paint over the effects of my broken sleep.

"Elena? Seriously! I'll be so late if you don't get a move on!"

Whatever. After last night's little escapade, she owes me big time. So, she can wait a while. On the plus side, at least she had come home alone this time, meaning I wouldn't have a repeat of the incident from a fortnight ago. The one when I stumbled into the kitchen first thing, to find a naked stranger parading his bare arse around the room while helping himself to my expensive blueberry yoghurt. Small mercies, especially given this specimen didn't even have an arse worth writing home about. Moments like this are all too common, living with Lindsey.

It's eye-opening at times, and not always for the right reasons.

I put the finishing touches to my face with a thick, charcoal-hued flick of liner on each eye, then stand back to examine my work in the mirror, careful not to rush things. I add a spritz of Ghost Sweetheart to my wrists and emerge from the bathroom to see Lindsey's panicked expression, her mousy hair frizzed with static as though she had been electrocuted.

"Finally! What took you so long?"

"Don't exaggerate, I wasn't that long," I say airily. "And maybe don't try and break into my bedroom like a stalker next time?"

"Sorry. Thought it was my window? You missed a great night, Elena. I swear I'm never drinking again."

Here comes that promise, the one she trots out with every passing hangover. How long this time, two days? Good job I am so forgiving.

Her life may be chaotic, but she is sweet, loyal and one of the few people I like rather than tolerate.

It's time to wheel out the sympathy. "Poor you," I cluck, keeping my voice as neutral as possible. Lindsey is my friend and has stuck by me over the last six years, through all that badness at work, the accusations and guilt I thought I would never move on from. I don't want to judge her, but I cannot help it sometimes. "Maybe have a quiet night in tonight?"

Lindsey nods, wincing at the pain coursing through her forehead.

"Get some peppermint tea down you. Don't put any Sambuca in it," I add with a wink before slipping away to select my outfit. Choosing my work clothes is always one of the highlights of my day, and I deliberate for several minutes before settling on a black leather miniskirt, a pink and black printed shirt and knee-high boots. My shoulder-length blonde hair is well-brushed and shiny and kept out of my eyes with a pink diamante slide.

I look good. Better than good.

I decide to let Lindsey know I'm going. No hard feelings. And any excuse to mention my incoming good news.

"I'm off!" I call through the closed door. "Got to be on time today, big day!"

She appears, toothbrush in mouth, foam clouding her upper lip.

"The job?" she splutters.

"Yup. Paula's going to make the announcement this morning."

"Oh wow! So exciting! Good luck!" Lindsey reaches out and folds me into a toothpaste-y hug. "Although I don't need to wish you good luck because I know that job is as good as yours!"

"Thanks," I say, extricating myself and glancing at my shoulder to check she hasn't dribbled any Colgate on it. Lindsey reaches out to dispense another hug, but I step back. "Got to go!" I tell her as I dodge her grasp and make for the front door.

My mood instantly lifts as I close it behind me and set off to my favourite place.

For over two years now, I have worked on the entertainment desk of Spark, a news and pop culture website with a hefty focus on showbiz, entertainment and lifestyle topics – and I've never had so much fun at a job. We cover TV, film, music, the lot – although there's more emphasis on showbiz than on arts and culture with our team.

In many ways it's like any other job – the admin, the office politics, the water cooler gossip, the argument over who gets the first week of August off when we're all booking our leave. Away from the daily routine we get to be starstruck among big names on red carpets, run around capturing quotes at celebrity-packed parties, and pose for hastily snapped selfies with reality TV stars, splashing them across Instagram for everybody's approval.

Otherwise, we're chained to our desks until all hours writing up everything from controversial celebrity comments to reality stars toilet training their puppy on social media. Or writing such incisive headlines as:

ICONIC INFLUENCER STEPS OUT WITH OWN FACE PRINTED ON T-SHIRT

US REALITY LEGEND ADDS EXTRA STOREY TO MALIBU HOME TO WIN BET WITH CO-STAR

I never stop to think that I could be helping people in poverty, or finding a cure for some communicable disease, instead of spending my days analysing what one WAG has said to another on Twitter in the name of journalism. The popularity of our site suggests we're doing things right.

I do, on occasion, think we should try to introduce more discerning content. Maybe a few more arts-focused stories about theatre – that recent West End hit everybody described as *Jude the Obscure* meets *Ghostbusters*, for example – or some ancient marble statue that's been found floating at the bottom of some Highgate banker's ornamental carp pond. Because let's be honest, this stuff isn't for everyone. My colleague Nathan, for example, openly finds a lot of the tittle-tattle he has to write about beneath him. How he survives in our office without being able to name a single Real Housewife is beyond me. Yet somehow my good intentions never seem to work out that way. Maybe my occasional support for producing a higher class of story has more to do with my secret crush on Nathan than any great desire to change our editorial direction. Does anybody need to know that my heart flaps like a trapped sparrow every time he comes near me? Certainly, my boyfriend Daniel should not. Why shouldn't I admit I find Nathan attractive though? After all, just because you're on a diet doesn't mean you can't look at the cream cakes in the shop window.

Since the departure of our deputy editor a couple of months ago, my manager Paula's looking to fill the post, and judging by the way she's been talking, it sounds as though the job is as good as mine. I have scored more exclusives in the past couple of months than anybody else, have deputised for Paula enough times when she's been away – and considering she recently announced her pregnancy, the stakes are even higher, as whoever gets the job (ME) will no doubt step into that role too, once she goes on maternity leave.

We all know where that job is going, and I'm more than ready for the challenge.

NATHAN

Fucking hell. Late for work again.

It's not my fault this time. It's not my fault. How did I know there'd be a swan on the track outside Canada Water? That I'd drop my phone in a puddle on the way to the station? That I'd go upstairs to try and fix the TV ariel and get stuck on the roof?

Except *none* of that happened. I overslept. Again. I can't worm my way out of that one. Instead, I'm knackered from yet another four o'clock night, losing track of time as I sat up working on my novel, in the vague hope I might find a publisher someday. I'm sure I could cope with those when I was younger, the all-nighters I pulled on my dissertation because I'd spent too much time partying and not enough on work. Not any more, it seems.

If I run from the Tube, it'll save a couple of minutes. I could say the lift wasn't working, I forgot my ID card, or anything to make my arrival sound plausible. Oh, who am I kidding? Little Miss Flawless Elena Robins will notice in a heartbeat if I'm late, however much I try to hide it.

She sees everything about me, what I'm wearing, what time I go to lunch, and is always mooching around my desk, trying to get me to talk. I ignore her most of the time. She's got some little schoolgirl crush on me, and I'm not reciprocating. I don't like women who try too hard.

9

Besides, what is there to say to her? She always comes across as a vacuous clothes-horse, obsessed with pretty outfits and the showbiz world we write about, like I give seven shades of shit about any of it. She's so tooth-rottingly saccharine at times she could give a man cavities just by glancing at them, and she must surely know from my attitude I'm only doing this job to keep my head above water. The stuff we cover is such bargain basement drivel. I swear if I have to write any more 'woman wears bikini' type stories this week, I'll stick my head through the office window without bothering to open it first.

Maybe today she'll be busy. Maybe she won't notice I'm wearing the same T-shirt I had on yesterday. *Maybe* I couldn't be bothered to do the laundry. Whose business is it anyway?

Not like I go within a thousand-mile radius of these people outside of work. So, I smoke a stealthy joint on the walk from the Tube, knowing it's the only thing that'll keep me sane today, and eventually reach the glass doors of the Spark building. The view of London from the windows on the fourth floor is the best thing about this place. Everything else is a means to an end.

And so, another week on the hamster wheel begins. What fun. Although today could get interesting, given Paula's finally stopped preening herself in the office toilets for long enough to announce the new deputy editor, the job that Elena has set her heart on. The one she didn't stop banging on about all last week.

I'm guessing she's heard the news by now. It's on the rota. And even if they hadn't someone as organised as Elena will have seen it. She strikes me as the type who colour co-ordinates her sock drawer and has a row of fucking plush bunnies lined up on her pillow. She probably has names for them all.

What a disturbing thought.

ELENA

The office is as quiet as expected for eight o'clock on a Monday morning. There's an air of hushed busy-ness when I walk in. To my right, there is no sound above the clacking keyboards. The early shifters on news have little time for conversation and even less time for us showbiz hacks. Those setting the agenda in the adjacent lifestyle team just look weary. Coffee cups compete for space on their desks among the jumble of beauty products, chocolate bars and press releases about chocolate bars.

I, however, veer left to the showbiz and entertainment desks, which are situated in a tidy corner right in front of the kitchen, meaning we bear the full brunt of anyone who decides to microwave broccoli or last night's fish for their lunch – and we all know that death is too good for any despicable sub-human who does either.

A glance at the Spark Showbiz Shack, as we've come to know it, reveals that we have put our stamp on it more than any of the other departments, who take a more corporate approach; News, for example, would never dream of livening their desks up with anything more daring than a pot plant. We, on the other hand, asked for, and got our own disco ball, winking at us from its spot on the ceiling. Meanwhile, the corner features our treasured life-size Dolly Parton cardboard cut-out – the subject of many a cheeky selfie – alongside a neat red sofa and a couple of tatty-looking teal-hued beanbags, popular with late shifters when the tiredness threatens to overwhelm them. We've also been screened off with a set of glass doors – allowing us the freedom of conversation and music while we work.

It's this I hear when I open the door to our office, the sounds of some radio-friendly wail confirming that James is already at his desk. He's floral-shirted as usual, clutching a giant Starbucks cup in one hand as he taps along to the song.

"Morning, babes!" he bellows, his round face bursting into a Cheshire cat grin. "Looking good today – rocking those boots!"

I may be 'rocking' my footwear, but I am beginning to regret wearing heels to the office, my arches feeling the strain of the hike from Canary Wharf to our Docklands retreat.

"Thanks, James." In my haste to sit down I drop everything in a puddle on my desk.

"Had to make the effort, given it's such a big day."

"Of course! I'm so proud of you darling, you've worked so hard for this! I know you're going to absolutely own that job."

The Cheshire cat is not wrong about that.

The glass door opens once more, and Nathan slopes in, seven minutes late, with the customary hangdog expression that suggests he would rather be anywhere but here. "Morning all," he mutters almost inaudibly, trying not to draw attention to himself. Although it's impossible to miss the smell of something light and citrusy, as fresh as if he'd sprayed it on in the lift between the third and fourth floor. What is it with him and his superior resting bastard face? Nathan's such a handsome creature, with his unruly mop of dark blond hair, those sapphire-blue eyes, the cute little dimple in his chin- and I could listen to that adorable, Irish-with-a-streak-of-London accent all day. He looks like the disreputable member of a boy band, the one who ends up in the papers for stumbling out of a nightclub at four in the morning and peeing into someone's letterbox on the way home. Yet I know almost nothing about him. In the two and a half years I've been here,

I've tried everything to get his attention – but apart from polite small talk, peppered with his sarcastic comments about the most lowbrow parts of our content, he's been a closed book.

Maybe he'll open up once I have that new job title under my belt.

"Morning, Nathan!" I shout a little too enthusiastically. "Good weekend?"

"Yeah," he says, offering no other information. As uncommunicative as ever. He doesn't bother to ask me about mine.

Nathan slips off his coat and slings it carelessly across his desk, my lip curling as I clap eyes on the black bird's wing tattoo peeking out from beneath his left sleeve – leading me to bask in a brief but vivid fantasy of him caressing the back of my neck before we get down to business on the bank of desks. The image crumbles into dust as he sidles up to me.

"What's on the agenda today – usual?" he drawls. He stoops to avoid the disco ball, standing so close to my desk that his groin unintentionally winds up nine inches from my right elbow. I feel myself flushing under my blusher as those impure thoughts return. Must remember to look him in the eye. Not elsewhere.

That shouldn't be as difficult as it sounds, mind, since all he wants to do is bang on about work. Nathan's pretty face wears an air of exhaustion, his T-shirt crumpled and stained, as though he's slept in it. Does the poor boy need someone to do his washing? I could add that to a long list of services I would happily provide if he'd let me.

"Honestly, Nathan, I've only been here five minutes," I tell him. "I expect all your showbiz favourites, as usual." I brace myself for the usual caustic reply.

"Grand," he quips. "Reality star wears her brunette tresses in a ponytail to buy cat food. I can't bloody wait."

"I can tell you're thrilled," I hit back. I admit I love him secretly, but his attitude sometimes boils my piss. Maybe that's a good thing, as I cannot imagine any world in which he'd be interested in the deputy editor's chair. Time to break the news while he's still hovering.

"Oh, there is one other thing," I add, unable to hide my excitement. "We've got a team meeting at half-nine. Paula is going to announce the new deputy editor – who, I believe, will be me."

Nathan gives me a strange look.

"Are you sure about that?".

"Of course, why wouldn't I be?" For the first time this morning, I have an uneasy feeling.

"Maybe you'd better take a look at your rota." Without a word of explanation, Nathan slides into his chair, flicks on his computer and slumps back into silence.

I want to ask him what he means, but I am not sure I will like the answer. Instead, I switch my machine on with a sense of urgency and type in my password – which I get wrong because I never can remember where the capital letters are and the exact location of my 'special character'. It takes me four attempts, my anxiety rising with each one, before I locate the rota icon on my home screen, open it up and scroll down to our section. There, lurking in the previous vacant 'Deputy Editor' slot, I see what Nathan was talking about.

WHO ON *EARTH* IS KATJA LAKE?

KATJA

My dad used to tell me that you can get anyone to believe anything you say if you smile.

That's always been my shtick. Turn on the charm, flash that dazzling grin so nobody will ever know what you're thinking. Wear the best clothes you can afford, do your hair and make-up, remember your manners. Say please and thank you to everyone, always be kind. Even to the Starbucks lackey who gave me the wrong macchiato this morning, much as I wanted to roast him like one of his coffee beans. Because you never know what kind of day someone is having.

As it happens, I am having a world-beating day.

There's no need to plaster the fake smile on and pretend everything is OK. Heaven knows I could do with a few more like this. They have been in short supply in recent years. It's OK because plenty of fabulous days are coming, now that I've bounded into work, even more exuberant than usual, and told my manager the news I've been sitting on for weeks.

"I'm handing in my notice," I announce, barely able to wipe the ecstatic grin from my face. Celine looks horrified. I feel guilty for a moment. I worked my socks off to achieve it. I deserve this. "I'm sorry. I've loved working here," I say. "But this new job is so amazing, I couldn't say no." For a moment, I think she's about to break down and weep on my shoulder, begging me to stay. I won't though. Not for all the pay rises in the world.

My dad would be so proud of me today. It's a shame he's not here to share in this triumph, and in happier times, he would have been the first person I called. Yet I feel as if he's taken up residence in my head, his face wide with joy as he learns what his daughter has achieved. What a big moment for our family.

How sad I have to celebrate it alone.

I know my current colleagues will be sorry to see me go by the way my desk mate's face falls when I tell her I'm leaving. Like I care. "I'll be sorry to leave you all. It's too good an opportunity to pass up," I tell her, peeling a speck of fluff from the new salmon pink blazer I bought on Saturday because I know how awesome it'll look in my new role. She'll miss my cheerful anecdotes about the weekend, my habit of bringing a *Colin the Caterpillar* cake in every time someone has a birthday, even the help and support I've given her with her frankly appalling writing. I've lost count of the times I've had to return work to her because it's incomprehensible. Her last piece was so inept that removing my eyeballs with a rusty spoon would have been less painful than trying to make sense of it. At least I would have been spared having to look at the damn thing then. And yet, somehow, I keep smiling through it all.

She knows nothing about me, truthfully. The sweetness and light I radiate – the one which means nobody ever suspects me of being anything other than the wholesome cartoon princess type, has served me very well over the past few years. Feeling a bit sad, a bit under the weather? Talk to Katja, they all say. She's such a good listener; so sympathetic.

Nobody here needs to know what I've been through. They see what they want to see: the girl who never seems rattled, never talks about her past, always has a single glass of Chablis at after-work pub trips and then goes home before the conversation can turn to anything other than idle gossip. I can't imagine I will stay in touch with any of them once I'm gone, but I'll have to try and make my last weeks here count. I want to leave them with nothing but positive memories of me. That's very important, ahead of what comes next.

The fact is that I didn't need to leave. It's not that I didn't like my current job – it's always been my dream to write about the world of entertainment and showbiz – but I found something better. A step up the career ladder at a little website called Spark, with more money, more power, and a truckload of prestige.

And someone who I've had in my sights for a long time.

Who fills me with even more pure, unbridled rage than my co-worker's inability to understand the English language.

I settle down to my day's work, wanting to scream into the void when I notice she has once again spelt actor Robert Pattinson's name as 'Patterson'. It's been on the live site since midnight and the rest of her garbled word vomit seems to blur on my screen. I realise my mind isn't on the job today. It's on how a certain person will react when she learns the news herself.

What a shame I won't get to see the look on that little she-devil's face.

ELENA

I stare at the rota, unable to comprehend what I am seeing as the unfamiliar name stares back at me.

Katja Lake.

IN...THE...DEPUTY EDITOR...SLOT!

Up until now, I had thought it was as good as mine. Who is this woman? What's she doing with my job? More importantly, why wasn't I told? I put myself through the interview process, sat up until the small hours slaving over my perfect answers – and this is how I find out that the post isn't even mine? I see it on the rota?

Talk about a slap in the face.

"I don't understand," I begin, turning back to Nathan, slumped in his chair, staring blank-faced at his computer. "Who is this person?"

Nathan shrugs. He does that a lot, a sort of 'Who, me?' reaction as though us addressing him is a personal affront. "No clue," he insists. "What, nobody told you?"

"No, they didn't say a word. Thank you for the heads up though; I appreciate it."

"You're welcome." With that Nathan jams his headphones on as an indication that our exchange is over. And he has left me with only a crumb of sympathy.

Is this another one of those HR fuck-ups? Should it not have been mentioned to me before the news went public? But how come her name is so unfamiliar to me? I have been working in this industry long enough to know most of the people doing similar jobs on rival sites – had one of their names shown up in this way, I would have been happy for whoever it was. But a total stranger? I'm not sure what to think. I fire off a line to James on Squawk, our in-house message board. He is as shocked as me:

Elena
Have you seen the rota?

James
WTF!! They didn't tell you first????

Elena
No! I can't believe they've done this.

James
Darling, this is horrible! ☹
Who is this Katja woman?

Elena
Never heard of her

James ushers me out of the office into the nearest stairwell.

"I don't believe this!" he tells me as soon as we're out of sight. "For one thing that job was as good as yours – for another, to find out like you did?!

"I know." I bite my lip to stop the tears. James wraps his arms around me. "I don't even know who she is. Have you come across her at all?"

"Nope, never heard of her!" James replies.

Now that is unexpected because there are very few people in this narrow industry of ours that he doesn't know. If Katja Lake is unfamiliar to him, I wonder where they found her.

Never mind, Paula will be here soon. I'm sure she'll explain everything.

Paula explains nothing. She sweeps into the office on the dot of nine, looking immaculate as ever – and promptly sweeps out again before I can grab her for a chat. Maybe she has a meeting or something. I'll wait. It turns out I'm left hanging for ages. When she eventually reappears I approach her desk, but the words "Paula, can I have a quick word?" barely leave my mouth before she replies: "Sorry, Elena, I don't have time now."

She is fobbing me off with excuses, I know it. She returns an hour later and claims to be going into another meeting, yet I can see her from where I'm sitting, working alone in one of the glass-fronted rooms that run along the side of the office. James keeps messaging me to say I should go and talk to her, but something is holding me back. I blast off a note to HR, wondering if I should make a formal complaint about how it's been handled. No response. I get through several coffees and most of my gel nail extensions, which cost me half a week's wages.

They look like I've spent the last hour scrabbling at a cliff face. And they taste like shit. I scrape them into the bin and try to focus on my work, But Paula's avoidance is very much on my mind.

After she comes back, sees me and disappears to the bathroom for ages, claiming to have been struck down with morning sickness, I decide enough is enough.

"Paula…could I have a word, please? I think you know what it's about," I say when she resurfaces, not looking in the least bit green around the gills.

"Can't it wait?" She can see from the look on my face that it cannot. Reluctantly, she pulls me into one of the deserted meeting rooms.

"Look, I know what you want to talk to me about…and it's quite awkward," she tells me. "I had planned to tell you this morning that you hadn't got the deputy editor's job, but it seems you found out quite – unexpectedly. Our HR department has been a little too efficient on this occasion, so I do apologise for how you found the news out. I've been trying to find out why that happened as I had no idea they were going to update the rota that fast. Katja only signed her contract on Friday."

"And you didn't think to…" I begin. But Paula is quicker than me.

"I want you to know you did very well at the interview. You're a very valued team member, and you bring a lot to the department," she tells me, hands on her tiny, non-existent bump. "But we were concerned you lack the managerial experience required to be my second in command."

"You're saying I wasn't good enough after all the work I put in," I snap. Paula holds up a hand to silence me. I feel like I'm in *The Apprentice* boardroom, cowering in silence after my teammate has failed to sell enough musical toilet brushes. She'll point a finger at me next to tell me I'm fired.

"Please don't take this so personally, Elena, It's not a reflection on your skills."

I switch off while she says the next bit, reeling off a whole lot of corporate flannel that she has doubtless had planned for weeks. What she is saying is inaccurate, I have run the show on more than one occasion in the absence of a deputy editor. Would those hectic Saturday night late shifts covering the big TV shows have gone so well without me? Did we not have one of our biggest stories of all time – the one about the social media legend whose pet marmoset escaped – when Paula was lying on a beach in Turkey, leaving me to hold the fort? None of these platitudes are going to work. Someone higher up doesn't like me. It's obvious.

"This should not deter you from applying for positions in the future," Paula concludes. Or at least I think she does since I have long finished listening.

"So, who is Katja Lake?" I stammer.

"Katja impressed us both at the application stage and her interview," Paula responds.

"She is very experienced both as a manager and in a journalistic sense – and she seems like a lovely person. If you have any other questions or concerns though, please email me and we can arrange a further chat."

She inches closer, squeezing my hand in an unexpectedly personal gesture.

"Don't let it get you down, Elena. You're very talented, and still a valuable part of this team. And I think you and Katja will get on very well indeed."

I doubt that. I haven't even met the woman yet, and I dislike her already.

Katja 'highly experienced all-round awesome human' Lake turns out to be the only subject

James and I can talk about at our usual Monday lunchtime badminton game, usually a hive of gossip.

"Maybe she won't be as bad as we suspect," James insists. I race to the corner of the court and return his shot, sweat bubbling up on my forehead as I smash the shuttlecock over the net. Like everything else, I am determined to succeed when I get on court. James may be good at it, but I am better. He returns my shot with ease, damn it, and I know that the gift of serving – and notching up the points – won't be coming my way from this rally.

"Paula couldn't stop raving about her. Did you notice?" he says, continuing the chat about our incoming colleague.

I didn't like what I heard. The words 'managerial skills' and 'lovely person' flew over my head, vague attempts to keep me quiet. In a past life, I might have employed a few underhand tactics to unseat the newcomer. I am above such behaviour now – especially after what happened last time. I'm not going to tell him that. Nobody needs to know about my past.

Besides, I'm wondering what I'm going to say to Daniel when I see him later. He's booked a table at the Shard to celebrate what he assumed would be my promotion.

I haven't yet had the heart to tell him I don't have the job.

Seven Years Ago
LAURA

I never thought about what falling through thin air would feel like.

It's not exactly something you expect to happen. And yet, even though I know the outcome, it feels oddly surreal, pleasant even, twisting in the wind among sparkles of glass, as though I'm at some glitzy awards ceremony surrounded by trophies. The sort I'll now never have the chance to win. It's equally surprising how frosty the air is when you're tumbling through it at this height – no wonder they don't allow you to open the windows on planes. You'd be turned into a stalactite before you'd even unwrapped your crappy complimentary eye mask.

A falling shard of glass has slashed me. There's a searing pain in my right arm confirming this, as if I didn't know already, and the skin around it feels damp and sticky.

Odd how I'm only noticing the trickles of blood now. If one of those pieces lands on me when I hit the ground, I'm done for. Who am I kidding? I'm done for anyway. Who knew it would end this way, when I walked into that office all those months ago, full of hopes and dreams, to undertake the career I'd wanted since I was ten years old?

It's true then, that your life flashes before your eyes right before you die. Because I can still remember what I wrote in my beloved diary on that first day so clearly:

FEBRUARY

I couldn't have been more excited when I woke up this morning, the day I took my giant leap into the world of employment. I still can't believe it. Me, a junior reporter on a sparkly teen website, where every page is decorated in squiggles and coloured stars, in which vaguely famous people are asked what they have for breakfast on the first Tuesday of every month, or whether they've ever thrown up down a neighbour's window. OK, so it's not the most prestigious publication in the world but everybody has to start somewhere. Don't they?

You couldn't put into words how excited and proud my family were of me today – my mother was calling all our relatives for weeks, telling them how her little girl landed herself such an exciting job. I wish she wouldn't, even though she means well. I get we are a close family, but my parents need to remember I am no longer that 10-year-old child, making up stories in her bedroom, but a working woman – although I still make up stories in my bedroom.

I thought for one heart-stopping moment they would photograph me on the doorstep on my first day in the same way they snapped me in my too-big uniform when I started secondary school, standing on either side of me while holding a makeshift Good Luck banner above my head.

I managed to dodge that one by leaving for the office before they surfaced, telling them I didn't want to be late on my first day. So, instead, they bought me this diary to write down my innermost thoughts as I embark on this new stage of my life. I'm hoping I'll be able to fill it with lots of happy memories.

So, what of my new employers? Gleam is a tween-friendly site whose accompanying magazine gives away a dubious unbranded lip gloss free with every issue. As a junior reporter, I expect I'll be doing the little jobs at first, writing the news round-ups in an over-excited tone of voice or conducting phone interviews with soap actors who aren't quite famous enough to warrant a 1,000-word spread but are eager to tell you all the gossip about how their co-star nearly burned the set down trying to set light to a fart. I don't mind not bagging the big exclusives just yet. I know my place, and I'm certain this will give me the break I've been looking for, and lead to bigger and better things.

I'm still amazed I got the job. Confidence has never been my strong suit, and I took a bold risk when applying for this one by submitting an actual physical letter (everybody emails these days, but I thought it would stand out) on bright yellow paper. It did the trick.

Although my soon-to-be-boss admitted that if I'd written it on red paper, I wouldn't have done.

It's all in the details, folks.

Today went as well as you might expect. I spent most of it in the care of the editor, a whirlwind of training and office tours and the like, to the extent that I didn't have much time to meet my other colleagues, but I'm looking forward to getting to know them better. One girl in particular seemed to dominate the office. She's all smiles and chatter, and the others flocked around her, hanging on her every word. Apparently, she's Gleam's star reporter, and very well respected in the company.

I can't wait to have an actual conversation with her rather than stare admiringly across the office.

I have this feeling we're going to hit it off.

THE PRESENT

Daniel is, as usual, on time for his date with Elena, waiting for her at a small table in the Shard's Sky Lounge bar. He's sitting by the window, the one offering a spectacular thirty-fourth floor look at the capital's skyline, now bathed in indigo twilight as night falls. It's getting crowded out there, he thinks. Too many skyscrapers by half, cutting off the view from one part of the city to the next. You used to be able to see across town from here on a clear day; now all he can see are rows of shiny windows like some dystopian sci-fi nightmare. So many offices have left their lights on despite being empty: the eco-warriors would have a field day at such a gesture of defiance. Daniel feels uneasy at this height, but knows Elena loves it here, even if the view down to the ground is enough to give you vertigo. There wouldn't be much left of you to pick up off the pavement if you fell from here. At least he can rest easy knowing that the windows are sealed shut. He knows this for a fact. He checked them all when he arrived.

He and Elena met by chance through his job in the legal department of Spark's publishing company. He spends his days telling the lowly hacks that they cannot use photos of celebrity houses taken by someone hiding in a bush or why they can't suggest someone is racist, gay, or pregnant without providing compelling evidence to back it up. It's complicated and stressful – but Daniel does it brilliantly, and knows it too. He is well-respected in the department and a ridiculously popular mentor to younger colleagues who are practically queuing at the door of his office to benefit from his wisdom and experience. One day, Elena – single for over a year and wondering if any man would ever understand the demands of her work schedule, and fed up waiting for Nathan to notice she existed – was working on a complex story which needed the legal once-over. Having wandered into the department, Daniel gave her the answers she was looking for. They got talking, and the next thing she knew, he had asked her out for dinner. She had nothing to lose by saying yes.

The champagne waits for Elena alongside two pristine, chilled flutes. It doesn't occur to Daniel to pour himself a glass, preferring to wait. If he is laying on this treat for his other half the least he can do is be polite, in public anyway – because if they were at home, he wouldn't hesitate to start on the wine before his companion could get there.

Daniel is optimistic that Elena is the one he has been looking for all this time. He has been through many girlfriends, massaging them with the expensive gifts and other benefits their exes might not have been able to afford. He knows that with his good looks and designer suits, he is regarded as a catch. They never stick around once things start to get serious and Daniel gets confused. He expects a certain level of commitment from his partners, and he expects it quickly because if they love each other, what's the point in hanging around? It's not as if he asks for much in return, as long as the woman in question meets his standards in terms of physical attributes, dress sense and intelligence, and isn't going to do anything to make him look bad in public. The idea of a partner who swears, or drinks too much, or says stupid things, or is untidy, is a huge turn-off for him.

Yet he's watched one relationship after another end in tatters, and he can't understand why they would turn down the life of luxury he's offering in return for what he's asking. Surely it was a no-brainer?

Elena is different though; he knows she is. She's beautiful, funny and clever, even if she is obsessed with pop culture. She needs to grow up on that front, but he's prepared to tolerate it as long as she doesn't talk showbiz gossip (who wants to bring their work home with them, after all?). The fact Elena is prepared to satisfy his every whim makes up for it.

He can see a future with her. The sort he wants, on his terms. And he's confident she'll agree to it, given how smitten she seems. He won't bring the subject up tonight, even though, after six months of dating, he can't keep his intentions to himself forever. For now, let Elena think he's thrilled with the promotion, that her future as a hotshot career woman is all mapped out. Keep her on side. She doesn't need to know his feelings about it are rather more mixed, in terms of what he has planned for them. He'll cross that bridge when he comes to it.

ELENA

I'm half an hour late arriving at the Shard, having been ambushed in the office by a last-minute story about a performing chipmunk who's been nominated for an Oscar. It's sweet of Daniel to organise this little celebration, even though I don't have much to celebrate. Given that he's gone to all this trouble the last thing I want to do is cancel. Besides, I could use a drink.

Six months into our relationship and everybody thinks Daniel and I are a perfect match.

OK yes, it's true he is good for many things – little gestures such as taking me out this evening.

And I admit the size of his wallet thrills me – I love having a man on my arm who can afford to give me the best of everything. You could do a lot worse, and indeed I have, many times.

What I'm not so sure about is whether he is the one.

My parents would like to think so, and I'm sure Daniel would too. They may have a point since I'm informed by those close to him that I've lasted longer than most of his exes. But I often worry something is missing between us, that he's too busy trying to be a grown-up and think serious thoughts about serious subjects when all I want to do is laugh myself stupid over a ridiculous TV show or dance till I drop at a friend's birthday party. He is seven years older than me, and I sense he is ready to marry and have children – viewing me as the person he wants to do those things with.

The fact is, I'm not ready to get married – least of all to someone I have only been dating for six months and am having doubts about. As for children, they're the last thing I want. It's not that I dislike kids – as long as I can hand them back to their parents at the end of the day and return to civilisation – more that I was born a career woman, and motherhood would stand in the way of that. So, kids are not for me. Not one iota and however much people tell me I'll change my mind. It would take someone beyond perfect in my eyes to do that, and I'm not convinced that person exists.

Or that person is Daniel.

I see him now at a small table in the corner, dark waves of hair sculpted into place, a frown crossing his face as he checks his phone. He is handsome with sharp features, gleaming white teeth, the faintest hint of lines under his eyes to betray his almost fortysomething status, and charisma you could lick like treacle dripping off a spoon. He's too neat and tidy in some ways, forever fussing with his tie and worrying about getting a spot on his designer jacket or getting upset if a bird takes a crap on the windscreen of his bloody James Bond-style Jag penis extension. He's the kind of person who always wears his socks in bed, even during sex.

I'm not sure how to feel about that.

He greets me with an oddly formal hug when I arrive. "Hi," he breathes, enveloping me in a cloud of Tom Ford Noir (his favourite fragrance on account of the bottle matching his bathroom). "How's my little superstar deputy editor doing?"

"Forget it, Daniel." I fling myself down into a plush leather arm-chair and grab the champagne, resisting the temptation to swig it straight from the bottle. "I didn't get the job."

There is a beat while Daniel's face registers the shock. "You're kidding," he gasps. "Who did?"

"Some new woman none of us have ever heard of." I pour myself a glass of champagne, bubbles frothing their way up the glass, threatening to spill over the top. "Her name's Katja Lake. Complete mystery to us all." I drink deeply from the froth. "And you know how I found out? I saw it on the rota."

Daniel grabs my hand and squeezes it. "What? That is awful," he insists. "Why didn't you tell me sooner? I can't believe they did that to you."

It's rather touching that he is leaping to my defence in this – albeit OTT – way, but the irony of Daniel holding me in such high regard is not lost on me. If he knew about my past, how I behaved in my previous job, I am sure things would be very different. I can see he thinks I am perfect though, so I won't disappoint him. At least, not tonight.

"I wanted to tell you in person," I explain. "Not by WhatsApp. Can you believe Paula stabbed me in the back like that? She'd better bloody well give me a pay rise to make up for it."

"I'm amazed you're thinking of staying there," Daniel says, sipping his champagne. "If that had been me, I would have been out the door so fast they wouldn't have known what hit them." For a second, I see his face flicker into a smile and wonder what is going through his head. Is he hinting I should hand in my notice? Why would he do that?

"I can't just leave," I point out. "Where am I supposed to go? I love my job, you know that. And anyway, I can't afford to; we're not all as loaded as you." I take another sip of my drink and I notice a look of distaste cross his face as a drop falls onto my blouse.

"I mean it's crap, I know it is. After everything I've done for them. But there's nothing I can do. I'm sure it'll all work out fine."

If only I believed it myself.

The conversation becomes stilted as I fish for things to talk about. Daniel is so work-obsessed that it can be hard to get him to take an interest in anything else, and he tends to shut down if I so much as mention what I've been writing about – but he's not usually as distant as this. He seems lost in thought, checking his phone constantly while claiming he needs to keep in contact with work, although I can't help thinking it's an excuse to cover those awkward silences.

Things are no better once we get back to his place, with him dumping his clothes half in the laundry basket and half on the floor, as usual (does he expect me to pick them up?) and virtually ignoring me until we're in bed. The more I stay at his, the more I wonder whether the champagne, kind words, and extravagant dates are just for show. There are times when he seems like a different person from the one who first swept me off my feet, one who merely wants a woman willing to wait on him while he keeps buying her affection with expensive presents and Bollinger.

He perks up at the prospect of sex, but it turns out to be predictably unsatisfying. I feign enthusiasm while he gets himself off, under the assumption I'm enjoying it too. He's so self-centred in bed, failing to locate my erogenous zones, and receiving the usual, oh-so- predictable blowjob from me without returning the favour. I like a bit of fellatio as much as the next person, but there's only so often you can give someone a birthday present and get nothing from them in return. At least, not without wanting to commit murder and throw their twitching body into the nearest skip.

All the while, I have to endure a running commentary of what he's doing which is about as erotic as listening to the bloody shipping forecast. I bet things wouldn't be like this with Nathan. I'd put my life's savings on him knowing how to please a partner. He's got a filthy look about him, and heaven knows my sex life could do with a bit of added filth these days. Sometimes, when I'm doing the deed with Daniel, my mind wanders to Nathan, to liven things up. Last week, that extended to a fantasy of us going at it on my boyfriend's precious marble kitchen

33

island, and I got so excited that it thrilled Daniel to think he had turned me on so much.

He has no idea.

My mind is elsewhere tonight as I just want to find out about Katja. I wish he'd bloody well hurry up and finish already. He always falls asleep when he does, arm around my waist in such a clinical way that I'm anchored to the bed, and I have to peel him off me without waking him if I want to use the toilet or move. Or pop to the bathroom with my Rabbit to finish what he didn't even start. God, I'm bored. Does he honestly think the longer he's inside me, the more I'll be taken to the heights of giddy nirvana? If he keeps this up, the only thing I'll be moaning about is thigh chafe.

I fake my orgasm, as usual. What else can I do? It does the trick since he gives a yelp of satisfaction about seven seconds later and falls onto me in a sweaty, weighty heap. He isn't even that big (in any department, as it happens), yet it's still like being crushed by one of those giant, Indiana Jones-style boulders. Well done, Daniel, now go the fuck to sleep.

It's only later, as he's lying comatose with his arm flung across my stomach that I have the opportunity to investigate my new colleague. Stretching out as far as I can without waking Daniel I unlock my phone and fire off a few WhatsApp notes to friends:

> We've got someone called Katja Lake coming to work for us. Has anyone heard of her, only none of us know who she is?

The scant handful of people still online at this hour draw a complete blank.

Who on earth is she?

KATJA

Spark's HQ is gigantic compared to the last place I worked, its glass-fronted structure towering over Canary Wharf. It's a gorgeous building, all pale marble fittings and purple circular sofas, with headlines from the company's many publications beamed onto a giant screen by the main entrance. I am so thrilled to finally be here. I even keep the smile plastered on when the sweet-but-dim receptionist fails to grasp I am new and takes several minutes rifling through papers and tapping on her keyboard before she can find someone to come and collect me.

So, I get to meet my new co-workers for the first time. James is a friendly guy who never stops talking – barely giving me time to reply before he's off again. He's pretty annoying in that respect, and I'm not sure I need him yapping crap in my ear all day. It's a relief to learn I'll be sitting at the desk opposite his. Perhaps if he can't see me over that giant monitor it'll be an incentive for him to shut up. He's well-meaning and harmless though, and I feel I could form a happy alliance with him – which will be much-needed once I put my plan into action. He's the face of Spark's YouTube channel, a fount of bitchy gossip about the showbiz world and the company. He has invited me to co-host one of the shows with him before I've even had the chance to take my jacket off. Maybe, I say. He doesn't need to know I've seen it already, and I think it's shit.

The person I am most keen to see has not yet arrived, having been delayed by some trifle, so I attempt to acquaint myself with the rest of the team while I wait. Molly, the junior writer, appears too busy to talk, furiously typing while taking hefty bites of an apricot Danish, which she appears too stressed even to chew. But she looks dull as ditchwater anyway, so I am happy to be spared an introduction. While it's hard not to notice how attractive Nathan is, he's not remotely my type. Which is just as well since the last thing I need right now is a distraction. I know a lot of women can't resist the bad boy look, but I've always been sceptical. I'm convinced men like that are over-compensating for shortcomings elsewhere, like being penniless, or a terrible shag, or hiding the fact that their mum still does their washing.

Nathan seems initially reluctant to talk to me, although he does open up a little when I introduce myself, appearing shocked that someone is paying him some attention. He tells me in his laid-back Irish lilt how he came over from Dublin to go to university in London and ended up staying. I nod and smile and act like I'm interested, even though my colleagues personal lives are of no importance to me. What I want to say to him is, *that earring makes you look a bit of a twat*, but I think better of it.

I'm laughing about something inconsequential with both boys when she walks into the office, and I clap eyes on her for the first time.

I have to be honest. Elena Robins is not what I expected. I had images of some fierce ballbreaker type stomping in and shouting orders left, right and centre, writers scurrying back to their desks in a bid to avoid her venom. Instead, she looks rather delicate, with a mass of iron-curled golden hair tumbling around her shoulders, Bambi-like doe eyes and a sickly, apologetic smile. She looks like she would snap in two if the wind changed direction.

For a second, I feel a flash of empathy towards her.

Those thoughts don't last long. I can tell straight away what sort of person Elena Robins is. The sort who had a lovely middle-class

Home Counties upbringing with adoring parents who gave her every-thing she wanted – private school, fucking violin lessons and ski trips.

Spoiled as hell, in other words. Unlikely to have ever suffered a day in her life. Time to put my plan into action. *Part 1: Charm incorporated.*

"Hello!" I say to her in a bright voice, extending a hand. "I'm Katja. I'm joining the Showbiz Shack today! You must be Elena; James has told me about you."

Elena looks taken aback, as though she wasn't expecting me to be so upfront.

"That's right – welcome to the team," she says, eyeing me closely. I knew it. Her semi-posh tone confirms my suspicions about her perfect, trouble-free childhood. It's the human equivalent of listening to a sheep bleat. She skipped the pink on this occasion, instead wearing black cigarette pants and a black shirt festooned with a red rose print. I recognised that garment as I saw it on a recent shopping trip and was tempted to buy it myself. Except I would never sully my wardrobe with something so cheap.

James butts in. "That's right, this is Elena!" he shouts. "I've been telling Katja how the office would fall apart without you. There is nothing Elena doesn't know about this place. If there's anything at all you want or need, she's your woman."

"Wow, high praise indeed," I say, beaming in her direction, dental veneers on full display. Elena doesn't miss a beat. "Oh, James, you do flatter me," she says with an irritating giggle, voice soaring to a cre-scendo as it becomes ever more patronising. "It's great to meet you, Katja – have we met before? You do look a bit familiar. Maybe we spoke at an event?"

Shit. She doesn't know who I am, does she? If she does this will be over before it begins.

I realise I have switched off my dazzling perma-grin, and I'm rapidly blinking as I attempt to wriggle out of this obstacle. "No, I don't believe we have," I say. "Maybe we've both covered something at the same time. You know how it is, you go to so many events when you're in this job, our paths may have crossed at some point." I reach up to push a stray hair off my face, giving her a good view of my tattoo, the purple flower which curls a garland up my wrist and snakes up the inside of my right arm. Not a flicker of recognition. Thank heavens for that.

At that moment, Paula arrives and saves me from any further awkwardness by sweeping me off for content management training and a tour of the building, which keeps me occupied for most of the morning.

That could not have been timed better.

When I return in the afternoon, all is quiet apart from the sounds of clacking keyboards and a Taylor Swift song from James' speakers. Nathan leaps up to greet me, loyal as a puppy.

"How are you settling in?" he asks. Cute. Does he fancy me? Poor, sweet, innocent lad, he wouldn't be the first. I'm far too accustomed to men telling me I'm gorgeous. But this is one crush I don't have time for.

"Oh, everything's great," I tell him. "Everybody's been so wonderful, I feel so at home already. And now it's time to get to work."

I fire up my computer. Our short exchange is over.

Nathan looks a little crestfallen, and I notice Elena throw him a look of solidarity, which he ignores. Just as I thought. She does like him. Maybe I should get to know him better after all.

I'll save that for later.

I log into our system for the first time and head straight for her byline page on the website. For the next hour, I can't stop looking at it – all the stories she's written, all the interviews and exclusives. The ones she is so proud of. There's something unutterably smug about the lot of them.

By half past five we are the only ones left in the office, Elena having stayed late for a Zoom interview. I can see her in the meeting room from where I am, laughing and chattering away with easy confidence as she lays the groundwork for another one of her oh-so-scintillating exclusives. No doubt whoever she is talking to is lapping it up. Whatever your opinion may be of Elena Robins, you have to admit she is good at that kind of thing.

I can feel my anger rising and push it back down.

It's only my first day.

ELENA

Two weeks into Katja's reign events take an unexpected turn.

The day begins much like any other with the outfit selection, as I go for a cherry-pink blouse, figure-hugging black trousers, and black patent boots, which will be bearable on the commute but still look dynamite. With a late winter chill still in the air, I toss a black wool coat over the whole outfit and set off.

On my way out, I pass Lindsey, who is hurrying towards the bathroom, her hair up on end in the manner of Christopher Lloyd in *Back to the Future*, and toast crumbs on her dressing-gown.

I do worry about Lindsey sometimes. Once, we were the dream team at the website where my career began. Now I have moved onwards and upwards, and Lindsey is still there, staring down at her eighth year there, only a minor promotion or two under her belt, and knowing that the longer she stays, the harder it will be to move on. I respect her choices, but that doesn't mean I understand them. Who wouldn't want to rise through the ranks and make something of themselves?

My new deputy editor is someone else who has been on my mind a lot this weekend. I am convinced there's something fake about Miss Lake. She has wasted no time stamping her influence on everything since she arrived. Our stories are shorter, our weekly meetings are longer, and she's obsessed with making our interviews sound different from everybody else's, even when our rivals get almost identical quotes. "We're Spark," she keeps telling us. "And we should have our unique spin on everything."

I have to admit, she is good at what she does. That doesn't mean I have to like it, and I can't shake off the feeling that I've seen her somewhere before. That tattoo, the way her smile switched off like a tap when I asked her if we'd met, was suspicious. Yet despite the déjà vu she is invoking in me, I still know nothing about her. Apart from the fact she's a stunner, as the sexist, sweating hacks at our sister tabloid publication might say.

It seems I also have a rival on the clothing front. There was an incident this week when I ditched my pink for a canary yellow blouse, the sort of thing that as a rule would stop James in his tracks. But on this occasion, he barely even noticed, his eyes instead lighting up when Katja walked in in a pink frilly top and pink plaid trousers which screamed 'children's TV presenter'. The same thing happened with the red dress she wore at the end of her first week.

She has already stolen my job from me.

Now she wants the office fashion victim crown, too?

Seven Years Ago
LAURA

I'm bleeding, thanks to that shard of glass. I can feel it now. It's pulsing from the wound and trickling down towards my wrist. That may not be the only place affected, given I smashed through the window in a shower of shards. There's a rip in my jeans that wasn't there before. My left knee, exposed to the unforgiving air, is stinging like a bitch.

If only these cuts were the least of my worries. The likelihood of hitting the ground at speed and ending my life so prematurely is of far greater concern right now since my clothes have been torn to ribbons by the glass.

I'm not even going to look stylish when I die.

The fact I am even thinking that way shows you the impact the place had on me. I was never able to keep up with the clothing obsessives at Gleam, which wasn't my fault – I couldn't afford much on my meagre junior reporter's wage and I've never been that interested in fashion anyway – but the snobbery over who was wearing what on any given day was quite unbearable. I bet if it was her falling to the ground and not me, she'd be well-dressed for the occasion: no shredded jeans for her, she'd be wearing some perfect, fitted dress and her favourite shoes, not a hair out of place on her windswept head as she fell.

And if she did by some miracle survive the fall, she'd doubtless be begging for a dry cleaner as they loaded her broken body into an ambulance.

Why do I feel I'm falling so gently when I know the outcome will be anything but? It's like one of those slow-motion sequences in a blockbuster movie. My thoughts…are all…rushing at once.

And they've turned to my diary once again.

ELENA

The message burns a hole in my retinas: "Looking for a job. Can you help?"

It's my freeloading step-cousin, Weird Nina – with her semi-annual plea to help her find work, probably the fault of my over-enthusiastic uncle, who's been pushing her onto me for years.

At thirty-five, Nina is surely more than capable of getting out of her mum's basement and finding work herself, although I made the mistake of engaging her in conversation when I was round at Mum and Dad's last weekend, I'm not sure how her failure of a life is my problem since we're not technically related, my family reluctantly inheriting Nina when her mum married my uncle ten years ago. Even at their country house wedding where we were both bridesmaids. I looked resplendent in a dark green dress while Nina looked like she'd donned the suit bag the dress came in. She wouldn't shut up and spent the day dropping such hefty hints about a job that I nearly threw myself into the venue's tiered fountain to get rid of her.

Considered throwing her in too, come to think of it.

She hasn't stopped since. I can't tell her what I'm thinking, so I fire off a quick 'Send me your CV and I'll see it gets to the right person' as I stride to the office.

What I mean is 'Send me your CV, I'll make sure it goes straight in the bin.' There's no room at Spark for someone like Nina, whose knowledge of anything showbiz-related is so limited she'd lose us millions of readers at best and get us sued at worst. I don't know what it is about this job that anybody with an opinion about any celebrity thinks they can do it, and I have little time for anybody who only wants to get close to me, so they can call in favours.

But I know if I don't reply to her message, she'll be calling me at work and launching into the sort of long conversation I can't afford to have in office hours – if I don't want Katja breathing spearmint fumes down my neck.

I pick up my usual vanilla cappuccino and make my way to the office, arriving on time.

James doesn't even look up from his work as I stride in. Nor does anyone else. What on earth is going on?

Katja arrives ten minutes later looking fabulous as always in a dusky pink trouser suit.

She's balancing a thimble-sized coffee cup with her morning macchiato – an espresso with a pointless bit of foam on top – in one hand as she chats away on the rose gold iPhone pressed to her ear.

"Promise me it'll be an exclusive, right? No sneaking off to our rivals behind our back? Love you too. Ciao!" She snaps the phone off and announces her arrival with a bright "Morning all!"

It's at this point that my colleagues perk up. "Morning!" yells James in that ultra-friendly voice he used to reserve for me. "Looking amazing today, lovely – those boots!"

My gaze moves down to floor level – where I see she has on the same pair of black patent boots I am wearing this morning. I cannot put into words how mortified I am. It's bad enough that Katja is stealing my signature colour, for my love of pink is well-known. Copying my footwear and getting James' attention when he barely gave mine a second look is another matter. Katja thanks him and lifts up her feet to give him a closer analysis. I say nothing and slump into my office chair, the oddness of the situation not lost on me. Maybe this is a temporary thing, the novelty of the new girl. I focus on my work, knowing it will take things off my mind.

I have no shortage of tasks to get to grips with, kicking off with an interview with a WAG who allowed me to ask any questions I liked as long as I included one about the horrible protein supplement she is promoting. It was one of the best I've done in ages. An hour later, I am deciding which quote would be best suited in the headline when I receive a Squawk prompt:

Katja
Hey

What the fuck? It is a known fact that any message on any shared board that starts with 'Hey' is never followed by anything good. My work is so well-written, so accurate and ahead of deadline, that it is unusual for me to receive one. I respond with a cautious 'Hello', only to receive the next part of the message:

Katja
How's that feature doing? Would be great if we can have it live by 10 am 😎

Elena
I'll do my best to have it to you by then

Katja
Great

No more smiley face is forthcoming.

I wasn't expecting that. I continue to write, the piece going live just minutes after ten o'clock. With Paula in a meeting, it's down to Katja to sub it, and I see her looking pleased as the link arrives. Our next exchange, however, takes me by surprise:

Katja
Hi

She says it again and my anxiety levels rise.

Katja
About your piece…would you mind taking another look at it please? Only seem to be quite a lot of typos in it.

Typos? Me? I hesitate before typing back:

Elena
Are you sure? I ran it through a spellchecker before I submitted it.

She returns it, as an attachment, with the words:

Katja
See for yourself.

I open up the document and I'm baffled by what I see. The piece is riddled – as Katja suggested – with spelling mistakes. Sloppy, careless ones too. I give an audible gasp. The errors are live on the site and winking out at me from the photo captions and the main headline, where the name of the WAG is spelled incorrectly. Getting an interviewee's name wrong is fatal, and I cringe.

I fire back:

Elena
I see what you mean. Sorry about that, I'll have another look at it.

I make the corrections before receiving a reply:

Katja
It's OK, don't worry. Maybe double/triple check your work before submitting it to me next time, because it doesn't make us look great if you're making so many mistakes.

With that, she turns her attention to a story James has just filed about celebrity dog-walkers, smiling as she scrolls briefly down the text. Out of the corner of my eye, I see her make just the smallest of tweaks before shutting the story and continuing with her work.

I'm confused – because I don't remember making those mistakes – but put it down to experience. We all make mistakes, after all. Even me, the person who once got out of bed at seven o'clock on a Saturday morning to ring the duty editor and point out they'd put 'Barman' in a headline instead of 'Batman'.

It doesn't end there. The following day brings more spelling errors and more awkward questions from Katja.

Tuesday:
She returns a Netflix release round-up I've written, claiming it is 'completely factually incorrect'.

Wednesday:
A story I've written with a strict embargo goes live hours before it should, and the PR is so enraged when she calls to complain I half expect her to burst out of the handset and throttle me.

Thursday:
An expensive pap snap appear in one of my stories. One which our picture editor had ordered us not to use as it cost so much he'd 'have to sell his firstborn to pay for it'.

I have some explaining to do. Except I don't know what to say. Because I didn't make those spelling errors, I didn't break the unbreakable embargo, and I don't remember using *that* picture.

What on earth is going on?

Lindsey coaxes my concerns out of me, noticing I am quieter than usual during a Friday night in front of the TV.

"What's up?" she asks, filling my glass to the brim with cheap, lemony Pinot Grigio, which I hate.

"How do you mean?"

"You're stress-eating," she says, gesturing to my Chinese takeaway box. "Didn't think to save me a spring roll?"

I stare at the cardboard container. There were six in there when it arrived, now it's empty. It didn't even occur to me.

"Something bothering you at work?"

"Yes…kind of…"

Before I knew it everything had spilled out. Lindsey listens in silence. She is a good friend despite her chaotic lifestyle. I shouldn't lose sight of that.

"That does sound weird, but you know what? It's her first few weeks and she's got to prove herself; I bet she's doing it to everybody. Have you asked anybody else at work if they've had the same problem?"

I admit that I haven't. Why didn't I think of that? "Not exactly," I say. "I got the impression she was only doing it to me – but maybe you're right, maybe I need to speak to the others."

I take a big gulp of wine and blanch at the taste. Lindsey earns good money, why does she always have to buy wine that tastes like she found it festering in a recycling bin?

"Honestly, I would have done, but you know, since I didn't get that job, I feel like I shouldn't complain, in case they think it's just sour grapes or something. Everybody else seems to love Katja, and I feel awkward."

"Don't," Lindsey says. "Monday morning, go and speak to James. He's your best friend in the office, right? He'll be able to reassure you. Oh, and Elena," she adds. "I'm sure it's nothing personal, because I worked with you long enough to know how talented you are. More than me at any rate, or I wouldn't be stuck at the old place." She huffs theatrically and spears a mass of noodles, which cling to her chopsticks like tentacles.

It had never occurred to me that Lindsey might feel stuck in a rut, having always seemed content with her lot. But she's been spot on with the advice. I'll talk to James on Monday morning, and find out what's going on.

I'm sure I'll feel a lot better knowing it's not just me.

KATJA

My dear Elena, it is just you.

I am delighted with the way things are going with part two of my plan: *Tighten the screws.*

It has taken little more than a week for my new colleague to wonder what's going on.

When I first returned that story to her, the look on her face was satisfying enough. To keep it going has been a masterstroke. I have never seen someone so confused, and the fact it's her, someone who prides herself on perfection, makes it even more joyous.

She has no clue I overheard her this morning. I snuck out into the corridor that leads to the stairwell and pressed my ear to the wall as she discussed me with James, thinking she had some privacy there. As if. That voice of hers is shrill enough to shatter glass. (Which, thinking about it, is entirely appropriate). He gave her short shrift. "I think Katja's great," he said. "So supportive and helpful, knows exactly what she's doing – and most importantly she loves my work, so she must be a woman of taste."

Wow. How's that for praise? James, that is the correct answer, and you win all the mediocre gin and tonics at the next team outing to the Bull and Terrier, that hideous old pub you all go to after work, which smells so rank you want to ask them where the bodies are buried.

Elena interrogated him further, pushing him for answers about whether he had had any work returned from me, and he got annoyed with her repeated questions.

"It's happened to us all at some point, Elena. Just because you've managed to avoid it so far doesn't mean you're immune," he told her impatiently. Another correct answer James, you win a bag of cheap crisps to go with the crap G&Ts.

I listened for another minute or two as Elena concurred that she had been too sensitive.

Sadly, I had to return to my desk as I they walked back to the stairwell door.

I'm at my desk, face impassive, staring at a screen of text without looking at it when they come in. Although the conversation has moved on to lighter ground.

"Sorry I haven't done badminton for a couple of weeks," James says.

"My diary has been nuts – but we should arrange something for the week after next," Elena tells him.

Badminton, eh? Interesting. I'm partial to a game of badminton. My vast experience with cocks definitely extends to the shuttle variety. It sounds like Elena and James play often. In that case, I might have to muscle in on something else she holds dear. Given his little attempts to get on my good side I daresay Nathan can be persuaded to make up a four. He's forever asking me if I want cups of tea or popping over and asking me how my weekend was. It's almost comical how smitten he seems. In this case, his desire to do stuff for me could prove useful.

He's a gym bunny if the sports bag he keeps under his desk is anything to go by, so getting him on court should be a no-brainer. Besides, I wouldn't dream of asking Paula to play in her condition, and Molly doesn't look equipped for anything involving sudden movement.

Speaking of Molly, I stare over to where she sits in silence, preoccupied with her work and the breakfast pastry sitting on her desk. She stuffs away an awful lot of unhealthy food, that one. Anyone would think the job was stressing her out.

Perhaps Nathan isn't the only one around here who might prove helpful.

ELENA

I wake up on Monday morning to a message from Katja telling me to get to work as soon as possible as Molly is ill and won't be in today. That in itself is not unusual. We're all prone to the odd sickie, so I'm not sure why our junior reporter's malaise should provoke such urgency.

Hungover, probably. Day on the sofa in her PJs watching *Bargain Hunt*, and she'll be fine. I could not have been more wrong.

"Molly's in hospital," Katja tells me before I've even had a chance to put my bag down. "She's got food poisoning."

Wow. Poor Molly. Death by Danish pastry would be a horrible way to go. Food poisoning is the worst, I speak from experience. I'm not sure what all this has to do with me.

Katja drones on for another few minutes, the sympathy dripping from her voice as she suggests sending her some flowers and organising a collection among the team. Does she care that much or is she trying to win brownie points?

She drops the bombshell.

"So, Elena, I'll need you to take on some of Molly's work," she says.

Wait, what? I don't want to be picky, but I have a mile-high pile of my own work to get through today. How much is she thinking?

It is nigh on seven o'clock and I should be going to meet Daniel, but instead, I am still in the office. Katja didn't explain that the extra work would involve writing up some interviews due to go live today – nor has she delegated anything to the rest of the team, who sauntered out on the dot of five as usual. I had planned to leave then, pop home, fix my make-up and change into a pink dress that I love even if Daniel isn't so keen (he isn't the one wearing it, though).

Now I'll have to go straight from the office wearing smudged mascara and a creased white blouse with a biro mark on the collar. And even then, a whole bunch of extra work is waiting for me tomorrow. Great.

I am about to log off, freshen up and meet Daniel when the WhatsApp comes from Katja:

Hey have you seen this?

A US TV star not terribly well-known in this country has died after drowning in a vat of his own-brand tequila. Tragic but not the most interesting of stories to our very UK-centric audience.

I reply:

No, I hadn't seen that – that's awful
Have we covered?

No. Why would we? It's not our target audience

I think we should. Just because we haven't done something before doesn't mean we shouldn't do it now

I beg to differ and am about to tell Katja, when she continues:

Are you still in the office? Any chance you could pick it up before you go?

I was just about to leave. Can our late shift person not pick it up?

I think we should get this up as soon as we can. None of our rivals have it, and we could do very well out of that if we take advantage now. Besides, I know you'll do a much better job of it 😃

I will myself to stay calm as I weigh up my options. I could refuse – but I can't be sure if I do, the next message will not come from Paula, ordering me to write the piece. Besides, I have already stayed two hours late; what harm will another 20 minutes do? I reply:

No problem, I'll get that done

Thank you! 🖤

Any notion that I am doing Katja a favour is quashed when she sends me yet another message:

And get on to his publicist and the local police department while you're at it, we'll need some statements from them too

She has got to be kidding. Surely this is just one of those 'get it live in fifteen minutes' jobs – hence the reason I agreed to stay on a bit longer, and do it? Apparently not, and so I sit back down and crack on. My dinner reservation is at eight. I'll probably still be stuck here then. All because of a story that I am convinced no one will read. This is turning into a nightmare of an evening.

I cannot help but think that it's all Katja's fault.

Seven Years Ago

LAURA

The screeching of the wind matches my screams. It's occurred to me I am screaming, as if I was going to fall through the air to my death in complete silence. Plus, we can add the pain of the wind rushing through my ears to everything else I'm currently suffering. It's like jumping out of a plane, only to realise about halfway down your parachute has a hole in it.

I can't think straight.

Too many memories coming back to me about that first month now for me to process them all.

Boy band interviews…

               Press conferences…

Soap stars…

               More press conferences…

Blonde hair…

               Crimson ankle boots…

Queen Bee…

That was what I called her from the start.

MARCH

If I play my cards right, I could fly up the ranks here. Imagine being the editor one day, and being able to emulate all the wonderful work she does. What a thrill that would be, to succeed doing a job I love and having a proper career.

So far, the people have been friendly too, with the senior members of staff only too willing to take me under their wing and allow me to learn from them, happy in the knowledge I may be one of them sooner rather than later.

It's a shame that I cannot say the same for the other members of the team. I suppose at a place like Gleam, the heavy work schedule is bound to take over at times, but it is a little concerning that those closer to me in age and position, haven't made as much effort. It hasn't been for lack of trying on my part, as I have done whatever I can to feel like one of them.

My biggest disappointment has come from the site's star reporter – the one I admired from a distance as she strutted around the office like a queen bee. She was wearing a spectacular pair of crimson ankle boots on my second week, her long blonde hair tied up in an elaborate plait, and I thought I would compliment her on her style and ask her how she did her hair. She stared at me as though I was radioactive. Like she wanted nothing to do with me.

Maybe she was having a bad day, I thought. But it hasn't ended there. She and her best friend went out to lunch earlier this week, clattering back two hours later, and laughing as they glanced in my direction. I don't like to be paranoid, but I can't help noticing how their voices drop to a whisper when I am nearby or how the odd sly chuckle is cast towards me if I walk past while they are gossiping. I even heard a comment about plaits the other day. Were they talking about me? I have no idea.

I am being ridiculous, I know I am. I have often been convinced people are talking behind my back, but just because the two of them behave like this does not mean it has anything to do with me. As the most junior member of the team, there are bound to be certain aspects of the workplace that are not my business. I should leave them to it, and continue to be my usual friendly self towards them.

I'm sure if I do that, any issues will fly right out of the window.

THE PRESENT

Daniel inwardly fumes when he learns Elena will be an hour late to Sushisamba. He hates to be kept waiting, and tonight is a big deal for him. It's the night he's going to discuss his intentions for their future, and he wants her to take it seriously. Yet her work has got in the way of what should be a special evening for them both. And not for the first time.

He stares impatiently at his Patek Philippe watch as he tops up his wine, gazing at the salmon sashimi in the centre of the table, looking as fresh and shiny as if the chef personally caught it from the Regent's Canal. It's Elena's favourite – no surprise, given it's as pink as one of her dresses. He took the liberty of ordering some other dishes – black cod, sesame asparagus, black truffle rice and edamame, even though Elena hates them. What was it she called them, 'vomit from Satan's Garden?' It's not his problem if she doesn't appreciate decent food. Besides, he doesn't trust her to pick the good stuff off the menu. He's seen those Chinese takeaways she orders on a Friday night and knows they're a heart attack in a carton.

All he wants is for tonight to be perfect.

Except it's all spoiled now. Should he wait for Elena? She messaged some time ago to say she was getting ready to leave and decides to tuck in anyway. The food won't taste nearly as good at room temperature, he thinks, spearing the first piece of salmon off the plate. Besides, it's her problem if she doesn't show up when she's meant to. He could understand it if something big had happened, but he checked the Financial Times website while he was waiting (because he would never read something as downmarket as Spark outside of work) and the world seemed to be much the same as usual. So, what could have kept her?

He's five pieces of salmon down when she reaches Heron Tower, face flushed with exertion as if she's run a 100m sprint from the office. Her hair's not as neat as usual, and there's a mysterious black mark on the collar of her blouse as if she hasn't made an effort for tonight's date. At least she's not in pink. Daniel can't stand the colour. That'll be the first thing he'll persuade her out of once he's talked her into making the commitment he wants.

"I'm so sorry," Elena says as she kisses his furrowed brow. "I got caught at the office at the last minute. My new deputy asked me to pick up a celebrity death story, as I was packing up." She pours an oversized glass of Bordeaux from the pricey bottle Daniel has ordered (which cost more than the food) and takes a deep swig of the velvety liquid.

Daniel notices the look of disappointment on Elena's face as she sees that most of the sashimi is gone. Well, that's what happens when she prioritises work over everything else.

If he has his way, that won't happen for much longer.

"Isn't that what you have a late shift person for?" he asks.

"It's complicated," Elena says, sounding guilty as sin. "The late shift person was on their break, and she wanted it written, there and then. No idea why, when it wasn't a story we would normally even touch. And it took ages, so…"

Daniel looks serious for a moment. This could be easier than he imagined. "You know, Elena, I know it's the nature of the job, but all this working the whole time is not doing much for our relationship, is it? If it's not staying late to finish something, it's prancing off to some party or premiere."

"What's wrong with that?"

"Look, I know how dedicated you are, but I wonder whether it's even worth your while since they didn't promote you…you know I want us to move in together, take things further. And you know I see marriage and children in our future, don't you?"

Elena looks confused. She doesn't know where this is heading. Or perhaps *doesn't* want to know. Daniel is undeterred. "I've been thinking," he explains, with a sip of wine. "Maybe it's time for you to leave; let me look after you for a bit. I earn enough money that you don't need to work if you don't want to. We can start planning our future properly. I'm nearly forty and I don't want to put off having kids much longer. We're committed to one another, and I see you as the mother of those kids."

There, he's said it. Easier than he thought. Yet Elena's reaction is not what he expected.

He has been playing the moment over and over in his head, imagining a scenario in which she flings her arms around him, covering him with kisses as she tells him how grateful she is to be rescued from her thankless employers.

Instead, he is met with silence and a strange, wide-eyed look from Elena, who downs the remainder of her wine in one go. That bottle cost over £250. Why is she knocking it back like it's some cheap plonk she picked up at Tesco Express?

"Sorry, what are you saying?" she asks.

"I don't want to pressure you into anything, I know it's a difficult decision," Daniel says.

"We've been together a while now, you're moving in, and with things not going so well for you in the office – this would seem like a good time to consider our options for starting a family. You don't have to be in a job where you're not appreciated. You won't need to anyway. It's not as if you can be out doing red carpets every night when you've got a little one at home."

Elena looks horrified – not the reaction Daniel had bargained for. "You don't like the idea?" he asks, sounding irritated.

"I…" Elena pours another glass of wine, drinking half before he can say any more. "It's a tough one. You know I can't just drop everything and leave, right? I'm going to have to mull it over for a while, you know – decide what I want to do."

Daniel appears crestfallen, as if he had been expecting Elena to walk into the office tomorrow and tell them where they could stick their job. "Right, I get it," he says, "I won't rush you into a decision. Don't leave it too long, will you? I'm serious about us starting a family, and I see us doing it within the next year if things go well between us." He ignores her shocked reaction as he ushers the sashimi towards her, one solitary piece now sitting on the plate. She waves it aside in favour of more wine. Shame to let it go to waste. Daniel grabs it before she changes her mind.

The evening does not go as expected. Elena makes little effort to talk, eating almost nothing and focusing more on her wine than anything else. All Daniel's plans for a celebratory night have gone awry, and it's made worse when she declares half an hour later she has developed a headache and wants to go home. Alone.

Serves her right, he thinks, as she speeds away in a taxi. She'll get no sympathy from him if she's hungover later. Or was she just trying to get away from him? Was he being a bit naive about this? Did he really think she'd go straight back to his, chuck away her contraceptive pills and start the business of baby-making there and then?

Maybe he was a little too hasty. Someone as sweet and delicate as Elena was bound to be overwhelmed by the suggestion. Of course, it's a lot to take in. She needs time to process things.

He gets that. She's the one who'll be up to her neck in nappies and soft play, dealing with toddler tantrums and sleep deprivation and watching that godawful *Peppa Pig* thing on a never-ending loop while he's out earning money. Which is going to be a big change from what she is used to.

Having kids will please his parents no end and Elena can always return to work once they're older and more independent. It shouldn't be that hard for her to pick up her career where she left off.

He knows she'll make the right decision.

ELENA

I hardly slept last night after Daniel's proposal. I knew at some point the chat would come about babies – the ones I don't want – but I didn't expect it to be so soon. The way he has mapped out a future for us, without stopping to think whether I might be singing from the same hymn sheet, is shocking. All I could think about was getting as far away from him as possible because my head was churning with panic.

Daniel is asking me to give up everything I've worked for to be his baby-making machine. He has no idea what he wants me to sacrifice. Surely someone who claims to love me – even though I'm not sure the feeling's mutual – would insist I do whatever makes me happy and support me in those endeavours? While he may have enough money to buy me anything I want, is that going to compensate for enduring decades of unsatisfying conversation and even less satisfying sex?

The problem is I have no idea how to let him down – and there's a part of me that wonders if it would be so unthinkable to give everything up. I know he treats me like a housekeeper sometimes, doesn't share my joy for the lighter things in life, and ate my food without asking last night. Not that I was hungry anyway after his suggestion.

Equally he would ensure I never want for anything again which could make up for those shortcomings. Nobody's ever going to tick every single box, right? I'm so confused. I need to think about this properly. Only I'm not sure I'll get the chance to do that today.

To my horror, today is even worse than Monday. Paula is furious when I arrive and proceeds to rip shreds off me for not staying to complete the story last night. "Do you think it's OK to leave a story unfinished like that, especially when Katja asked you to do it?" she asks. "Have you thought about how bad that makes us look?"

I try to explain, saying that passing a story on to one of the late team to complete in such circumstances has always been acceptable. It only makes things worse. "Not any more, it's not," she snaps. "Katja is clamping down on that kind of thing. Weren't you listening in last week's meeting when she announced it?"

I remember that I was out at a press launch for a hot new Sky drama, and tell Paula so, a note of triumph in my voice – but she only half believes me. "OK then," she says, "but I don't want to hear this has happened again." Even then, she's not done as I slump to the door, conscious of my colleagues straining to hear my interrogation. "Oh, Elena," Paula tells me, "I think you'll do a lot better with Katja if you shed this – resentment – you've got for her. I know it's been tough for you, but you should be used to her by now; she's been here nearly a month already. I'd like to see you make more of an effort, please and I don't want to have to talk to you about this again."

Resentment? I want to ask who she has been speaking to, but I can't bring myself to do it at ten o'clock on a Tuesday morning, and the fight has gone out of me already.

I feel as if I could sleep for a week.

I struggle to keep my eyes open when I arrive at work on Friday, wondering if Starbucks can hook me up to an intravenous drip of coffee. The days have been getting longer and longer – and it could be another week before Molly is back. Last night I didn't finish until ten, sharing a Tube home with happy people returning home from nights out, clearly having had a much better time than me. Daniel only lives five minutes' walk away, but all I wanted was my bed, not to be kept awake for hours discussing our future. Besides, in the wake of our chat the other day, he doesn't need another excuse to suggest I should quit.

Today has to be better. It's the end of the week, and the team is going on an office night out to Sleek, a new cocktail bar near Harrods that has fast become a celebrity haunt. The PR is very friendly with Team Spark, and we have all been looking forward to it for weeks, given she is treating us to a VIP table, a free karaoke booth, and all the free fizz we can drink in the space of an evening. I love karaoke. My 'Bat Out of Hell' is the stuff of legend, and James and I have been making plans to perform it together tonight. I might not be in the mood, but I am determined to be there.

No amount of work is going to spoil this for me.

KATJA

"Morning, Elena!" I say in a bright voice as I stride into the office.

Her look of despair tells me everything I need to know. She cannot bring herself to return my greeting.

What a wonderful week it's been, watching her perfect façade begin to crumble in the face of so much extra work. The late shift freelancer told me in the handover that she was here until ten o'clock last night. Even then, she still didn't get everything done, having saved some of Molly's less urgent content for the morning. Poor Molly. I hope she enjoyed the handpicked bouquet I sent her. Ever the perfect, supportive colleague.

I hope she's not back anytime soon, because I'm having way too much fun with this.

Time to activate part three of my world-beating plan: *Elena No-Mates*.

We're all meant to be going out tonight to Sleek, a hot new bar in town with an actual fountain behind the DJ booth – a health and safety disaster waiting to happen. None of us can wait. I know Elena is looking forward to it, so she can drive us all to distraction with her dreadful caterwauling. I had quite enough of that in my first week here. James was playing one of Beyonce's albums one afternoon, and Elena couldn't stop singing along. I swear every dog in the neighbourhood stood to attention hearing that high-pitched wail. But it's OK. I don't think I'll be listening to that tonight.

With a bit of luck Elena will be far too busy with her workload to go.

Things are off to a cracking start. I have deliberately attempted to up-stage Elena by wearing one of my favourite dresses to work – a floaty grey number that cost me a week's salary. But money is no object for me when it comes to clothing. On the other hand, Elena hasn't made much effort. Her pink frilly shirt looks like something she swiped from her nan's wardrobe, and I can see a cream stain on her black leather trousers. I say leather, and I mean 'cheap PVC that would go up like a Catherine wheel if you set a match to it'. Now, there's a thought.

Nathan appears, as enthusiastic as ever, perching on my desk and dunking an almond croissant into a steaming cup of tea. He wants to discuss some gig he's keen to review for the site, suggesting that kind of content can only be a good thing. I smile politely and say I'll think about it. Bless him for trying so hard. It's like having my very own emotional support Labrador at work. Except I don't need one. He must know he has no chance with me. But Elena doesn't. Let's have her think I'm going to steal him from under her nose. Nathan continues his idle chatter, but we are both distracted when we hear Elena pounding at her keyboard in frustration.

"What's she doing?"

"Forgotten her password again." He shrugs. "She does that all the time."

Interesting. For a so-called intelligent person, she's not very bright. Maybe she should staple it to her forehead. That way, she wouldn't forget it. I'm sure it wouldn't hurt that much.

Nathan and I watch in amusement as it takes her five attempts to log into the system – but that's not nearly as much fun as seeing her dismay at the amount of work she has to do. There is no way she'll get through all that by the time we leave.

And if she does?
I'm sure I'll think of something.

ELENA

I'm going to be buried alive by work today.

Katja doesn't seem bothered by this turn of events. She's chatting with Nathan without a care in the world, as though I don't have double my usual number of stories to get through. What is it about her and her ability to win over every person in the world except me? Why Nathan, of all people? If I didn't know better, I'd say she was doing it on purpose.

No. I'm being paranoid. Nobody knows how I feel about him. More importantly, she must know all of this will take me so long there's a possibility I won't break out of this cell before Saturday morning, much less make it to Sleek.

That won't happen.

For the next eight hours, I speak to nobody except when I have to, my fingers flying across my keyboard in a bid to get everything done. I churn out wire copy in twenty minutes flat. I triple check everything for spelling errors and mistakes. I badger PRs and publicists until they give me the quotes I need. I work through lunch to get it all done. I even ignore Weird Nina when she calls me, which feels more satisfying than usual.

By 5.15 p.m. I hit the publish button on my final story of the day, finish up the dregs of the coffee cooling on my desk and sit back, a small smile of triumph crossing my face as I wonder what Katja will make of my efforts. Until, seconds later, the blue screen of death appears, its eerie cobalt glow staring me in the face.

Nooooo! Having your computer suffer a catastrophic error moments before you're due to leave the office on a night you've anticipated for weeks doesn't bear thinking about. I gaze back in disbelief at the sad face emoji and the incomprehensible words about how my machine has suffered a 'fatal error'. It might as well add 'and what do you expect us to do about it, loser?'

It's fine, though – I saved everything before it happened, right? The machine reboots itself, only to discover it has shut me out of everything. My anxiety rises once again. I attempt to log back in so fast that I forget my password for about the seventh time today, my fingers falling over themselves in an effort to get the correct characters out.

Finally, I am in. The last four stories have evaporated to nothing but headlines – and all of them are live on the site. Katja, sensing my discomfort, wanders over to my desk.

"Everything all right, Elena?" she asks as she sees my shocked expression and glances at the screen. "That doesn't look right – where's the rest of the story?"

I can hardly muster up the words. "I – it – I had a system error, and it's wiped it."

"Oh well, it happens," she concedes. "Can you find a backup?"

I click into the content management system, and it is as I feared – the backup has vanished. "Afraid not," I tell her, trying to remain calm.

"That's frustrating. Just the one story, though? That shouldn't take you long to fix."

I will have to tell her. "More like – four." I cringe as the words leave my mouth.

"Four? How did that happen?" Katja looks as horrified as I feel. "You'll need to get those back – we can't have missing stories all over the site."

It's a head/desk moment. I drop to my keyboard in frustration, squeaking like a horrified kitten that's fallen into a bag of doggo treats. Katja remains unmoved.

"You'll have to stay and get this sorted. Come and join us when you're done."

I knew this would happen. I *knew it.*

Four hours later, I put the finishing touches on the last story I had to rewrite, each seeming to take twice as long. I am too exhausted to contemplate going to Sleek but equally devastated to have missed out.

Looking at Facebook, James has already been posting photos of the evening, showing him, Katja and Molly bathed in purple light, sipping expensive cocktails from frosted Martini glasses. Katja looks radiant, having added a sparkling choker to her grey outfit while James has flung his arm around her shoulder. He used to do that to me, not so long ago.

"Been wanting to go to Sleek for the longest time," he comments, "and now it's happened, thanks to this lovely lady Katja Lake."

It all looks fantastic, and the *FOMO* is real. Under normal circumstances, I would have been the first to the bar. Now I feel like I am a stranger in my own world. How did everything go so wrong?

Fighting back tears I log off my machine. A familiar voice snaps me out of it.

"What are you doing here? I thought you were out drinking with the rest of the team?"

I turn to see Nathan. He's staring at me, his hair and jacket shimmering with rain.

Seven Years Ago

LAURA

I thought dying would be quicker than this.

I feel as if I've been falling for ages. Even the glass sparkles that surrounded me are fading, some descending to the ground before me, others dispersing into the sky.

My inevitable death no longer feels glamorous. The pain of all those glass cuts is made ten times worse by the freezing night air, and part of me is wanting to hit the ground so it ends.

And I've lost hope of being snagged on a tree or something instead. As if there's some mighty oak spreading its branches across this part of London, reaching up to save me. Knowing my luck, I'd land in a bird's nest and be pecked to death by a giant magpie.

And all of this because of some dumb show we decided to put on, packed with teenagers stupid enough to think the celebrities they idolise could become more than mere strangers on a stage.

If I could talk right now, I'd tell them that's rubbish. Those people don't care who they are, however many posters of them they might stick on their wall. I saw them come in with their banners, which they'll wave during the concert in the hope of a wink from their hero. "*Tyler Bard, have my babies*", one of them read. None of them stopping to think that if he took them up on the offer, they'd run a mile.

Tyler Bard, though. This is all his fault.

Because I was that person, the one with the ill-advised crush. On a man for whom charm was just a meaningless part of the job. She loved that, of course. I remember the diary entry like it was yesterday.

MARCH

I went to my first showbiz party the other night, and it's fair to say that it wasn't a success.

It started because I was sent to interview Tyler Bard, that pop star whose debut single Out There by Myself is soaring up the charts. It's such a catchy, anthemic little number. You'll either love it or it'll make you want to rip your own ears off and throw them over the nearest fence. Something so divisive cannot fail. I do not find Tyler attractive, with his eyebrow piercing, dark eyes and distinctive, freckled face, but went to do the assignment anyway. And wouldn't you know it, we hit it off – or at least I think we did. My editor was very keen for me to do it, entrusting me with such an important job, although Queen Bee wasn't happy about it, given she normally does our prestige interviews.

Which meant I got the usual snide remarks when I was getting ready to leave.

"I wouldn't get too excited," she snapped. "I've heard Tyler's a total wanker – he's rude to journalists and gives one-word answers to questions. What makes you think he'll be different when you go in there? It's not like you have a lot of experience, is it?"

Not listening to her. We all know I'm a better writer. She bats her eyelashes and wings it most of the time. Besides, she was wrong. Far from his moody public image Tyler was charming and flirty throughout, greeting me with a hug and asking me about myself as I fired questions at him. I had been nervous beforehand, the way I always am before interviews, but I was smitten when we parted ways. The record company said they were having a launch party for him the following week, and I jumped at the chance to attend. Maybe I would meet Tyler again.

The day dawned, and my excitement was running high. I had made an effort with my outfit – I do not own anything fancy clothing-wise but snuck out to New Look at lunchtime and bought a black lace top from the sale rack, hoping it would detract from my ancient jeans and worn-out boots. My hair was well-brushed, and I had put on more make-up than usual. But my colleagues still outshone me in the outfit department, Queen Bee dazzling in a lilac satin mini-dress. I'd look like I was in my nightie if I wore that, but it fitted her like a glove. And yet, for all their efforts to look good they seemed blasé about the whole thing. I had forgotten they went to parties like this every week and found them boring.

So much so that they insisted on going for a few drinks first and I had no choice but to join them. I wasn't planning to drink much this evening, so when they bought a bottle of rosé wine and filled my glass up, I had no idea how to react. I have never been much of a drinker, but it seemed rude to say no, so I accepted the glass, figuring it would give me a bit of pre-party courage.

I liked the wine, and drank more than I intended. Which was not hard since my colleagues made little attempt to involve me in their conversation – much of which consisted of bitching about colleagues and rivals or sharing the sort of scandalous gossip about household names which would get us sued if we ever published it. Who is a functioning alcoholic, who is secretly gay, which reality show judges are sleeping together. That kind of thing. Was any of it true? Who knows. My illusions of the celebrities I've been wanting to write about all these years have been shattered.

After two hours of this and two large glasses of wine down, we walked to the party a few streets away, at the kind of elitist club I would never have got into if I hadn't been an invited guest. I was hungry and sweaty, and my fuchsia lipstick had deposited itself on the rim of a wineglass. Any notion of stopping for food or freshening up vanished as we flashed our invitations at the door, paying no attention to the fans outside, hoping for *a glimpse of Tyler. Or even a wave, the sort of brief impersonal gesture guaranteed to make some of them die on the spot.*

The party was not what I expected. The entrance was bold and flashy and covered in thousands of lights, twinkling shards of glass in the night sky. Inside, though, it was far from glitzy. Instead, it was hot, noisy and thronged with people drowning out the DJ with their chatter. Everybody seemed to know somebody and have something to say to them. The floor was so sticky I had to prise my boots off it like Velcro, and while there may have been a bar somewhere, it was so murky and crowded it was impossible to find it. My colleagues had done, however, as about ten minutes later, a dark brown beer bottle, dripping with condensation, was handed to me. And just like that, they disappeared.

Leaving me to fend for myself.

ELENA

I am struck dumb at the sight of Nathan shaking the water from his hair, raindrops scattering across the hideous office carpet.

"Bit late for you to be here, isn't it?" he asks.

I try and reply, yet the words won't come.

Part of me wants to tell him what's been going on with Katja and the heaps of extra work I've been forced to take on this week. Yet, something is holding me back. The fact he seems to like her as much as everybody else, for example. Or maybe it has something to do with how alluring his perplexed face is.

"It's complicated," is all I can eventually muster up.

"I thought you'd be going to that godawful cocktail bar." Nathan perches on the corner of my desk, stretching his never-ending legs across the carpet, and my heart feels like it's going to beat out of my chest, like a lovestruck cartoon character. Oh help. Can he hear my raised breathing? Did he notice I turned as pink as my blouse the second he sat next to me? He's so close I can see how butter-soft the leather of his jacket is. All Saints, if I'm not mistaken. That can't have been cheap.

My mind races. I'm alone in the office with him. Anything could happen. It won't, though. After the week I've had, I feel about as sexy as a carrot. I finally find the words after an agonising silence, Nathan throwing me an expectant look. "I had a little – technical issue," I stammer, "and I've spent the last four hours trying to put it right."

"Bloody hell! That must have been some technical issue." He looks bemused by my confession. I try to swerve onto safer ground.

"So, how come you're not there having drinks with the rest of the team?" I ask.

"As if I'd ever do something like that!" Nathan rolls his eyes. "Do I look like I want to spend my Friday night drinking Martinis and gossiping about the Kardashians?"

"I don't know," I mutter, sensing his irritation. "I thought you might enjoy it."

"Because I work on a showbiz desk? And I suppose because I'm Irish, I also like Riverdance! Do you always stereotype people, Elena?"

He's being unfair now. What does he expect when I know so little about him? He has such barriers around himself, ones I've never managed to break. I compose myself.

"So, why are you here?"

To my relief, his tone softens. "Forgot my door keys, didn't I? Went to the gym on the way home," he says, indicating a duffle bag which I hadn't noticed, "got to the front door, left them on my desk. I had to come back here. I didn't expect to find you. Are you going to that cocktail bar then?"

And it occurs to me, the fact that he isn't out with the others, that I might have an ally after all. One who's been under my nose all this time. However annoying he might find me.

I hang my head. "No, I don't think so – it's so late already, and I've had the worst week, I want to go home and forget about it."

He raises an eyebrow. "That's not like you, Elena…what's up?"

"Oh, all sorts of things. Working late, picking up all of Molly's stuff…and today, as I was about to leave, my computer crashed and took half of my content with it. I had to stay and rewrite everything."

Nathan sounds sceptical at this point. "That shouldn't do anything to your content. It happened to me the other day and it resolved itself within a few minutes. Are you sure you didn't do something else that wiped it all?"

I cannot believe it. "You can't be serious…you mean I could have just got all my work back?"

"Of course. It's a pain when that happens, but it's no big deal."

"It's not the only thing that's happened over the past few weeks." My voice is quaking. I will not cry in front of Nathan. It is unprofessional. The look on his face changes to one of concern.

"You sound like you could do with a drink," is all he says.

I think he just read my mind.

NATHAN

I know I shouldn't get involved with Elena. On any level.

There was something about her tonight that got to me. She looked so sad at having her night out ruined. I mean, it sounded bloody awful, all of them getting shitfaced and talking bollocks all night. And don't get me started on karaoke. Given the choice of singing Bohemian fucking Rhapsody into a giant inflatable microphone or chewing my foot off, I know which would hurt less.

Elena was devastated, and I can't bear seeing anyone upset. Even when it's Little Miss Flawless, the irritating bane of my office life. I may not always be good, but I do try to be kind, and she needed a bit of kindness then. Besides, what harm will one drink do?

Twenty minutes later, we're sitting in ancient leather armchairs by the fire in The Bull and Terrier, a stone's throw from the office. It's seen better days, this place, but it's nearby, and at least it's cheap by London standards. Which is why Spark people pile in en masse after work or when someone's leaving or has a birthday. I prefer to celebrate mine somewhere that doesn't stink of four-day-old piss but whatever.

It's half-empty. The usual Friday crowds have gone. Elena orders a large glass of Shiraz, which surprises me. I didn't have her down as a red wine drinker, more that person who favours some pink fizzy shite with a paper umbrella. I once went out with a woman like that, whose opening line to her friends was always, "So when are we going for bubbles, darling?" as though they were arranging a trip to buy Radox. She couldn't understand why I ended it.

Perhaps I'm wrong about Elena. I grab myself a whisky from a bored-looking member of staff who slops half of it over the bar and join her at a small table in the corner.

"What's going on?" I keep my tone neutral. This is not a date. Let's not have her think it is.

Judging by her air of despair, I don't think she does.

"Well, everything's started to go wrong since Katja arrived," Elena tells me. "I've had so much work returned full of mistakes which I don't remember making. I've had stories go missing altogether. And then this week – well, you know Molly's been off sick? Katja's made me pick up so much of her work that I've been in the office until almost ten every night. I mean, I know it's all hands-on deck. I'm sure you've had to take on some of Molly's stuff, too."

"No, I haven't. I asked Katja if she needed me to take on anything else, but she said not to worry it was all in hand."

"She did?" Elena sounds horrified.

"Yeah. Maybe she thought you were the best person for the job."

"You don't think it's weird?"

"You're the fastest writer on the team. Everybody knows that. Perhaps that's why she didn't ask any of us to do any more work." It sounds as though I am fobbing her off with excuses, but what else can I say? She's not buying it.

"What about all the spelling errors I didn't make, the returned work…it all seems to have started since Katja arrived. Don't you think she's got something to do with it?" Her hand shakes as she lifts her wine glass. She's downing that faster than everyone at work moves when there's free Greggs steak bakes in the kitchen.

I won't have to buy her another one, will I?

"It does sound like you've had a rough few weeks," I admit. "You don't have evidence Katja's doing it on purpose, do you?"

"No, I don't, and she seems to get on with everybody else, even you."

Even me? What is that supposed to mean? Better 'fess up.

"Actually Elena, I'm not keen on her either. I'm only hanging around because she is open to new ideas and I'm hoping she might let me do some more film and music content – you know, something I enjoy for a change."

It's true. There's nothing wrong with letting Katja think I'm sweet on her. Not if it means I get some decent assignments thrown my way instead of all the usual showbiz crap. Elena is staring intently at me as she takes another big gulp of wine and asks the million-pound question.

"Why do you work for us if you hate it so much?"

Here it comes. The guilt-tripping moment about how I'm so ungrateful, stealing a job from someone who would kill to get on those red carpets. It wouldn't be the first time. The sad thing is they're right. Fuck it. I might as well tell the truth. I brace myself for her inevitable judgement.

"OK. You've sussed me out. This isn't how I would prefer to be spending my life. I have to eat, I have bills to pay like everyone else, and do you have any idea how hard it is to get a job in the sort of fields I want to be writing about? I'm thirty-two Elena, do you think I want to be crawling back to Dublin, admitting to my parents that I'm broke?"

Of course, I don't. "I'm not a trained journalist like all of you lot," I explain. "I fell into this by accident – I was freelancing while working on a novel, and I ended up doing some shifts for Spark, and they offered me a full-time job. I thought I could put up with the showbiz crap if I got to write about stuff that interested me. It's been over four years, and those bits are very few and far between."

I expect Elena to laugh or to make some sarcastic comment about how I should quit.

To my surprise, she doesn't. Instead, she nods, and offers me an apologetic smile.

"I'm sorry," she tells me. "It must be rough having to do a job you don't feel passionate about, to keep your head above water. I'm not sure I could do it."

I am taken aback and try not to let it show. Who saw this coming? "What's your book about?" she asks.

"It's a crime thriller set in Dublin, with an added soundtrack. Think *The Commitments* meets *American Psycho*. I'm editing it, and it's taking forever, so I'm late for work sometimes, I lose track of time. But I can't write until four in the morning when I have to be in the office by eight every day. So, it's a slow process."

"I hope it happens for you." She sounds like she means it. "I guess we're both in a tricky situation at work." She drains the last drop. "Maybe we should look out for one another a bit more."

Come to think of it, that might not be a bad idea.

"I mean – sure. I could use a friend at work. I keep to myself there because I don't think anyone likes me – James can't stand me, you know. Have you noticed how he always shouts, 'Did you bring the Evening Standard in with you?' if I'm more than five minutes late? I mean, what a wit, how original."

I don't want to reveal the real reason he doesn't like me. Judging from the look on Elena's face she doesn't know. Or she doesn't care.

"I'm sorry he does that," she says. "It stopped being funny ages ago. I'll have your back if you have mine."

"You have yourself a deal." I crack a vague smile as I clink her empty wine glass.

I guess we're friends now. Kind of. I've judged Elena too harshly. She's decent underneath all the fluff and silliness. Easy to talk to and didn't judge me for my life choices. She gets it, which is more than anybody else at work does. They think I'm that moody bastard who sits in the corner and says nothing all day. It'll be good to have someone there who doesn't.

She has to leave, and I walk her to the Tube before we part with a peck on the cheek. I tell her I'm on her side. I mean it, but we're only mates.

And I intend to keep it that way.

ELENA

It never occurred to me how lonely I was feeling at work until Nathan stepped in.

I have to say it was unexpected. He's never shown any interest before (and it wasn't for lack of trying). But he helped me in my hour of need and I learned that he's not the grumpy sod everybody thinks he is. "You have to start being a bit more pleasant to me in the office now," I told him as we parted at the Tube. "No more moody Nathan!"

So far, he's kept up his end of the bargain. I can only imagine what the rest of the team makes of our new-found friendship. Let them think what they want, though; nothing is going on.

The fact I have a boyfriend – as if I could forget – prevents such behaviour anyway. It doesn't stop me from thinking about it, mind.

I find him in the office kitchen. He's making a cup of tea by putting the milk in with the teabag. Before the hot water. Luckily, we're not an item because that would be a dumping offence right there.

"Morning!" He's so cute when he's all sleepy and bedheaded. His face lights up as he runs a hand through his unruly barnet, as though eager to smarten up in my presence. He's perfectly fine as he is. "How was your weekend?" I ask.

"Class. Went to a Nicolas Cage film marathon at the Prince Charles. Saw *Con Air* for the eighteenth time. I swear it gets better with every viewing!"

"Damn it! I love that movie! Why didn't you invite me?"

"Next time, I promise!" He ignores my wince as he removes the teabag and dumps it in the bin, leaving behind a mug full of beige, pallid liquid. It looks like he fished it out of the Thames. I half expect to see a shopping trolley floating on the top.

"Ready for our doubles match tonight?" he asks.

Nathan is joining James, Katja and me on the badminton court after work, and I cannot wait. Finally, it's my chance to destroy her at something.

"Of course – looking forward to it.'" The only thing I am looking forward to is wiping the grin off her smug face. "Do you play by the way?"

"Not for years," Nathan admits. "I'm pretty shite. That won't be a problem, will it?"

I haven't the heart to tell him.

The day passes without incident and my workload is reduced now Molly has recovered.

Weird Nina's CV plops into my inbox – a bizarre document, written in rhyme and covered in hand-drawn hearts, rounded off with a big 'THANK YOU' at the end. Does she think she's applying for a job teaching two-year-olds to finger paint? The accompanying letter is typical Nina, given she's tried to write it in verse. I say 'tried' because even the greatest literary minds in the world have failed to rhyme 'fever' with 'Justin Bieber'. So, why Nina thinks she can do it is beyond me.

It arrives at 10.50 a.m. and it's in my recycle bin and forgotten by eleven. Although by ten past she's already messaging me to ask whether I've passed it on. In Nina's world HR are so keen to get her on board they've dropped everything to read her mindless witterings.

I am jittery and impatient the rest of the time, waiting for the moment when I can bring Katja down a few pegs, but she doesn't notice.

Instead, she gets on with her work, only stopping to treat us to tuneless renditions of the 80s compilation album James has chosen for the day, sounding like a parrot on crack. *Now That's What I Call Murdering A Duran Duran Classic*, Katja. Maybe it was for the best that I missed the karaoke night.

Finally, the clock creaks around to five o'clock and it's time to head for the court. Even here Katja cannot help but outshine me. I am wearing black leggings and an ageing pink T-shirt.

She shows up in thigh-skimming black cycle shorts and a grey sports bra, her dark hair pinned back in a perfect high ponytail. She looks like she's just come from raving about a protein shake on Instagram. I've never felt more frumpy.

We mark our first doubles game with a selfie – me holding the phone up as I snap the four of us, Katja holding her racket aloft with a vivacious smile to camera. We choose our ends of the court – me playing with Nathan, Katja with James, Molly on hand to keep score – and our game gets underway, James serving a swift forehand into our side of the court. Nathan fluffs it with all the skill of someone who has never even picked up a badminton racket before. It's going to be a long night.

He soon gets the hang of it, supporting me as I race around the court like a woman possessed. So determined am I to outpace Katja that I dial up my regular gameplay, rosy with exertion, returning every shot, and winning us the serve on multiple occasions.

"Wow, Elena, you're on form tonight!" That is James, giving me one of the most encouraging comments I have heard in weeks. It forces a grin out of me as I dart to the front of the net to return a shot flying high into the air.

"Thanks," I pant, slamming the shuttlecock down and watching as it falls inches below the net on the other side of the court. Another point to us and we keep the serve. I can't help but look a little bit smug.

Katja, however, is having none of it – and she is proving to be a better badminton player than I imagined, fast and deft as she darts across the court. For God's sake, is there anything this damn woman cannot do? She and James nab the service back and win two points straight off the bat, leaving Nathan standing as the shuttlecock whizzes past his nose and lands in the far corner. Molly confirms what I already knew, that she and James have taken the lead.

I grow more frenzied in my bid to nab victory. I'm running rings around Nathan. He can barely get a look in as Katja sends volleys of shots my way. I smash them back, breaking their service and winning the next two points for us, forcing a dead heat. The next point is make or break. I send the shuttlecock over the net at high speed, watching as it gathers pace when Katja returns my serve. I smash it back with such force that my racket almost flies from my hand.

Seconds later, Katja cries out in pain. Her hand flies up to her face. Her racket clatters to the floor.

"Katja!" James screams. "What's happened?"

"My eye..." is all she can stammer. I stop in my tracks. Molly and James race to help her, alarm spreading across the court. Her breathing grows more panicked, and I peer at the shuttlecock, which has rolled back under the net towards me. I see why she is making such a fuss.

Because unless I am very much mistaken, it is speckled with her blood.

Seven Years Ago

LAURA

If I could turn back the clock, I would have done things differently that night. Actually, if I could turn back the clock I would stop myself from tumbling through the air at high speed to my inevitable doom, but you get my drift.

In truth, it was the night of the party that changed everything.

FEBRUARY

My head was telling me it didn't matter I'd been abandoned. I wasn't there for any of those guests, who had their heads so far up their arses they could see what they had for breakfast. I was there for Tyler. I knew he would arrive soon, remember me and whisk me off to whatever little table or area he happened to be occupying. I wouldn't be alone for long.

But I was. I stood in the corner by myself for ages. Not one person bothered to ask if I was OK. The longer I stood, the more it occurred to me that this party was little more than a glorified school disco made more credible with the addition of alcohol – and that any celebrities that might be there were very well hidden.

There was nothing left to do but drink. I finished the beer, hating the bitter aftertaste, and immediately looked around for another – which I found sitting in a giant cooler full of melted, slushy ice next to a cardboard cut-out of the guest of honour. People were posing with the two-dimensional version of Tyler, images that might later convince some of those fans out there that they had had their picture taken with the man himself. Except he was nowhere to be seen.

Until…

A commotion at the entrance, and there was Tyler! Black hair swept back off his face, matched by a black bolt peeking from his eyebrow piercing, and a midnight blue suit that looked as though it cost more than I make in a year. I stood on the sidelines and watched him gliding through the room, surrounded by a brace of buttlickers hanging on his every word. He was acting like a visiting pop legend instead of some guy from Staines-On-Thames who'd just gone into the charts at number eighteen.

Emboldened by the premium Pound Shop lager I'd been drinking (sell-by date: 11 months ago), I moved forward, hanging on the edge of the crowd, trying to catch his eye, waiting for him to recognise me. Tyler barely even glanced in my direction. He did not even stop to acknowledge the half-smile I gave him when our eyes met, staring through me as though I was a stranger.

Instead, he passed through the room to a roped-off area and that was the last I saw of him. Only then did the penny drop. Celebrity parties have hierarchies, and Tyler would have been taken straight to a VIP section, where hangers-on and people famous for pouting on red carpets were sheltered from the proles.

Any thoughts I had of spending time with him evaporated. I wasn't his friend. To him, I was another person doing a job on the day of our interview. Of course, he wasn't interested in me outside of that capacity. Why was I so stupid as to think he would be?

I realised I didn't want to be there. I wanted to be at home with my parents, sipping hot chocolate and watching a game show. Not stuck in this claustrophobic box with cheap beer and snobby, self-absorbed strangers.

I started to feel ill.

I had combined beer and wine, something my father had warned me about ('Never mix grape and grain,' he was forever telling me). The room was stifling. I hadn't eaten since lunchtime.

I needed to get out of there.

I skidded on a patch of water, fell to the floor, and ripped a hole in my only decent jeans.

Hands reached out, but I batted them away. Oh, NOW you're asking if I'm OK, I thought to myself. Bit late. I don't remember much about those few minutes apart from shoving aside those trying to help me. I may have sworn at people, something about the party being about as much fun as a root canal. I may have marched up to the Very Irritating Pricks entrance and demanded to be let in. I may even have ranted about Tyler being a talentless wet wipe who couldn't sing his way out of a roll of cling-film.

It was all a blur.

Eventually, I found Queen Bee, jumping on to the lap of a muscular blond man in a tank top. I muttered something about not feeling well, begging her to take me home – much to her annoyance. She ushered me out into the now-empty square. Before the party, she had begrudgingly agreed to make sure I got home safely, as she lives near me. Her manner was terse, as if leaving at this stage was a massive burden.

The last thing I remember was being sick on the station platform – much of it splattering over an expensive-looking briefcase belonging to a fellow passenger. To say he looked unimpressed was an understatement. My colleague apologised and attempted to clean it up with a sanitary pad while muttering something about my having food poisoning. Now I know why I have never been much of a drinker.

I have no idea how she got me on and off the Tube, but suffice to say my parents were waiting in the car outside. They offered her a lift home, and she spent it trying to make polite conversation with my folks as I mumbled and lolled and tried not to throw up once more. It's OK, though. I'm sure everybody else in the office has a similar story, and I'm only grateful that Tyler didn't see me in that state. I decided the best course of action was to apologise to Queen Bee, thank her for looking after me and laugh it off. Then everything would be fine.

It wasn't like she would shop me to my editor.

NATHAN

It's chaos in here.

Katja clutches her eye, wailing as though she's been shot. James and Molly are hysterical. Elena's shell-shocked. As though she genuinely caused some serious damage.

It's a shuttlecock for fuck's sake! Thank God there is one sensible person around here. I take charge, leading Katja off the court to reception for help, resisting the urge to tell the others to calm the fuck down. She's got a bit of blood around her eye, not a huge amount, but what a drama queen she's being. Now, if it had been a squash ball coming towards her at speed, that would have been another matter. Those little buggers could knock your block off.

Elena's gone pale and hasn't said much, although James and Molly staring daggers at her as though she's just graduated with honours from psychopath university hasn't helped. She seems pathetically grateful when I suggest that James should take Katja to A&E, while I take her home. He looks surprised that I'm siding with her. But what does he want me to do? I'm not leaving her in that state. Besides, this wasn't her fault. Anyone with an ounce of sense can see it was an accident.

Elena's deathly quiet in the cab.

"They all hate me, don't they?"

"Oh, they don't hate you. Maybe a little – scared of you, perhaps? You were quite fierce on the court. Even I was taken aback, and I don't scare easily."

"Thanks. I needed to hear that. Everybody seems to think I did it on purpose – you know I wouldn't."

"Of course." I reach out and give her hand a reassuring squeeze. Where did that come from? That was intimate. She doesn't push me away.

Elena's flat is on the first floor of a posh-as-fuck mansion block near Angel tube, all art deco looking with a wrought iron balcony and a lawn out front. We walk in, and within seconds, are met by a brunette holding one of those bloody awful cocktails in a can. This must be her best friend Lindsey, who she's mentioned a few times. Based on her anecdotes, I was expecting someone more dynamic. Not this woman in a dressing gown, swigging cheap Strawberry Mojito like it's tea.

"Elena! What the…" she begins, noticing how upset she is. No sooner has she ushered her to the sofa than she claps eyes on me.

"And who might you be?" she asks with a coy smile.

"I'm Nathan, Elena's colleague. We were playing badminton and there was an accident." I hover awkwardly in the hallway, and I can tell she's not listening.

"Why don't you come in? Anything I can get you? Coffee? Tea? Me?"

Oh, for fuck's sake. I start to apologise, saying I have to get going, but before I can she sweeps into the living-room. "Elena, who's the hot guy? You kept him quiet!" she shouts, loud enough for my parents back in Donnybrook to hear.

So, I've been reduced to the level of 'hot guy', have I? I slip away quietly before I can hear more. I shouldn't be surprised; it's a regular occurrence. Women have always been drawn to me like I'm luring them in with a giant comedy magnet. I ought to be flattered, although I sometimes wish they did so because they want to get to know me as a person. Not because they view me as a Dublin-esque Chris Hemsworth. Elena's the only one who's shown an interest in me beyond that lately.

A short time later, a message comes through from James on our group WhatsApp – the one meant for work messages but more commonly used by the others to gossip about which Love Islander has been pap-snapped without make-up. He says Katja is fine, beyond a couple of stitches and bruising. I message Elena directly to check how she's feeling now she's seen the news. She's grateful for my concern. The others thought it odd that I stepped in to help her. It was even more unexpected when I took her hand like that. I was only offering her support because she was upset.

Because that's what friends do for one another, right?

KATJA

"Does this mean I lost the match?" I squint at Elena from my remaining good eye. Its partner in crime is mangled is hidden behind a black patch. I look like a pirate. Fuck my life. Fuck bloody Captain Hook and the ship he rode in on.

But let's lull her into a false sense of security. She looks wary at first but eventually offers a nervous smile as it dawns on her that I'm kidding. Or at least pretending to.

"I'm so sorry, Katja," she says to me. "I got a bit carried away...hope it's not too painful."

It isn't, really, just a bit sore, enough to have me mainlining cocodamol by the fucking truckload. I assure her of this. She doesn't need to know I am focusing on the positive side of what happened. For one thing, my damaged eye is spared the disturbing sight of her candyfloss-pink skirt, its frills and flounces flying everywhere. What is she, six? This is an office, Elena. It's not a kids' birthday party at Wacky Warehouse.

For another, she fails to realise what a deep hole she has now dug herself into. The rest of the office is noticing Elena's odd behaviour – the things she's been saying about me, the accusations flying back and forth. All of which has fallen on deaf ears so far. I mean, why wouldn't it? There are perfectly simple explanations for my actions, all of which the others have accepted. Pity Elena hasn't.

Still, it's to be expected. She has been under a lot of stress lately and the badminton match is part and parcel of that. I think the others were shocked by her behaviour. I wasn't. I knew all along she has violent tendencies. How convenient the others have seen it for themselves. I note how they are avoiding Elena throughout the morning. James only speaks to her when he has to for work purposes. So sad to witness the end of a beautiful friendship, albeit a flimsy one constructed around footwear and Jägerbombs. Molly scuttles out of her way whenever she sees her, as though she's about to decapitate her with the nearest blunt object.

Nathan, on the other hand, appears unbothered by her presence. If anything, he seems to be treating her better than before. As I discover when I pop into that ghastly fruit fly infested kitchen for a peppermint tea and find them talking quite cordially – something about 90s gangster movies.

I am shocked. What is that all about? Nathan has never shown any interest in Elena before; he's been way too busy mooching around me. So why are they pals all of a sudden? This won't do at all. For my plan to work, I need to completely alienate Elena from everybody. I can't have her seeking solace in the office pretty boy.

I return to my desk, forgetting the tea, my head full of this latest dilemma. What to do? I turn to my inbox for some inspiration. There's a directive from Paula saying that the phrase 'a whole other mood' is now banned in headlines. Like I care. I'm only being nice to Paula, so she makes me editor after she fucks off to drop that bloody little crotch fruit of hers.

It's followed by the usual shower of emails from desperate PRs trying to get me to write about their Egyptian cotton pillowcases or woven Hessian coffee tables or something else that has no connection to showbiz. I've been invited to the press launch of a new body spray at London Zoo.

Maybe I could send Elena to that, as long as it comes with the added guarantee that she'll fall into the tiger enclosure at feeding time.

The next email I open up contains the answer to my prayers. It's too perfect. It has part four of the plan: *Abject humiliation*, written all over it.

So, Elena likes gangster movies, does she? She won't like them so much in a few days. Not after I've made her an offer she can't refuse.

ELENA

"You're not going to believe this!" I tell Nathan as he strides into the office, seven minutes late as usual.

I am fizzing with excitement, enough to stop him in his tracks. "Go on...I'm guessing it's something good, right?"

"Certainly is. Guess who's interviewing Freddy Taylor this morning?"

"Freddy Taylor? The actor?" Nathan's interest levels skyrocket. "That's brilliant news! But how? I thought Katja was doing it."

"That's just it, she can't. She's at the hospital this morning, dropped me a note before I got to work." I pull out my phone and read the message for about the seventeenth time, still thrilled:

> *SO* sorry but I have to have my stitches out this morning. Don't suppose you could pick up the Freddy interview for me? Questions on my desk. Any problems call me. K x

"For his new film? The one I saw the other week? God, I'd have sold a kidney for an interview like that! Wish she'd asked me!"

"Sorry. Maybe Katja wants me to prove what I can do. Sucks to be you, I guess," I retort with a grin. "Don't be too sad; I heard there's a big breaking story on the list about someone from *TOWIE* going swimming in a swimsuit. Sure, you'll have fun with that while I'm hanging out with the lovely actor."

I grab the sheet of questions from Katja's desk, not stopping to look at it. "Don't forget to mention they're living their best life," I shout, and am gone before Nathan can reply.

I should have shared the news with Daniel first that I've been handed the biggest interview of my career so far. He is my boyfriend, after all, and it might have proved to him how much this job means to me. But he's away at a law conference at the moment – which sounds about as exciting as unblocking the sink – and part of me thinks he wouldn't understand what a big deal this is. Or care.

Nathan got it, though. Which is why I told him before anyone else. And his reaction said it all – jealous as hell but still excited for me. He was so sweet after the badminton incident that it brought us closer together, and increasingly I find myself wanting to tell him things before I tell Daniel.

I wonder why that is?

It's not every day you get to interview a huge star like Freddy Taylor. He's one of the hottest British actors around – in more ways than one – and he's starring in a new gangster movie that is tipped to do great things. *Seven Bells* is your standard issue 'chirpy Cockney wide boy ends up in a heist gone wrong' type film – two hours of drug busts, car chases, swearing, and loveable but dim sidekicks accidentally setting themselves on fire. Plus, car chases. Did I mention those?

I mean, I hope that's what it is. I haven't seen it – I missed the screening that everybody else went to a couple of weeks ago – which in movie interview terms is a big no-no. But I've watched the trailer. And I've seen some of Freddy's other movies. I'm confident I can wing it.

Besides, these interviews are always the same. The film company takes over a suite in some fancy venue, staffs it with the scariest looking members of the PR team they can find, and instals the talent in a separate room, where they spend their day delivering five-minute identi-kit soundbites to the faceless parade of journalists who troop through. It's a lot more fun for us than it is for the stars, being sweet and polite as they recount for the twenty-ninth time how much they enjoyed working with their fellow actors. Even when it's a bold-faced lie. Bet they're secretly wishing someone would ask them something different for once, like who is their favourite Muppet, or which body part they'd eat first if they were stranded on a desert island.

There'll be none of that today. Given Freddy's been in the papers for all the wrong reasons over the past year – a trip to rehab, drug-fuelled benders, and cheating on his partner – they'll want to keep this one strictly business.

All I have to do is ask the questions Katja's written. So, I can't possibly get into any trouble.

I am met at the super-swanky hotel by a perky redhead who is holding the press event. She's all teeth and ponytail – not a day over twenty-one. "Hi!" she says in an upbeat tone. "Are you here for the junket?"

No, I just wandered in off the street after seeing the film posters in the foyer. But there is no way I am going to be that rude. "That's right, I'm from Spark. My colleague Katja had a hospital appointment, so she's sent me on her behalf. I'm Elena Robins."

"Oh dear, I hope Katja's OK?" The girl appears more concerned about her welfare than finding out more about me. "Tell her Lucia said hi – it's a shame not to see her today."

"Yes, she's fine. It's a routine thing. So, you have me, I'm afraid."

"No problem." Lucia crosses out Katja's name on her list of inter-viewers and writes mine in instead – spelling it 'Eleanor' but I haven't the heart to correct her. "You've seen the film, I take it?"

"Of course," I lie. As if Lucia needs the truth. She is merely the gatekeeper between myself and Freddy Taylor, who, as we speak, is probably having to push his tongue back in his mouth with his fingers from the number of soundbites he will already have given this morning.

"Great! It's good, isn't it?" Lucia is looking at me with expectant eyes.

"I've seen it twice in fact." How many times has a journalist perpetuated this myth about a TV show, album, to keep the PR sweet? Quite a lot, I reckon.

However, I have to keep up the illusion that I have seen *Seven Bells*, so this is the only logical answer I can give.

"Glad to hear that! "I'll need you to sign this release form." She returns to business mode: "I should mention that given recent stories in the, er, tabloids, we must ask you to stick only to questions about the film. Freddy will not be answering anything else."

"That shouldn't be a problem." My thoughts have drifted to the table in the suite, loaded with fresh coffee, pastries and the remains of a fruit platter. The free food never stops in this job – everyone is convinced they can win us over with complimentary pain au chocolat and melon slices. Two middle-aged men in the room, in matching *Avengers Endgame* T-shirts pay no attention to me loading up my plate as they are too engrossed in a discussion about Cannes accreditation. Film journalists I can spot a mile off. They're the only ones who wear promotional tat.

I'm not interested in talking, since I've not looked properly at Katja's questions. I run through the list and most of them are standard fare. Until about halfway down, I notice a question relating to Freddy's drug addiction. Was Katja not warned about that? Better let her know that one won't fly. I duck out into the corridor, swipe open my phone and dial her number, hoping she'll be done at the hospital by now.

"Elena!" she says, answering seconds later. "Everything OK?"

"Oh, hey Katja. I'm waiting to interview Freddy, and I'm not sure about one of the questions – this one about his rehab trip. I've been told to stick to questions about the film so I don't think I can ask it…"

I can hear the sigh, loud and audible. "Elena, I want you to get a unique line out of this interview. It's going to be super-boring if all we get are the same soundbites as everybody else…"

"I get that, but it could damage our relationship with the film company. They've got some big movies coming up and we wouldn't want to be shut out of those interviews, would we…"

"Are you questioning my professionalism here? You know if I ask you to do something you should do it, right?"

"But, Katja…" I'm abruptly cut off.

"You understand?" she says, her voice wearing thin with impatience. "I'd appreciate it if you ask him that question. All you have to do is keep him sweet, talk to him about the film and then slip it in. I've done that loads of times. I'm sure he won't mind."

"Katja, I…"

"Remember, this is a big interview for you, Elena – possibly the biggest of your career. Don't let me down. At least, not if you want to do any more." The line goes dead before I can protest further.

This doesn't sit well with me. It's understandable why Freddy might not want to touch on the rehab line unless he has agreed to it. I glance around the room at my fellow hacks, I cannot imagine any of them would put him on the spot with those I know full well I'll be the one who faces the wrath of the PRs if I ask that question. Not Katja. She'll waltz off scot-free, leaving me to pick up what's left of my career. My phone buzzes with a message moments later, but not from Katja. It comes from Paula.

Hi Elena. Katja has told me you're disputing some questions in the interview you're doing on her behalf. Please ask the questions she has given you, I have already discussed them with her. I am expecting you to come back with some

good exclusive lines. Not the same ones as everybody else.
P

I'm faced with a huge dilemma. Do I skip that question, risk a bollocking at the office and the prospect of never being sent to do another huge exclusive interview? Or do I ask it and risk a bollocking from the film company – and the prospect of being banned from ever going near another of their clients?

It's like asking me if I'd prefer to have gonorrhoea or syphilis.

Seven Years Ago
LAURA

There's glass embedded in me; I know there is. I can feel it sticking out of my neck. The ground's coming closer and the impact will only make things worse. Hopefully, it'll be a fleeting pain, over quickly as I succumb to my inevitable demise.

Yet none of it compares to the agony of the morning after that unmentionable party. The one where Queen Bee stabbed me in the back. The one where I realised I wasn't among friends.

And how dumb I'd been to believe I was.

Why did I ever assume landing my dream job would come complete with supportive co-workers who would welcome me into the fold? That the old notion of not taking kindly to strangers wasn't just a myth from creepy old horror movies? It just goes to show that you never know who your colleagues are. You might get on well with yours, gossip by WhatsApp when your favourite TV show is on, play tennis with them at weekends, or laugh about your peers over endless glasses of red wine down the pub after a trying shift. You might even refer to these people as your 'work family'.

Don't be fooled. Your co-workers aren't your family. Families don't go around pushing each other through plate glass windows. No, they're nothing but a disparate bunch of losers thrown together in unusual circumstances who you're expected to get on with. If your face fits, and you're one of the chosen ones, you will. If not, you can forget about the WhatsApps, the tennis, and those after-work trips to the pub to bitch about everybody who's not in their clique.

Because all they are to you are a bunch of evil wankers who resent you for existing. As I discovered that morning, they don't need much to turn the knife.

ELENA

"Elena, you can go through now."

Oh no. It is time for my interview. How do I fix this? I haven't a clue. I drag myself to the next room, dread gnawing in the pit of my stomach. It feels like I've been called in from the doctor's waiting room for some icky procedure.

Then I'm face to face with Freddy Taylor.

He is smaller in real life than he appears (they always are) but as handsome as I expected, dressed in dark blue jeans and oversized, ridiculous trainers that make him look as if he's about to take flight. "Hi!" he almost shouts, shaking my hand vigorously. How perky for someone who's set to spend the next six hours answering the same questions on a near continuous loop.

"Lovely to meet you, and you are..."

"I'm Elena," I tell him, "from Spark. "How are you doing?"

At this stage, I would put the subject at ease with a little light conversation, maybe empathise with them about how many interviews they have already had to do that day. I can't do it – and Freddy seems so warm and friendly that I already feel terrible. "I'm good," he tells me, "so happy to be promoting this film of mine. Sit yourself down, and we'll have a chat."

I do as he has instructed, leading to an awkward moment as I pretend to prep my questions, hoping he doesn't notice my shaking hands. He is so sweet and gracious as I launch into a chat about *Seven*

Bells and I relax, which I wasn't expecting. If these are pre-prepared answers to my formulaic questions, he certainly knows how to give them. Maybe I will get away with addressing the elephant in the room after all.

"Would you react to the situations in the movie the way your character does?" I ask him at one point, and he can't hide his amusement as he answers. We are getting along well. He seems like a lovely guy.

It is now or never.

"So, Freddy," I begin, offering him an apologetic smile, "obviously this film attracted a lot of attention during production because of issues in your personal life, er, you know…'

Instantly, the barrier comes up.

"What do I know?" he says. His expression is guarded. He bristles.

Shit. It's not working. "I'm referring to the reports of things that happened when the cameras stopped rolling, that attracted the wrong sort of attention."

"Ah," Freddy replies, "well obviously, there was a lot of camaraderie among the cast; we were all like one big happy family." The clever boy has swerved the question. I am determined to get my exclusive.

"I'm referring specifically to some of the recent reports about you in the tabloids," I tell him. "What can you tell me about the continued rumours of rehab that seem to surround you wherever you go?"

There. I've said it. That wasn't as bad as I thought. However, Freddy's friendly face snaps off. "I don't have any comment to make about that. And I'm not sure what it's got to do with promoting my film, which is why I'm here."

Fuck me with (seven) bells on. This is the exact outcome I was dreading. I have to claw it back.

"I understand. But this is about the film."

"The film? Are you sure about that?" Freddy's tone has changed from laid-back and flirty to hostile in a split second. He leans back in his chair. "What did you think of *Seven Bells*, Elena? You haven't told me yet."

He sounded like one of the gangsters in the movie. I half expect him to whip out a vice and stick my head in it. Help.

"Oh – I loved it, it was great," I say, but he is right back at me again.

"Only most people who have been in here today have told me how much they loved the movie before we started the interview." He leans forward, almost threatening. "Tell me, Elena, have you even seen the film?

A dreadful moment of silence follows. "Of course, I saw it," I stutter.

"Then which character's teeth did I remove with a croquet mallet?"

I look at him in silence, cheeks blazing.

"Oh dear, did you forget that bit? OK then, how many bags of severed human fingers does my character put in the basement freezer next to the oven chips?" He stares at me with a menacing look of triumph.

I have no answer for him, apart from the obvious.

"I'm sorry," I say. "You're right. I haven't seen the film."

He loses the plot.

"What the fuck are you playing at!?" he shouts, drawing himself up to his entire five foot-five. "How could you disrespect me like this? You journalists, you're all the same, coming in here to dish on my personal life!"

"No! No, you don't get it."

"Oh, I do. You're like all the rest, aren't you? I make this piece of…this piece of…*art* – and all you lot want to know about is that time I got laced at a premiere and set fire to my co-star's hair!"

There's your exclusive, Katja. But I can't use it. Because Freddy grabs my recorder and stamps on it with his expensive trainers. I gasp as it shatters into pieces. I paid for that myself.

It's been with me since my very first interview. Not any more.

"Try transcribing that!" he yells.

"Freddy – I'm sorry! I didn't mean it like that – I don't want to know about you setting fire to anything."

My pleas come too late because he's throwing the mother of all tantrums, ripping up the *Seven Bells* promotional stand behind him and throwing the pieces at my feet before kicking over the table my recorder was on. The glass tabletop shatters into pieces, narrowly missing me, followed by the cameraman's lighting equipment, which falls to the floor with an incredible bang. Freddy goes on the rampage like a designer-clad, pocket-sized Godzilla.

The commotion brings his agent, Linda, running into the room. Shit. Not her, as well.

She's terrifying. Middle-aged, wild-haired and with a face like a damp haddock. "What in God's name is going on!" She stops short when she sees Freddy smashing a succession of expensive hotel vases, one after the other.

"Get – her – OUT of here with her fucking personal questions!" he yells, gesturing in my direction.

"No, please! You don't get it!" I feel as if I'm nine years old again and have been sent to the head's office for hiding the science lab locusts in my teacher's desk. "I wasn't meant to do the interview."

She takes his side in an instant. "How *dare* you come in here and upset my client!" Freddy rants in the background, looking for something to break.

"Please, just let me tell you what happened!"

It's no good. Freddy stomps around, Linda calls security, and the next thing I know two burly guys who wouldn't have been out of place in *Seven Bells* – they look like the type who have a stash of severed fingers in their freezer – frogmarch me out of the room. A crowd of journalists from the holding room – all sensible-looking types who would never ask a serious actor such a forbidden question – peep around the door to see what's going on. I'm manhandled out, cheeks blazing with shame.

The last thing I clap eyes on is Linda, desperately pleading with Freddy not to wrench the TV from the wall.

The security goons march me down to the ground floor, through the foyer in front of all the paying customers, ignoring the hot tears of humiliation on my face before shoving me out onto the street in such a way that I trip and fall to the pavement. Seconds later my bag lands beside me, spilling my wallet, keys and my Charlotte Tilbury lipstick everywhere. My Airpods fly out of their box, and I watch in horror as one of them rolls down a nearby drain.

My head aches from the stress and the crying and being yelled at. I have had enough.

I pull myself to my feet, wincing from the pain of my fall, seconds before Freddy Taylor's TV hits the ground beside me with a resounding crash.

Katja has dropped me right in it. I'm sure she did this on purpose. When Paula summoned me to the nearest meeting room to find out what happened, blaming Katja was the last thing on her mind.

"Elena, what have you done?" she snaps as I sit there, head in hands. "We're facing a huge bill from the hotel for the damage caused – including, I might add, for Freddy Taylor's custom made, hand-painted trainers that he ruined because of you – and you can forget about Linda ever letting you interview another one of her clients. Or the film company either, since they've had to cancel the rest of the day's interviews. I understand you attempted to do the *Seven Bells* junket without having seen it first. I'm surprised at you, Elena, I thought you knew better than this."

"Paula – you don't understand," I tell her. I feel so weak. "I went along to do that interview on Katja's behalf – and I took the questions she had already prepared. The problematic one – I told her asking it would be a bad idea, but she insisted, and you did too."

"Which question?" Paula stares at me coldly.

"You must know," I insist. "The one about the rumours relating to Freddy's trip to rehab. The subject they told us specifically not to talk about."

She looks confused. "I'm sorry, Elena, I went through those questions with Katja beforehand, and I don't remember any such thing."

Sorry, what? Is she kidding me?

"I assure you it was there!" I tell her, my voice rising in pitch. "What on earth is Katja doing? Get her in here now!" I leap from my seat.

"Elena!" snaps Paula. "Control yourself! This isn't like you at all!"

"Why don't you believe me?" I am almost losing it again by this point. "Ask Katja to show you her questions. Then you'll see."

Paula gives an exasperated sigh and summons Katja to the meeting room.

I'm going to have this out with her once and for all.

KATJA

Elena was in tears when she came back to the office earlier. It seems the interview I sent her to do, out of the goodness of my heart, didn't go so well, and she's in a heap of trouble.

Oh dear, how tragic. Forgive me while I get out the world's smallest violin and play a sad concerto for her. I can't get over the irony that she's the one crying at work for a change.

Now she's with Paula in the meeting room to my left. Our beloved editor paces the floor, throwing her hands up as she speaks. She looks agitated. Not ideal in your condition, Paula. I'm desperate to know what they're talking about – but my patience is rewarded seconds later when Paula drops me a Squawk message asking me to join them.

This is going to be fun.

"Paula, what's up?" I ask, the picture of innocence as I slip through the glass door.

Elena's face is ashen and her hair is satisfyingly untidy, as though she's walked through a storm.

She has. Only in her case, it's a shit storm.

"Katja, I'm so sorry; I know you're busy, but Elena is insisting you told her to ask the question that got us in trouble at the Freddy Taylor interview," Paula says. "Could I see what you sent her off with, please?"

Woah. Blaming me for what happened? I mean, she's right. But even by her standards that is a new low.

Luckily, I expected something like this to happen, so I have come prepared.

"No problem," I reply in a smooth voice. "Happy to help Paula since, as far as I'm concerned, the whole thing's been a big misunderstanding." I hand her my phone with the original question document on it.

"That all looks fine to me," Paula tells her. "Sorry again to bother you."

She would say that, of course, since a certain controversial is question missing from that sheet. But Elena's having none of it.

"What do you mean it all looks fine?" she snaps. God, she's amusing when she's angry. It's like watching a toddler throw a tantrum because their sandwich is the wrong shape.

"Elena, Katja is not the one at fault here," Paula says in a voice dripping with irritation.

I've seen the questions she sent you on that email – which I might point out she also sent to you – and there is no mention of anything relating to Freddy Taylor's drug problem."

"But I don't understand, that's ridiculous! She must have changed it."

"Why don't you check your own email and see for yourself then?" Paula's patience is wearing thin.

I watch Elena open up her inbox, determined to prove me wrong – and the look on her face when she sees the email, minus the offending question, makes every moment of this endeavour worthwhile. Still, what do you expect when you take the sheet of questions off my desk instead of checking the ones in your inbox?

"I – don't understand. The question was on the sheet Katja told me to take from her desk," Elena stammers, and then it dawns on her. "Of course! That's it! I'll show you!" She rushes from the room before either of us can say any more.

Shit. I hadn't thought of that. The little minx has brought the question sheet back with her. If Paula sees that it's game over. She's staring at me, confused. I have to remain impassive. The seconds tick by. I realise I have nothing to say to Paula. Not a word. She's nothing to me. Just some bossy little harpy who got herself knocked up.

I'm mentally kicking myself for such a rookie error. Why didn't I check Elena's bag for the question sheet before coming? Because rooting through it in front of everyone would have looked seriously weird. Plus, that perfume she keeps in there, the one she's forever spraying around at her desk, smells of cat fart.

Maybe I could grab the sheet and read the questions to Paula, so she doesn't see what's on there. Or distract Elena, steal the sheet and make a run for it. As a last resort, I could wrestle her to the ground and watch as the questions fly out of that open window. When she asks why, I could tell her I spotted a poisonous snake in the corner of the room. No. That won't work. The only poisonous snake around here is her. My heartbeat is running close to the speed of light when she returns to the room.

Thank the Lord and all his little helpers. She's empty-handed.

"I'm sorry," she says to us both. "I – must have left the questions at the hotel."

That was a close one. I need to be more careful in future. But there's no denying I've played an absolute blinder.

Round two to me, bitch.

ELENA

"I don't know what to say," Paula tells me. "Your behaviour – well, I'm not the only one who's noticed how much it's changed in the past couple of months. Are you feeling all right? Because this is very out of character."

I'm unable to look her in the face. The resentment I feel at knowing I've been stitched up cannot be put into words. Katja planned this perfectly, from switching the question sheets to insisting I call her with any problems – meaning that conversation we had about the interview might as well not have happened. Why didn't I message her instead? How can I have been so dumb as to leave the question sheet behind – the one bit of physical evidence that might have doomed her? I'm kicking myself under the table. Literally.

Paula isn't finished with me though. "I'm not the only one who's noticed it. Some staff members have complained to me about your attitude towards Katja."

This is a real punch to the gut. Who has been saying things about me? I open my mouth to speak, but she won't let me get a word in.

"I'm aware that Katja's appointment was not easy for you given the circumstances, but that doesn't give you the right to go around bad-mouthing her to others and accusing her of causing trouble. Katja is only doing her job, and she is doing it incredibly well. I won't accept you saying otherwise just because you maintain the job should have been yours."

It is pointless trying to argue, so I mutter something about trying to do better and lapse into silence. Anything to get out of this situation. It seems to do the trick, as Paula's tone becomes more conciliatory. "Look," she says, "I get there has been a communication breakdown on this occasion because I know you wouldn't deliberately sabotage an interview. But you need to take on board what I've said about Katja. She's here to stay. You need to get used to it."

Paula's got it all wrong. Katja has been tormenting me over the past couple of months, I'm certain. The only reason others have not complained about her is because she is not doing the same to them. All the spelling errors she has picked up on, the additional workloads – none of these have been foisted upon other people.

It has only ever been me.

It's been the day from hell already, and I still have to get through the afternoon. The thought of sitting next to Katja for the next several hours is more than I can bear right now. Instead, I step out of the office for some fresh air and am surprised to see Nathan standing in a secluded alley around the back of the building. Even more so, a barrel of smoke from a hand-rolled cigarette partly obscures his face.

"I didn't know you smoked," I remark, edging closer.

Nathan's expression is that of a naughty teenager caught lighting up behind the bike sheds. "Ah yes…it's not that kind of smoking. I gave that up years ago. This is a little something else to get me through yet another day at the grindstone. Would you like some?"

He hands the roll-up to me, and a pungent scent fills the air. It's not tobacco but the offer could not have come at a better time. The weed hits the spot as I inhale, a warm, relaxed feeling settling over me almost immediately. I haven't smoked one of these for months, but it's much needed.

"Thank you," I say to him. "I'm so pissed off right now I can't even put it into Words. *Seven Bells*? Seven Shitting Bellends more like."

"The interview? Yeah, I heard about that. Quite the fuck-up by the sounds of it."

"I'm going to be blacklisted, Nathan!" I wail. "Freddy's agent works for one of the biggest firms in the country, and I won't be allowed to interview any of their clients! I won't be able to get near all those big names! What am I going to do?!" I lean against the wall, despondent.

"Is it that bad?"

"Oh, you know it is! The biggest interview of my career, and it was a disaster." I blink back fresh tears. "I hate Katja! Everything was great until she came along. I wish she'd disappear."

"Are you sure about that? You should be careful what you wish for." Nathan takes a final drag of the joint before dropping the remains to the ground and grinding it out with his boot. He locks eyes with mine. I flush scarlet and avert his gaze. Instead, I become fascinated with the diamond stud glinting from his left ear. Another thing I've never noticed about him before. He really is the antithesis of my current boyfriend, and that might be the appeal. I couldn't imagine Daniel, with his expensive suits and conventional good looks, having piercings or tattoos or doing funny smokes around the back of the building on a Wednesday afternoon.

I'm captivated.

"It was a crap film anyway," Nathan tells me, "Seven Bellends is about right."

"No, that's just the people in it. Maybe that should be the porn remake. Imagine the tagline: 'These hard men will put a stiff in your trunk'."

Nathan explodes with mirth at this. I've never heard him laugh before; he's always been too busy sulking. Fuck me, he's loud. He's like that person you don't want to sit next to in the cinema during a Will Ferrell comedy. And yet, it's charming. "That's cracking!" he shouts. "I'd totally see that!" Now I'm laughing, and it breaks the tension between us. The weed makes my head spin, and I stumble as I move away from the wall.

"Careful!" Nathan reaches out to steady me, and the next thing I know, we're tantalisingly close. So much so that I can smell the cannabis-chewing-gum hybrid of his breath. "I'm sorry you had a shit day," he tells me. "It's not fair. You're lovely."

"Excuse me?"

"Only telling you what I've been thinking for ages." His voice drops to a low, flirty tone. "I've been waiting for the right moment to get you alone."

Is he coming on to me? My God. He is. My legs begin to quiver so much I can barely stand up. I'm going to collapse right here in this alley; such is the effect he is having. Is it me, or is it suddenly baking hot out here?

"You have?" is all I can squeak in response. I feel as if I'm having an asthma attack.

Except I don't suffer from asthma. In a single heart stopping movement, he brushes my hair aside, takes his face in my hands and kisses me. Gently, tentatively at first. But when I don't try to stop him, he takes it further, his tongue probing my mouth, his fingers stroking the back of my neck like in those random daydreams of mine. I snog him right back, of course, every bit of desire I've ever had for him bubbling to the surface while fireworks detonate in my head. This is what being let loose in Harvey Nichols with a black Amex card must feel like.

I can't believe this is happening. I don't want it to end. After what seems like hours, we pull apart. "Does that answer your question?" Nathan asks, looking every bit as dazed as me.

I cannot take my eyes off him as I wipe the spit from my upper lip. I have lost the ability to form a coherent sentence.

"Er, yes, right…" I eventually stammer. "Do we – have to go back to work? I can't face it."

"Don't think so," Nathan says. "I'm meant to be going to a screening. I could always bunk off. You know," he adds with a wink, "pretend I've seen the film." He leans in and kisses me again, his hands snaking down to the small of my back and my entire body feels as if it's on fire, a million tiny electric shocks pulsing across me like pinpricks.

I want him. I want him right now. Screw how wrong it is. I'm done with being good.

NATHAN

I shouldn't have done that. I know I shouldn't have done that. I should have told her it was a mistake after the first kiss. That she should go back to work and pretend it didn't happen.

Except I didn't want to.

It's as if some fuse in my brain short-circuited, revealing what was staring me in the face all along. The fact that I've liked Elena all this time. Every pink-wrapped, sugary, vapid inch of her. Only I refused to acknowledge it. But it ends here. It has to.

Even though that second kiss was magic. Like nothing I've experienced before. If she notices how aroused I am now, it's game over. I try to think of something, anything else.

My local MP, romping naked through a field of wheat. The CEO of our company chairing a meeting in Speedos. That security guy at work with the missing front teeth, whose breath smells like coriander. Nope. Not working. Nothing's going to stop this hard-on.

Ah, fuck it.

"Do you know anywhere we could – you know – be alone?" I ask hesitantly. At best I'm expecting a quick fumble somewhere, like a couple of horny teenagers. Then a return to our desks, red-faced and awkward, like nothing happened.

The wicked smile on Elena's face suggests otherwise.

"As it happens, I do," she tells me. "My boyfriend's away at the moment – and guess who has the keys to his place?"

Sorry, what? Boyfriend? His place?

Just her – and me? That's taking it too far. I know it is.

I can't agree to that.

LAURA'S DIARY
MARCH

My office life has gone to shit since the unfortunate incident at Tyler Bard's party. I was mortified by what happened, not to mention additionally mortified to be in such a condition in front of my parents. Thank goodness I have such a forgiving family who pointed out that everybody makes those mistakes sometimes and that I had nothing to feel guilty about. I resolved to put it behind me and move on.

If only the same could be said for the reaction at work.

The press officer who had invited us was on the phone with my editor the next morning, complaining about the behaviour of a Gleam person the previous night – and it was clear who she was referring to. I don't remember anything, but it seems in my drunken state I harangued her when Tyler failed to turn up – and then became rude and aggressive towards her and several other people when he ignored me. Apparently, she told my editor that being invited to such an event did not give guests a free pass to hang out with the talent and that the way this person (i.e. me) had acted was unacceptable.

This did not bode well. My editor wanted to know what had happened, and when I couldn't bring myself to admit it, she summoned my two colleagues. I watched nervously as Queen Bee entered her office, her blonde hair streaming across her shoulders like a golden cloak. How could she look so fresh-faced after the amount she drank even before the party last night – while I was nursing the hangover from hell? Life is so unfair sometimes. She had a look on her face that suggested she was about to cause trouble for me –and I prayed that the pair of them would have my back.

My hopes were soon dashed as she told our editor how drunk and out of control I was, that she had seen me shouting and swearing at people (did she? I thought she spent half the time in the corner flirting with that blond guy) and that she practically had to drag me out of the club before returning me to my parents in a semi-conscious state.

All of this was bad enough. Even though I had hoped she might defend me, I could still cope with her telling my editor the facts because I deserve that much. She took it further and told her that I ran up to Tyler, tried to kiss him in front of everybody – and refused to let go of him when I was asked to stop.

This is a flat-out lie. And she has said it for no reason other than to get me in trouble. It is a cardinal rule we must always treat talent with the utmost respect – almost as if they are royalty. She made it sound as though I sexually harassed the poor boy, but I didn't lay a hand on him.

I crossed my fingers behind my back and hoped my other colleague would suggest none of this was true. She took her friend's side. Inevitable. If my colleague hadn't said that my editor might have fought my corner, pointed out that I was new to the job and that it was a one-time mistake which would not be repeated.

That little lie is going to do me some serious damage. Judging by the smug way my colleague looked at me in the editor's office as she tore the inevitable strips off me, she knows it too. For my part, I couldn't understand why she was so furious at the claim I had thrown myself at Tyler. I can't be the first journalist to have tried it on with a celebrity. I wouldn't put it past Queen Bee to have done so.

I returned to my desk, feeling as small as the dust mites on the carpet. I tried to overlook the brain fog of the morning after, to ask Queen Bee why she had said those things about me – and why it had provoked such a strong reaction,

"Oh, please, Laura," she sneered. "You wanted to do that to Tyler all evening; don't pretend you didn't – you haven't shut up about him since you did that interview, it's so pathetic."

125

Before I could open my mouth to reply, she dropped the bombshell I wasn't expecting.

"You're only getting what you deserve," she added. "What did you expect happens when you start going after your boss's boyfriend?"

ELENA

When I said eating out might be fun today, this wasn't what I had in mind.

No, this is a gazillion times better. Because I'm spread-eagled on Daniel's kitchen island and my knickers are draped over his horrible artisan mug tree, and Nathan has burrowed his head between my thighs, his tongue expertly teasing the sweet spot that my clueless boyfriend's always ignored.

As he whips me into a frenzy with each flicker, thoughts of that dreadful morning at work melt away. Fuck Katja. Just fuck her.

I bet nobody's licking her like she's a waffle cone right now.

Things escalated rapidly after that kiss. I told work I'd developed a migraine and was leaving, and we practically sprinted back to Daniel's place. We started snogging again the second the lift doors closed, hands sliding up tops and down trousers, as we did, and pretty much tore each other's clothes off in the flat. I've never felt so desperate for someone before.

What a fantastic release of tension. What a waste of an expensive silk shirt.

The more I writhe around the marble worktop, my excitement levels at fever pitch, the more enthusiastic Nathan gets – and seconds later, he makes me come with an intensity that takes my breath away, all of my nerve endings combusting at once. My legs have turned to custard. I may well be stranded on this worktop for life. Lord knows what any neighbour within listening distance must be thinking.

Not bad for a grey Wednesday afternoon.

Once I scrape myself off the ceiling and return to planet Earth, I notice the mug tree is on the floor. It's been joined by the latest issue of Daniel's dull-as-ditchwater *Law Society Gazette* scrunched into a ball.

My head whirls and my heart goes like the clappers. In six minutes, Nathan has achieved more than Daniel managed in six months. As I fight to catch my breath, he emerges from my crotch and leans in close.

"Was that good?" he says with a devilish grin I've never seen before. I throw him a look somewhere between tipsy and smitten and full-blown hero worship.

Does he need to ask? The mental pictures I'll have next time I lurch into the kitchen at six in the morning for a bowl of Frosties, don't bear thinking about. I'm euphoric and I sense we're just getting warmed up.

Several moments and a lot more fooling around later, we're having mind-melting sex on the faux fur rug in the open-plan living area, Nathan panting on top of me as I wrap my legs tightly around him and try not to think about the 'tingling intimate gel' I spilt over the tufts of fur. The damn thing cost a fortune, the finest floor decor John Lewis has to offer, but whatever. It's not known as a shag rug for nothing. We've already defiled the entire flat with a trail of lust anyway. That 'Living my Best Life' mug I swiped from work smashed to smithereens. My favourite leopard-print push-up bra knotted around the potted palm in the living room, and that tell-tale foil from the condom wrapper sitting between the guavas in the middle of the fruit bowl? Don't even go there.

The kitchen island was blissful, but this is on another level, and it comes without a soup ladle poking into my left butt cheek. All those filthy fantasies I've had about Nathan when he was sitting next to me in work meetings, and I was pretending to be engrossed in Paula's latest PowerPoint presentation have come true. And they're everything I hoped for. Daniel doesn't even cross my mind.

Until, when we're both on the brink, my phone – sitting under the coffee table where I dropped my bag – pipes up. Habanera from *Carmen*. Barely inches from us. Shit. It's Daniel.

That's his ringtone. Of all the moments, my conscience decides to wake up from its nap.

"Oh God...we shouldn't...we mustn't...what am I..." I gasp, my brain in overdrive, my hand inching away from Nathan's and towards the handset. What if I called him by mistake?

What if he heard everything? What if he's watching us, secretly via a long-range camera while attending a seminar about contract negotiation? It's too late to stop now. Not that I want to. Now I know what I've been missing all these months. My free hand makes contact with the handset to push it away, but as it does, my body floods with a sensation so stunning that my mind instantly shuts off like a Sky box in a thunderstorm. And as I lose sense of everything, letting off a high-pitched squeal and gripping the still-ringing phone so tightly it feels like it might shatter, Nathan reaches the point of no return. "God...Elena!!" he cries out before he collapses on to me, spent, covering me in sweat as he does. He's landed awkwardly on my left leg, and I can already sense pins and needles shooting all the way up it as reality once again descends.

However uncomfortable I might be feeling as we lie together on the floor in a clammy, breathless tangle of limbs, nothing else matters at that moment as he gazes at me in pure exhilaration and utters a single word: "Wow."

In that second, the phone falls silent, clattering out of my grip, and my guilt vanishes.

Never to return.

THE PRESENT

Daniel is surprised when his call goes unanswered. It rings several times before snapping to voicemail:

Hi, it's Elena. I'm probably out chasing a K-Pop exclusive right now, so leave me a message, and I'll call you right back!

This isn't like her. He's only been gone a couple of days. Has she forgotten that he hates it when she ignores his calls? He only wanted to ask her to water the palm tree and make sure the fruit bowl was stocked for his return tomorrow night. Knowing her, she'll have eaten all the guavas by now.

He hopes Elena will use the time constructively to think about his proposal. She's moving in soon after he gets back, and as far as he's concerned, the time is right to take things to that next level. Fingers crossed, a little separation will enable her to see that, too. Absence makes the heart grow fonder, after all.

Daniel calls again several minutes later, but the phone rings out for a second time. She's prioritising her work over him, by the looks of it. He's about to abandon his principles and leave her a message when his boss appears. Damn. The chat with Elena will have to wait until later since his boss is the only person in the entire world he has any respect for. He decides to give her the benefit of the doubt just this once. Perhaps she's in a meeting at work or out doing an interview.

Either way, it sounds as if she's got her hands full.

ELENA

Nathan and I are cuddled up on the sofa under Daniel's super-pricey Hermes throw, giggling like a couple of newlyweds as we smoke the remainder of the weed.

Afterglow. Another thing Daniel has never bothered with. He calls again. This time, the phone is within easy reach. I put it on silent after that little incident, yet here it is, buzzing on the coffee table. The sense of panic returns.

"Shit! It's my boyfriend! What if he knows about us?"

"Hey, calm down!" Nathan's voice is a contented murmur. "You said he was miles away! Tell you what…I'll talk to him."

"No! Nathan!" He can't be serious, and I move to block him. He gets there first, whisking the phone off the table. "Oh, hi there," he says into the handset, "I'm here on the couch with your lovely girl-friend. Did you know she squeaks like a guinea pig when she's turned on?" It's obvious he hasn't answered it. I'm done with his joking around and play-wrestle him into the cushions. The phone flies out of his hand. It skitters across the solid oak floor, coming to a rest in the corner and stops ringing.

"Behave!" I shout. He doubles up with laughter, but seconds later, we're kissing again, and I realise I can't stay angry with him for long. "I don't think Daniel would find that funny!" I tell him when we finally come up for air.

I swear the colour drains from his face. "What did you say his name was?"

"Daniel! Daniel Carrington from our legal team. Do you know him then?"

"Know him? Does banging his ex-girlfriend at the work Christmas party count?"

"Sorry, what? You're joking!" This is news to me. Nathan is serious. "How? When? He never said a word!" I can't decide if I'm horrified or amused. I ought to throw him out and send him a cleaning bill for the soft furnishings we've violated.

I'm itching to know what happened.

"OK," he says. "It was a few years ago before you joined the company. The party was the usual crap – close-up magicians, casino tables, people jumping around like idiots to that Mariah Carey song. And then this gorgeous woman, Andrea, walks up. We got talking. She said she was pissed off with her boyfriend, that she'd only been with him a few months, and he was already pressuring her into having his kids or something."

I can't speak. That's what he's been doing to me.

"I'm taken aback by this whole *Handmaid's Tale* shit he's got going on. I showed her a good time – champagne and tequila shots. They had this freaky playroom for the guests and we wound up doing coke in the ball pit.'

"You did cocaine at a work party? That's a sackable offence!"

"All right, Judge Judy! You think nobody else was?"

"Do you often do that kind of thing?" I can cope with Nathan being a pothead, but nose candy? I'm not sure what to think.

"Well, I don't go home on a Monday night and do bumps off my neighbour's arse in front of *News at Ten* if that's what you're thinking," he says, sounding indignant. "What, you've never done anything like that before? Oh, I don't touch drugs, she says while smoking my expensive weed! I bet you would if I served them on a solid gold platter and cut them with a platinum credit card."

"Stop it!" I tease, snuggling into his shoulder. I've never been with a man like Nathan, someone so dangerous and yet so wonderful. He could confess to selling crystal meth to pensioners from his mum's basement, and I'd still be entranced. "What happened next?"

"Oh, I went back to hers, and she fucked my brains out," he says, with all the casualness of someone telling you they've stuck the kettle on. "Daniel caught us. He was raging. He kept threatening to deck me. As if. Dude looks like he couldn't punch his way out of a crisp packet. Then he started chucking all my stuff out the bedroom window, so I escaped, slid down the drainpipe. Left half my stuff behind, had to flag down a cab in my pants. Never did get my trousers back. Not my finest hour." He shrugs, exhaling a plume of fragrant smoke across the blanket. "Seriously though, what are you doing with that desperate fucker? Andrea said he's shit in bed too."

I'm horrified. "I don't see how that's any of your business!"

"Oh, come on! You don't strike me as the cheating type. You're so sweet and proper, and you were the one who suggested this! Just saying. I don't think you'd have dragged me here and ripped my clothes off like a crazed animal if he was meeting your needs on that front."

He's hit the nail on the head. I've never cheated on a partner before. "You know, I'm a decent listener," he says in a softer tone. "If there's anything you want to talk about."

"OK, I admit it," I say. "He's asked me to give up work and have his bloody kids, and I don't want to. And after what you've told me, I'm even less convinced."

"I'm not surprised! He claims he loves you, and he wants you to quit your job? The very essence of you? As if anyone would suggest you do that! I hope you said no."

"I'm so confused. He could give me a great life I'd never want for anything. But it's all on his terms. See, I'm about all things being equal. It's the same with kids – he'd be so busy being rich and important I wouldn't get a shred of help. That's what worries me most."

Nathan says nothing, and pulls me closer, a gesture that says he gets it. I wonder if there's any going back for my relationship after this. Maybe I can still salvage it. I can chalk it up to a moment of madness that Daniel need never know about. Mistakes happen, as Nathan has pointed out. I can ask him to leave, tell him I got pissed off and carried away. I could blame the events of earlier. It was Freddy Taylor's fault. Mrs Damp Haddock. Katja Lake. The axis of evil.

If only I could bring myself to do it.

"What do you think I should do then?" I ask.

"That's up to you," Nathan says, toying with my hair. "Promise me you won't do anything stupid."

"It's too late for that." I move in towards him, and seconds later, we're smooching so passionately I half expect steam to rise from the sofa cushions.

I'm powerless to resist. "Do you want to stay here tonight?" I ask. I mean what the hell.

That's when he claps his eyes on the mantelpiece clock.

NATHAN

Help! It's one minute to five and Elena is kissing my neck like she wants to go in for round two.

Doesn't she realise it's one minute to five? Seeing the clock brings me back to reality with a jolt.

I need to get out of here right now.

"Shit!" I tear myself away, spring from the sofa in a panic, and head for the bathroom to clean up before she has time to register what's going on. Everything feels surreal. The smell of her perfume all over me. The fact that my dick feels as though it's been through a spin cycle. The realisation that this happened in the first place. It might have been the most mind-blowing shag of my entire life.

Thank fuck for a power shower to wash my sins away. All of it down the plughole like it never happened. I rinse my mouth out, steal some of Daniel's Tom Ford because he's such a rich bastard he can afford gallons of it, and try to locate my clothes as quickly as possible. Elena calls me from the living room. I ignore it, as bad as it makes me feel. I need to get back before I have to face any awkward questions. She's not the only one who's had a crazy time on an overpriced rug with the wrong person.

I'm dressed and in the middle of retrieving my left boot from a dark corner when I see her standing in the doorway, wrapped in a pink satin robe. God, she's gorgeous. That blonde hair, those stunning green eyes, that fantastic body that she's kept hidden under those outfits of hers the whole time. How did I never notice any of this before? Imagine what we could get up to if I did stay. No. Stop it, brain. This is not the time.

"Nathan...what's going on?"

"Elena...I'm so sorry, I forgot I have an appointment." We both know that's bollocks.

She looks wounded, as though I'm rejecting her. It's killing me to go, but what choice do I have?

"Yeah...OK." There's a pause. "Did I do something wrong? Is that why you're leaving so abruptly?"

Damn it. "No! No, of course not!" I pull her into an awkward embrace. "You're amazing. I'm glad you had fun today. I did, too. See you at work tomorrow, yeah?"

I kiss her on the forehead, and I'm gone. Knowing I didn't handle that at all well.

At least, not if I don't want her to suspect something.

The Jubilee Line home is noisy, stifling, and packed to the rafters. I'm convinced every person in my carriage knows what I've been up to. Screw them. I was meant to be back an hour ago, but I have to get my story straight:

1. *The film I didn't go and see turned out to be a four-hour fantasy epic.*

2. *I craved a kebab from that local place where the shawarma comes with a side of salmonella.*

3. *My best mate asked if I could come round and help him assemble an Ikea bookcase.*

4. *I was abducted by aliens.*

I'm rambling. I can't think about much else except Elena. Little Miss Flawless. The last person I ever thought I'd end up fucking. Except I don't want to call it that. It didn't feel like some fun but meaningless encounter, like all those others.

It felt…incredible.

Would I have slept with Elena if I had been happy with my circumstances? Doubt it. I sense she isn't happy with hers either. I don't think Daniel's treating her well. That worries me. I can tell he's the type who doesn't have a fork out of place in his kitchen and only ever has stupid organic rabbit food in his fridge. A no-fun zone, in other words. No wonder his girlfriends find him such hard work.

What happens now? I know I can't be Elena's boyfriend. Although I'm not sure she would want me to be, if she knew the truth about my situation. That doesn't mean we can't have a little fun, and if we do, maybe those difficult questions won't have to be answered.

I make it as far as the walk from the station before I'm messaging her, trying to make out I have nothing to hide:

Missing me already? What are you up to?

The reply arrives moments later:

I'm lying in bed, watching *RuPaul's Drag Race*. And I've just eaten all the salted caramel ice-cream in the freezer. I was so hungry – best thing I've put in my mouth all day

Cute. Typical Elena. I'm typing out a flirty – but not too flirty – response when another message comes through, one which makes me practically spit out the water I'm drinking. It reads:

Actually, make that second best

ELENA

"You can't let it go, can you?"

I am taken aback by James's curt response to my latest whinge about Katja. Seeing him trot off to do yet another interview that should have been mine over the past couple of weeks has got to me. I thought if anybody would understand, it would be him. Apparently not.

"I thought, being my friend, you would understand."

"Look, I'm sorry you're stuck in the office, OK? Blaming Katja because you've got some – agenda – against her is wrong, Elena. She doesn't have anything against you. You're struggling to get used to her way of working, that's all."

"James…"

"Enough now!" he snaps. "Nobody else has had any problems with Katja and her working methods. You need to stop this. You've done enough damage to your relations in the office as it is."

With that, the glass office door bangs and James is gone. I am left desolate in his wake, looking for something to improve my day. I get it when I return to my desk and see the magic words: '**Nathan Flynn is typing**…' flash up on my Squawk board. The message arrives seconds later:

Nathan
Ignore the bastard. Lunch?

139

Hell yes. I know what he means; it doesn't involve any actual lunch. I'm still smiling at the thought of our first afternoon together, even if it did come to such an abrupt end. I didn't intend for it to happen again – but it did, in spite of myself. A few days later there was a repeat performance. By our fourth secret encounter, I was so hungry for him I'd given up trying to resist. If Daniel is a tiny portion of nouvelle cuisine, Nathan's an all-you-can-eat buffet, the sort you want to fill your plate at time and time again. I know which meal I prefer.

Does he care that I still have a boyfriend? It doesn't seem that way, especially given he lost any respect he might have had for Daniel after finding out his intentions for me. Which might explain why I emerged from the bathroom after one lunchtime tryst last week to find him naked in the kitchen, parading his bare arse around the room while helping himself to Daniel's expensive blueberry yoghurt. It's different when I do it, OK? And besides, I wasn't exactly complaining about the view. I couldn't help thinking it was his way of punishing Daniel for his behaviour. That yoghurt was hand-fermented from Himalayan Yak's milk cultures, not easy to find in Tesco next to the Petits Filous. But I am fast learning that Nathan does what Nathan wants without too much concern for what anybody else thinks.

As for the sex, I've never known anything like it. We can't keep our hands off each other, and we don't want to, doing it all over the flat (or at least most of it – I can't bring myself to go near Daniel's bed) in positions that would make a porn star blush. I swear he almost had me standing on my head at one point. Our chats on the way back to the office from our 'lunchtime workouts' are just as revealing as we're learning so much more about each other. We don't see eye to eye on everything; my idea of a great holiday is sizzling by a pool some- where – the hotter the better – whereas he regards anything over twenty-one degrees Celsius as an unbearable heatwave. "I crisp up like a lobster," he told me. "It's not pretty." And I can probably live without his *Game of Thrones* obsession or his Saturday afternoon habit of chucking two hours of his life down the drain watching football.

But there's so much we do have in common. If I'd known all this time, the guy sitting two desks away loves decent red wine, and stand-up comedy, and the same Noughties indie bands I loved at uni, I'd have got to know him a lot sooner. Then there's that shared love of 90s blockbusters, the one which led to us spending a whole afternoon quoting lines from the Nicolas Cage movie marathon to one another via Squawk.

Of course, that conversation made a sweetly innocent change from his more X-rated messages. They might make me shiver with antici-pation, but I've had to ask him to use WhatsApp instead after one particularly salacious note flashed up while Paula was standing next to my desk, and I closed my browser with seconds to spare:

Would you miss that lace thong of yours terribly if I ripped it off with my teeth?

I almost fell off my chair with embarrassment. Not that I was quite so bothered when he actually did it later on.

I can't shake the feeling he's hiding something from me though. He seems reluctant for us to meet anywhere other than Daniel's flat dur-ing our lunch breaks, fobbing me off when I suggested we go to his place – saying he's got the builders in or there's a problem with the drains. Anything to keep me away it seems.

Lindsey was equally suspicious when I confessed the fling – and Nathan's odd behaviour – over margaritas a couple of weeks ago: "Oh my God, Elena! Are you sure that's a good idea? He sounds like he's got a girlfriend already. Or wife. And you're still with Daniel."

Don't I know it. I've been trying to end things with him since my fling with Nathan started. It's the right thing to do under the circumstances. Whenever I try it's as if there's a golf ball stuck in my throat. I've had no choice other than to move in with him because Lindsey's rented my room out to some pot-smoking tree-hugger from Gleam's HR department, but I can't keep this up forever. Despite Lindsey's warning, I can't bring myself to give Nathan up either. Being with him is intoxicating, like a drug I can't kick. To me, he's more than a friend with benefits. He stimulates my mind and other organs, listens to me when I'm in rant mode, and makes me laugh. I can't remember the last time my actual boyfriend did that.

Nathan gives me the best news I've had in months when he pops around to see me on a day off. I'm waiting for him in that pink satin robe he likes so much (and not a lot else), and when he walks in, I leap into his arms, wrapping my legs around his waist as I cover him in kisses. We waste no time getting busy – because you can't when you only have an hour for lunch. It's only after we've tumbled on to the sofa that he tells me.

"The nominations for the Publishers' Awards are out," Nathan says, "and you're on them."

I sit bolt upright. "You're joking. For what?"

"Exclusive of the Year, the one about the TV judge, obviously. Well done you!" His hands disappear up my robe, every millimetre of my body standing to attention, as usual.

But for once my mind is elsewhere.

I'm staggered by his news. The Publisher's Awards is the company's biggest night of the year. Everybody from the people in the boardroom upstairs to those who work on our more – shall we say, specialist – websites at that mysterious office in the provinces put on their best clothes and gather under one roof to honour the year's biggest achievers. We get fed, we get well watered and it all ends in a tacky but brilliant disco, with no cheesy dancefloor filler left unplayed. If you haven't ended up in a conga line with the chief sub of *Salmon Fishing Gazette* by the end of the night, consider yourself to have failed in life.

This year, I'm one of the nominees. For one of the most hotly contested awards of the whole damn event, no less. That story was huge, a scoop I picked up about a presenter leaving a certain TV show following a financial dispute that the producers tried in vain to cover up. Maybe this will be the thing that finally forces Katja to respect me.

I play the scenario in my head, the one where I take the prize, looking as smug as hell on the podium as he sits there, crushed. It's cut off as Nathan pulls me in close. My robe drops to the floor next to his long-discarded T-shirt. "What do you want to do today then?" he asks in a breathy growl that makes my spine wilt. Straight away, I know the answer.

I want to think about which shoes go best with pink.

THE PRESENT

Daniel finds Elena on their bed, shoehorning on a pair of shiny nude heels. They are getting ready to join her family at a pricey Sunday lunch for her dad's birthday, although Daniel is more interested in the food than the company. He finds Elena's folks tedious and will have to endure a whole afternoon of them asking her which celebrities she's met lately, something they seem to find fascinating above and beyond everything else. Like his job, for example.

It doesn't matter. He has nothing to say to them anyway. He has no intention of stopping Elena from seeing her parents once they are married. She will be birthing their grandchildren after all. But he will use his powers of persuasion to ensure his family gets the lion's share of their time. He doesn't trust Elena's mum – who looks like an older version of Elena, with the same perfect hair and make-up, but none of the intelligence – to look after their baby for a second. She'd probably drop it. Goodness knows how she managed to raise a daughter.

"Is this yours?" he asks Elena, who looks up at him with her sweetest smile. Bless her. So devoted. He hasn't had to lift a finger around the flat since she moved in. Long may it continue.

"What's up?" she asks.

"Wondered if this was yours? I found it under one of the sofa cushions just now."

He extends his hand to reveal a small diamond ear stud.

Elena looks mystified as if she's never seen it before, but Daniel persists. "Nice diamond, that one. Wouldn't want you losing it."

"I – oh no, that's not mine. It's Lindsey's, she must have dropped it when she was here the other day. I'll give it back to her when I see her next."

He doesn't question her explanation. "No problem," he says, handing her the little sparkly stud. "Shame I missed Lindsey; you should have her round for dinner one night."

As if. That's one invitation that won't be forthcoming. Daniel can't stand Lindsey, and senses she doesn't like him much either. If she came for dinner she'd be drunk and making boorish jokes before the garlic baguettes had even been served. You couldn't take her anywhere.

But he'll say anything to keep Elena sweet. He is pleased to see she is wearing the dress he bought her, a long flowing number in a deep indigo blue. Much more flattering than all those pink things she insists on wearing.

"We'd better get going," he says, disappearing into the ensuite, "We don't want to hit traffic."

He means it. Daniel hates being late for anything, and it'll take them at least forty-five minutes to get across London to lunch in Jermyn Street. Forty-five minutes, in which he'll have Elena all to himself, with a whole lot to discuss – and no means of escape like she had from Sushisamba.

Good.

ELENA

My heart thumps so loudly I'm surprised Daniel can't hear it in the ensuite. I don't need that kind of thing to happen. It'll send my blood pressure through the roof.

The earring Daniel found has to be Nathan's. It must have fallen out during our session the other day. Thank God, he believed me about it being Lindsey's, although I hope that dinner he suggested doesn't happen. For one thing, they barely tolerate each other. For another, he might be confused if he notices she doesn't have pierced ears.

I take several deep breaths, grab my phone, take a stealthy snap of the stud, and fire off a message to Nathan:

Lost something?

The reply comes in seconds:

Shit, thank you! I've been looking for that everywhere, my parents bought it for me! Hope that fuckwit boyfriend of yours didn't see it

The words blaze onto the little screen as Daniel walks back in, and my hands shake so much that the phone drops to the floor. He doesn't see what Nathan has written as he returns it. I heave an inward sigh of relief.

My shattered nerves, on the other hand, may take longer to fix.

I have Daniel alone as the Jaguar purrs through the streets. We're en route to my dad's birthday lunch, and the last thing I want to do is ruin his big day by dumping my boyfriend. But when will I get as good a chance as this to address my feelings – or lack of – for him?

He gets there first. though.

"Elena," he says, voice soft and meaningful, "I don't suppose you've thought any more about my suggestion from the other week?"

Something jolts inside me. "Which suggestion?"

"About moving on from Spark?"

I knew it. He was waiting for a moment to get me alone. "Ah…Daniel, I don't think now's the best time. You know Paula's pregnant, which might mean another shot at promotion, and I've been nominated for that big award. Why should I walk away now?"

I can hear the note of exasperation in his answer. "You know, Elena – it would have been lovely to go to your dad's party today and give them some news about starting a family. You know how much your folks want that and I do too. So, what's the problem here? It feels like you're fobbing me off."

I don't want this. I don't want any of this. I see frown lines sketched across his face and wonder whether his family is pressuring him to settle down. If that is the case, I wish he'd told me sooner, back when I thought we still had a future. We might have been able to work through it together. It's too late now. I won't have him snapping his fingers and expecting me to fall in line.

"I don't know if it's the right time."

"When will it be? You know I'm ready for this, Elena, it – disappoints me that we don't seem to be on the same page. What is it you're worried about?"

How about I don't love you and you won't support me, for starters?
The uncomfortable silence that follows his question hangs between
the gear stick for ages.

"What is it then? You care more about your career than about us?"
The restaurant looms into sight, much to my relief. Daniel is not
done. He pulls the Jag into a side street and activates the child lock so
I can't escape. "I don't get it Elena, what is it about your job that you
can't bear to give it up? I mean, if you were negotiating world peace
in the UN or helping victims of oppression, I could get it. But all you
do is spend your days writing crap about what Z-list talent vacuums
have said on social media. Hardly a worthy use of your time, is it?"

The fury is rising so far up my throat I can't find the words. Instead, I content myself with mental pictures of Daniel driving his beloved car off a cliff and being reduced to a small blob of plasma in the
ensuing fireball. The scent of Tom Ford Noir is overpowering. I'm
starting to hate it.

I'm not expecting what comes next.

"I'll make the decision for you then," he says. "I know it's a lot to
think about, but I've given you so much time already. I know you're
excited about the awards – so how about we talk about this again once
they're over?"

I struggle to hide the anguish on my face. The awards are less than
a month away.

"What I mean is, you will have an answer for me by then Elena,
I've waited long enough. If you love me, you'll say yes, otherwise I'm
not sure we have a future. Given Lindsey's rented your room out I'm
wondering where you'll go if I don't have a place for you in my life
any more." He peers across to my impassive expression, the one dis-
guising my true feelings, and clasps my knee a little too hard. "I'm not
sure someone of your high standards would cope well with being
homeless. Think about it."

He zaps the car doors open with his remote key fob like he's in bloody *Fast and Furious 27* and hops out as though none of this had ever happened. He doesn't see me gripping the leather seat so tightly I might put a fist through it.

There's a new thought racing through my head now. *I don't fucking want your fucking kids Daniel. Because I'm so fucking disillusioned with your fucking emotional blackmail that I'm fucking your arch fucking enemy.*

In your fucking flat.

KATJA

I'm starving. Who wouldn't be after days of eating grey scrambled eggs and dried-up quail's egg sandwiches in that listeria-laden work canteen?

You can't blame me for wanting some proper food now it's Sunday. So here I am, sitting in a lovely West End restaurant, innocently sharing a Bloody Mary and a plate of smoked salmon with my best friend, Alexandra. Waiting for a decent Sunday roast. A sirloin of beef with mustard and some goose fat roast potatoes ought to do it. Maybe a side of cauliflower cheese made with extra mature Cheddar. And a Yorkshire pudding. I could murder a Yorkshire pudding. I haven't had one in ages. I wonder if there's another diner I can persuade to fork out their credit card? My question is answered seconds later when who should walk through the door, but Elena.

She's surrounded by people, chatting away as she clings to the arm of some well-dressed guy. Is that her boyfriend? I know him, he's that uptight twat from our legal department who wouldn't let me run a story about two soap stars having a secret fling. Said the photo was too blurry to prove it was them. Stupid know-it-all.

Wait. She's seen me. The look on her face suggests I was the last person she was expecting.

"Elena? What are you doing here?" I shout, with the same look of surprise I give my doctor when she tells me I need to keep taking my meds. There's nothing wrong with me that ruining Elena's life won't cure. "What a coincidence!"

Coincidence my fanny. If she doesn't want me to know she's going out for a lovely family lunch, don't bloody discuss the details on the phone with Daddy Dearest in the office kitchen. She's too stunned to reply. What the hell is she wearing? It looks like a blackout curtain. Somebody save me. My cheeks hurt from all this fake smiling.

Luckily, the guy next to her dives in. "Is this a friend of yours?" He gestures to me.

This must be her dad. Wow! Sexy older man! Bit of Martin Kemp about him. I'd ride him into next week if I had half the chance.

"Is this your dad?" I ask. "Couldn't help noticing the family resemblance! I'm Katja – Elena and I work together. Lovely to meet you, Mr Robins!"

"You too! I've always wanted to meet one of Elena's colleagues! How bizarre you should be here!"

"Oh, I love this place. Best Sunday roast in London."

At least TripAdvisor thinks it is. I've never been here, but there's no harm in doing a little research to make it look like I have. That's the cue for the rest of the family to gather round me, and soon, we're the centre of attention. I notice how much Elena's mum looks like her. She's as overdressed as her daughter usually is, with too-bright lipstick and suspiciously orange cheeks. I still can't help feeling sorry for her. Imagine having to push someone like Elena out of her raddled old clunge.

For a moment, I think they're going to walk past to their table, and that'll be it. A brief exchange, enough to unsettle Elena during her family outing but not to do any real harm. Until the unexpected invitation tumbles into my lap.

"Would you like to join us?" her dad says as he edges up to our table. My face lights up with fake delight.

"Oh, that's lovely of you – but we wouldn't want to intrude!"

"I promise you, you wouldn't be! "It's my birthday – the more, the merrier! Any colleague of Elena's is a friend of ours."

"Well, as long as you're sure." Her dad helps Alexandra and I move our table until it joins theirs. Out of the corner of my eye, I can see Elena's look of pure fury. It occurs to me I could have taken a different tack here. I could tell Elena's family what kind of person she is before strutting triumphantly from the room in slow motion, my hair buffeted by a wind machine and applause ringing in my ears.

But where would the fun be in that?

Elena's on edge. The Sunday roast is as delicious as the reviews suggested but she's pushing her food around her plate and eating very little. She's getting through a lot of wine, though. I pretend not to notice, as I've been too busy feigning interest in her uncle and his appalling dad jokes. He keeps trying to sell me a story about his next-door neighbour, whose brother's cousin is a magician who auditioned for *Britain's Got Talent* and is doing panto. As if I'm interested. He can fuck right off and take his end-of-the-pier shit with him.

He's harmless, so I let him chunter on while I turn my attention to his daughter Nina, a greasy-haired sad sack wearing a knitted hedgehog jumper. I've never met someone more likely to be a virgin in my life. Nina appears to be the sort of person who spends her days sitting in a darkened room arguing with strangers on the internet about which order you watch the *Lord of the Rings* movies in. But she claims to be close to Elena, which it's hard to believe. As if she would ever tolerate such a sorry excuse for a human.

"So, what do you do at Spark?" she asks. I spear a piece of charred broccoli from the plate on the table. It's Elena's favourite, or so I'm told. I'm sure she won't mind me helping myself since she doesn't want it.

"I'm the deputy editor," I tell her with a broad, fake smile. "I've only been there a few months, but Elena's been wonderful."

"I'd love a job like yours," Nina adds. "I find it so hard to keep jobs. I've always wanted to work somewhere like Spark."

Another loser who thinks they can do this job. If I had a pound for everyone who's ever said that to me, I'd be living it up on a Caribbean island right now. Not eating a £100-a-head Sunday lunch with these abysmal people.

Her next comment catches me off guard. "I sent my CV to Elena a few weeks ago," she tells me. "I was hoping she could help me find a job there, but I've not heard back from her.

Maybe you could put in a word?"

Wow. She's known me for five minutes and is already asking me for a job. She's either dumb or desperate. Or both. I open my mouth to reply but luckily, Elena's dad saves me. "More wine?" He tops up my glass without waiting for a response.

"I never say no to more wine." I flutter my eyelashes, long enough for Elena to notice, look horrified that I'm flirting with her father and reach for her glass. Nina drones on about her worthless life, and I pretend to listen while planning my next move. It comes moments later when Elena and whatever-his-name-is leave the table. She looks annoyed about something, he follows. Interesting. Not my problem. I slide into her seat next to Elena's parents. I chatter away to them about what an asset their daughter is to the team, and notice she's left half her roast beef uneaten on the plate. What the hell, I think, tucking in to her leftovers. I know Elena's grubby paws have been all over it. But I'm reluctant to let decent food go to waste.

She's got a face like thunder when they return a few minutes later. Trouble in paradise?

She sees me sitting in the place that ought to be hers.

"Katja – my seat?" she says. Like I care. The only thing concerning me at the moment is her disgusting perfume, Eau de Pensioner's Dressing Table. The sort of lavender-scented crap someone gifts you at Christmas, and you wear to be polite before encasing it in a hermetically-sealed box and throwing it into the English Channel.

"Oh Elena, I'm so sorry!" If I widen my eyes any more, they'll fall out onto her plate. "Your dad told me about your journalistic ambitions as a child."

"That's right!" he says. "When Elena was seven, she used to play a game where she'd pretend to be the host of a chat show, and we'd be her guests. She put us on the spot with some of her questions! I always knew she'd end up doing what she does."

"Oh, that doesn't surprise me. Elena's our star interviewer, always meeting the big names. Who was that one you met recently – Freddy Taylor, wasn't it? Lucky you – bet the girls in the office were jealous!"

Elena turns puce at my little jibe as though her head is about to combust. Before she responds an enormous cake piled high with macarons, chocolate curls and lit sparklers arrives at the table. The twat collective sings Happy Birthday. Quite the distraction, and I sing the loudest of all. As though I mean it. Once the chorus of cheering and shouting of 'speech!' finally comes to an end, I realise Elena is not there.

"Shame she had to leave," I hear her dad saying. "She did seem a bit off today. Something to do with her work, maybe."

That's the gorgeous moment when I know my plan is working. I carve a huge slab of cake – chocolate fudge, my favourite – and tuck in. Might as well have Elena's since she isn't here to eat it herself. Besides, I have reason to celebrate. Today couldn't have gone more perfectly.

What's coming next will make it look like a tea party.

Seven Years Ago

LAURA

I need to plan my funeral. It should be a celebration of my life. Everyone wearing orange and sharing their memories of me.

First things first, what songs should I have:

You Raise Me Up? No, never. Unless they change the title to *You Push Me Down.*

Flying Without Wings? Well, that's obvious. If I had wings, I wouldn't be in this mess.

Defying Gravity? Not funny.

When I'm Cleaning Windows? Stop it now, just stop it!

What about a song called Falling? That gives me a few choices. Alicia Keys? The theme from *Twin Peaks*, that show my dad used to watch? The murder victim was called Laura. How ironic.

Why am I bothering coming up with a falling song when I'm too busy doing it for real? I can't exactly leave my family a note about my dream funeral, can I? If I could though, the one thing I would wish for is that she isn't even allowed near it.

Not after the events that followed the party from hell.

MARCH

My reputation at work has been destroyed. It's all Queen Bee's fault. Things might have blown over if she hadn't lied about my behaviour. However, the suggestion that I made a pass at my boss's boyfriend has been too hard to ignore.

How was I supposed to know that she was dating Tyler Bard? I'm not a mind-reader – and nobody told me before I went to interview him. Tyler didn't say a word either. I can only think that my editor told him to keep quiet. Or I was just one of the faceless parade of people who interviewed him that day – and he had no idea who I was.

I wasn't going to stand for this. I went to see my editor and told her Queen Bee had been lying, saying she had left me alone for much of the party, that I would never approach someone like Tyler in that way, and certainly not if I had known his status. I claimed she had been trying to make trouble for me since I arrived. She almost believed it. I could see her through the office's glass door, giving Queen Bee a proper grilling over my accusation that she was a troublemaker. She looked pissed off when she returned to her desk, which gave me a brief moment of satisfaction.

It didn't last long. The next thing I knew, I was called back in, but the look on my editor's face told me it wasn't good news. Instead, she berated me, accusing me of telling lies myself to get out of trouble – telling me I wouldn't get far at Gleam, or indeed in life, with that attitude.

I was stunned. I thought Queen Bee had been getting what she deserved. And now this?

She warned me not to be so underhand in future, and I returned to my desk, bruised and crestfallen.

It was then I learned what she'd done to save herself.

"I thought I was in trouble there for a minute," she told everyone. "Good job my dad was on hand to have a word. It took a while – I had to remind him not to threaten her with the press – but we got there in the

end. I mean, that's what dads are for, isn't it? Have to admit the old guy has his uses."

She saw me staring in her direction, horrified by what she had done to perpetuate her lie, and threw me a look of pure disdain.

ELENA

"Katja isn't my friend, Dad."

I've told him this about ten times already since that awful birthday dinner, and he still doesn't get it. This is why it's coming up again like a dodgy takeaway, during a hasty chat on my way to work.

"That's a shame," he says. "She seems like such a lovely person. I can't think why you wouldn't get along."

"It's complicated."

"Well, you know her better than me. Remember, you can always come to me and your mum if there's a problem."

His voice is so gentle and reassuring that I start to well up. I almost give in and tell him everything. But I need to be a grown-up and solve these things myself, rather than run to Daddy as I have done so many times.

I've barely spoken to Katja after her stunt in the restaurant, ruining a day which Daniel had already trashed beyond repair. He was appalling that afternoon, ordering the roast beef well done before I could ask for it rare and questioning how much wine I had. "Don't you think you should consider cutting back?" he said at one point, "to increase your chances of getting pregnant when the time comes?" I had to drag him out at that point and have words given how close I was to throwing the entire glass in his stupid, smug face. And then Katja lobbed in that Freddy Taylor grenade, and I couldn't stay another minute. Not even for Dad's birthday cake.

Instead, Daniel and I drove home in silence. Did we speak? Did we have a civilised discussion about ovulation charts and upping my folic acid intake? Did we hell.

His ultimatum has knocked me for six, and I don't know what to do. If I cut my losses and end things; where do I go? Yet if I stay, I lose everything I've worked so hard for.

Once I've given in my notice or fallen pregnant with the spawn of Daniel, there's no going back. The thought sends chills through me.

I daren't say a word to Nathan. If I did it might blow our fling wide open, and given the pair don't exactly like each other, who knows how that would end? Nathan's a lot taller and broader than Daniel, who despite his handsome face has an air of the geeky kid who always got pushed into a ditch on the school field trip. If things turned physical between them, it wouldn't be a fair fight. Besides, the thought of the two of them scrapping over me, like something out of an *EastEnders* Christmas special isn't one I want to entertain.

Nathan is so protective. He's got my back at work. He's always sending me cute messages at one in the morning to check I'm OK. Right now, I only forget my troubles when I'm wrapped in his arms during those idyllic stolen lunch breaks. He's acting like a boyfriend would, in other words. So, why isn't *he* my boyfriend? Maybe it's time I raised the issue once and for all. If he can't – or won't – commit, then so be it. If nothing else, I'll know where I stand with him. Even if I don't want to hear it.

At least I also have the awards to distract me. One last night of freedom and celebration.

I'm not looking forward to it as much as I was. And even though I don't want to think about the direction my life might take once it's over I'm going to make the most of it. I've bought a stunning new dress – pale pink chiffon and showered in sparkling sequins. I have silver shoes that are so shiny they'll light up the venue's walls. I'll be waxed and curled and made up to within an inch of my life. I've paid for all of it myself, rather than asking Daniel to fork out, and made a massive dent in my bank account. Guess I'll be bringing in leftovers for lunch for the next fortnight instead of going to Pret.

It'll be worth it. However, I'm feeling on the inside, at least I'll look a million dollars on the outside. Nobody – not Daniel, not Katja – will take that away.

I reach Spark HQ, feeling less excited than I used to about the day ahead. But I am determined to press on. I can hear James's music – louder than usual, when I arrive. I'll be as sweet as I can to him today. Maybe we can pick up where we left off before Katja swooped in and sabotaged my life.

Full of good intentions, I march through the office door – and I am struck dumb. Weird Nina, my step-cousin, is there.

Peeling an orange all over the desk next to mine.

KATJA

I hear the commotion long before I've reached the office. No need to ask what's happened – I already know.

It's that Nina woman. The one I gave a job to. The sort of inept being I would never normally employ because I doubt she can even make a cup of tea without asking where the hot water goes. No matter. She's here, and gripping Elena in a vice-like hug when I walk through the door. "I got a job here! Thank you SO MUCH!" she shouts.

Must feign surprise. The look on Elena's face is indescribable.

"I – how?" She's close to boiling point.

"You should know, I sent you my details," Nina says, puzzled. "I was talking to Katja when we met at that lunch – she offered me a job a week later! She said she needed someone who could come in and help her. I couldn't believe it!"

Who, me? Oh, dear Nina. I can't cope with the flattery. I'm sure you'll be an asset to the team. I'm sure there's plenty I can teach you. Like fashion sense, or social skills, or how to use mouthwash, for example. As for Elena, she could stand to learn a thing or two. Such as emptying the recycle bin on her computer so it isn't full of half-wits' CVs.

"NO!" she screams. "This is NOT happening!" How can she do this?! WHY is she giving you, of all people, a job?"

Nina is taken aback. "I – I thought you'd be pleased," she says in a small voice. "She said I could have this desk next to yours."

161

"Pleased? NO!" Elena's causing a racket now. She needs to pipe down, or we'll have half the staff here. "Why would I be happy she's hired a pointless freeloader?!" She freaks out, grabs the mug from Nina's would-be desk and flings it to the floor. It doesn't break. She can't even do that properly.

Is she trying to have a tantrum? It's comical to watch. The mug is followed by a pile of papers, which cascade everywhere, and the remote control from the office TV. The batteries fly out and roll under the kitchen counter. Oh, Elena. How are we supposed to watch *Come Dine With Me* re-runs with the sound turned down so as not to disturb the news desk now? I'll add it to the list of things you've damaged, shall I?

The anger makes her face even uglier than usual. She's eyeing the printer in the corner as though that might be next in her trail of non-destruction. Instead, she starts on me.

"You did this on purpose!!" she shrieks with a fierce scowl.

Oh, quit it with your conspiracy theories already. Why shouldn't I give Nina a job? There was something about her which tugged at my heartstrings and made me want to help her. I admired her enthusiasm and persistence. She's clearly close to Elena, given how often she calls and messages her. And after the kindness Elena's family showed me by stumping up for my expensive lunch, the least I can do is give them something in return. At least, that's my story, and I'm sticking to it.

Because it sounds so much better than "I drank too much wine and thought, fuck it, that'll piss Elena off big time." It's true. I've never seen her this riled. Maybe flames will shoot from her head. That'd be fun. "I don't want you sitting next to me, Nina!" she's now screeching, "And I don't want you...IN...THIS—"

"Hey Elena, calm down!" James has walked in. My right-hand man, just when I need him most.

"Don't get involved, James! Katja's given her a job – my stupid family member who's incapable of doing a damn thing!"

Oh God, now Nina's crying. It's ear-splitting. She sounds like a rhino forced to listen to power ballads. What the fuck is wrong with this family? James has his arm around Nina, trying to calm her down, and Elena is ranting and swearing like a trooper. "What are you siding with her for?" she roars as I stand, quietly surveying the chaos I have created. "Stay out of this, James! It's her. She's done this because she hates me!"

"Elena! What is going on?!"

Shit. Paula has waddled in, instantly stunning Elena into a quivering silence.

"Paula, I'm sorry about this," I say before anyone else can speak. "It's Nina's first day, and she and Elena had an argument. She got upset." I am wearing my most innocent look. The one I've spent hours perfecting in the mirror so I can throw it out in situations like this.

She sides with me, of course. "Thank you, Katja," she says. "James, do you want to take Nina outside, till she's calmed down?"

"Of course. Come on Nina, come with me, darling. Let's get a cup of tea and have a chat, shall we?"

Nina pipes down and mops her eyes with a filthy shredded tissue. The sort that looks like it's been tucked in her junkyard of a handbag for months. She follows James meekly.

Paula focuses on Elena, eyes like meteorites.

"Right then," she says, "do you want to explain what the hell is going on?

If the news desk were here I would know what they'd say:

BREAKING NEWS

Star showbiz reporter in meltdown:
Spark's Elena Robins loses the plot.

THE PRESENT

Paula removes Elena from the scene of conflict, whisking her to the coffee shop across the road.

Mainly because she knows she won't make a scene in public.

The picture Katja has given her is not good. Abusing a colleague, damaging office property, throwing wild accusations around, disrupting the other desks with her behaviour. This latest outburst is far from ideal, especially given Spark is still paying off the bill for the damage done at the Freddy Taylor interview. They've had to downgrade the teabags in the office kitchen from Teapigs. The standard Spark cuppa now tastes like mouldy gym socks.

By rights, she should sack her on the spot. Yet something is stopping her from doing it.

Elena has always been a model employee – punctual, polite, brilliant at her job and has never damaged so much as a stapler during her time with them.

She can't possibly have changed her character to this extent in such a short space of time unless something was seriously wrong. Personal problems, perhaps? She's been taking longer lunch breaks than usual, coming back late a few times all flushed and full of apologies – which is very unlike her.

"Elena, I'm concerned about your behaviour," she tells her, getting straight to the point. "The way you've been conducting yourself the past few weeks – it's not normal."

"Paula, I'm sorry – truly I am," Elena says in a subdued voice. "Things have become very difficult for me since Katja arrived, and I don't understand why. It almost feels to me as though she is doing it on purpose."

"I don't understand. Why would Katja go out of her way to make your life difficult?"

"That's just it – I don't know."

Paula sips her oat milk decaf latte. Elena gazes into her cup in uncomfortable silence. She looks exhausted. Overworking? It wouldn't look good for her if that were the case. The last thing she needs is to face awkward questions from HR. She's meant to be taking care of her staff, not letting them get into this state. At the same time, she can't ignore what Elena's done.

"You know what I think?" Paula says. "I think you're suffering from severe stress, and you've convinced yourself it's Katja's fault. Elena, this needs to stop. Katja has done nothing that would suggest to me she is behaving in the way you claim. I think you've been working too hard and let your imagination run away with you."

"No, Paula. You don't get it."

"I think I do, Elena. I can't claim to know every little thing that happens in this office – but I do know if you carry on like this, you will make yourself ill." She unlocks her phone and begins scrolling through it. "I would suggest you book in with the in-house counsellor, who is excellent when it comes to mental health issues."

"That's ridiculous! My mental health is fine! I don't need to see any doctor!" Elena bats at her coffee cup in a burst of temper, and it tilts sideways sending a pool of cappuccino cascading across the table.

"I beg to differ," Paula says, observing the chaos. She leans in closer. "Otherwise, I'll send you home right now. If I do that you won't be coming back."

166

Elena looks indignant. She is pushing Paula to her limit, although Paula's confident she'll go along with it.

She knows she doesn't have any choice.

ELENA

So, it's come to this. See the work counsellor. Or get fired.

I chose the counsellor, of course. Anything else would give Katja way too much satisfaction. Plus, I'd be playing right into Daniel's hands. Which means before I knew it, I had an urgent appointment to see Donna. She's the sympathetic-looking woman who sits in a swanky office on the top floor comforting traumatised creatives with low self-esteem.

I've never seen a counsellor before, not even after that horrific incident at my last job.

Secretly, I'm terrified. Donna is of similar age to me, a whirlwind of ombre hair extensions and satsuma-hued fake tan. Her room is filled with cushions, blankets and vanilla-scented candles that blaze away alongside a box of tissues on the coffee table. Others might see it as comforting.

I see a fire hazard.

I'm so full of resentment at being sent here that, at first, I decide to brazen it out. Maybe Donna will decide there's nothing wrong with me and send me packing.

"I'll be honest with you – I shouldn't be here," I tell her as I slump onto the sofa. It's a good opening gambit, except Donna doesn't look surprised.

"That's what they all say," she quips.

Excuse me?

"Nobody thinks they need help. That's the trouble with depression – often you don't know you have a problem until it's too late."

"I'm not depressed!"

"I spoke to your line manager earlier," Donna says, glancing down at a file on her lap.

"She has been concerned about your behaviour towards a new member of the team at – Spark, and says you've been acting erratically and accusing her of having something against you. I understand you applied for the same job and didn't get it?"

I am too stunned to speak. Donna rustles in her chair.

"Missing out on a promotion can be difficult to come to terms with," she says gently.

"Tell me, Elena, how did it make you feel?"

Oh, enough already. Like this is going to make a blind bit of difference. Yet I'm drawn in by the soothing tone of her voice. She doesn't seem like she's against me. I can't stop staring at her nails, their French polished tips layered with rows of tiny, shiny pink gems. She's giving me manicure envy. Although good luck going to the toilet with those claws, love. Maybe I will confide in her after all. I spend an hour trying to explain things, telling her about everything that's gone wrong for me lately – from the work mistakes through to what happened with Weird Nina. It's not as horrendous as I imagine. She listens and makes the right noises of support, even if she still seems sceptical.

"You've had a hard time lately," she admits. "It sounds as if the situation in the office isn't helping."

She's not wrong there.

"You know, sometimes when you're faced with something like this, the only person you can rely on is yourself." At that moment, when I finally start to feel I have someone on my side, the alarm goes off on her phone.

In a split second, Donna's manner becomes brisk, as though she wants me out so she can move on to someone whose problems are more urgent than mine.

"OK, we'll have to leave it there," she says with a broad, fake smile, "come and see me again next week. You've done well in opening up today. Make sure you relax tonight. You need a little self-care."

Damn it. Just when I thought she was on my side. What a waste of time. Although I can't stop thinking about the last thing she said. That sometimes you have to rely on yourself when nobody else will step up to the plate. Maybe, if I want to find out what Katja's really up to, I'll have to take matters into my own hands.

NATHAN

Elena isn't herself today.

We've managed to sneak some morning time alone in the guest bedroom, as she has a late shift tonight, and I'm at a press conference. Or at least, I've claimed to be. I mean we're press, and we're having a conference. That's my story and I'm sticking to it. She was fine when I got here, as passionate as ever. It's only after we finish that I noticed something's up. I sneaked off to the kitchen and made us some peanut butter toast because I know how starving she always is after sexy time. She's hardly touched it.

"Everything OK?" I ask her, ripping off a chunk of sourdough, the one Daniel bought from that artisan bakery in Borough Market. Whatever. He can buy another one.

"What do you mean?" She's on the defensive.

"You've not eaten anything. That's not like you. Not hungry?"

"It's fine, Nathan, don't worry. Got a lot on my mind."

She looks as if she's about to cry. Oh God, what's happened now? I slide the plate over to the bedside table and move closer, slipping an arm around her shoulder. "What's wrong?" I ask. "You know you can talk to me, right? I'm not only here for the fun things in life."

Please don't let it be Katja. Or that boyfriend of hers again.

It's neither of them. It's me.

"Why are you so secretive, leaving so abruptly on our first day together, not letting me round to your place? Are you married? Tell me!"

171

Shit. I knew this would happen. Only I wasn't expecting it so soon.

"No! I'm not! I swear!" I mean it. Why would anyone want to marry me? It's not enough to deter her.

"Then why are you so furtive the whole time? I've been upfront with you about my situation, and yet all I get in return is a wall of nothing! Why won't you tell me about your personal life? There's something going on here you don't want me to know about, and I don't know how to feel about that."

She's right, damn it. I should be able to tell her. I wish I could. Except I know it would be game over if I did. I feign confusion. "I don't get it. I thought this was a no-strings thing. That you were happy with our arrangement."

"I am, Nathan. You make me happier than anything…but that's just it. How long are we supposed to continue like this, with you behaving so oddly? Am I not worth more than that?"

She is. Of course she is. There's an unbearable silence. What do I say? How about the truth?

"All right," I tell her. "I do care about you. I love our time together. I'm coming out of a difficult situation, and I don't feel ready to talk about it. With anyone. Please understand that, Elena, it's nothing you've done wrong. You're helping me so much. I think we both need that."

"Helping you how? By getting your rocks off every few days?"

"That's not quite what I meant."

"What is it then? If you're in some sort of trouble…"

It's no good; she's not buying it. For one brief second, I wonder what would happen if I did 'fess up. My phone lights up with a message. It's Paula, asking for an update on the press conference. Fuck. Worst timing. On the other hand, it's provided me with an escape.

"I…I have to get to work." I jump up to locate my clothes before Elena can say anything else. As usual, they've been scattered across a wide berth, and I scrabble around for jeans and socks while ignoring the way she's staring at me. She looks small and confused, and I feel guilt-ridden.

"Elena, I'm so sorry," I tell her as I grab my things. "Honestly, I'm fine. I don't want you to worry. I promise we'll have this conversation. I need more time. Please."

"OK," she says, not sounding OK about it at all. "The thing is…"

"What?"

"No. It doesn't matter. Please go. Get to work."

I'm shaking when I leave.

Outside, the nausea hits, and for one horrible moment, I think I'm going to throw up in the nearest bush. I manage to claw it back. The last thing I need is for Daniel to turn on the CCTV and see me puking his expensive sourdough into the hedge. If this is a panic attack they can keep it. It takes a few minutes of deep breathing before I feel less light-headed.

What brought that on?

ELENA

Now, I'm even more confused.

I tried to get Nathan to commit to me, and I failed. I'm not sure there's any future for us if this is how he's going to be. I can't trust him if he's hiding some dark secret. What could be so bad that he can't confide in me? For a few seconds, I contemplate calling him to end things.

Perhaps getting the inevitable over with will hurt less if I do it sooner. I stare at my phone, at the messages we've sent one another – explicit ones, funny ones, cute little asides for no reason other than to brighten each other's days. The sort of messages a proper couple might exchange.

I can't bring myself to do it.

For one thing, he's not the only one keeping a secret. I haven't told him about Daniel's ultimatum. I wanted to, so badly, when he asked me what was wrong. To tell him everything and have him save me from my problems. To break Daniel's grasp over me. But I was scared of how he might react, so I kept quiet.

If I ditched him now, I'd be the biggest hypocrite going. There's a bigger reason to hang back. Ending things with him would break my heart into a billion shards. However much we try to dress it up as a casual fling, it's so obvious. I've fallen in love with Nathan – big time.

My stomach somersaults when I think about him. I don't so much get butterflies as *Silence of The Lambs*-sized moths when he walks in the room.

When I'm with him, he makes me feel like a goddess. As if nothing else in the world matters. I die a little on the inside every time we have to go back to the office. Or when he leaves work and goes home to whatever – or whoever – he's hiding. I've never felt like this about anyone before. Not even when I was ten and Simon Pepper from 6B scorched my name into the lab desk with a Bunsen burner. So why wouldn't the words come earlier when I tried to tell him?

Maybe it's for the best.

After the way he's just behaved, I'm not sure he loves me back.

Seven...Years...Ago

LAU...RA

...Help me...

...tell my mum and dad...I love them...that I didn't do this to myself...think straight Laura...how is anyone going to do that? Shut up brain...how can I think straight...when I'm about to die? People will think...what they want to think...they'll assume I threw myself out of the window...

...I mean I've got form...when it comes to throwing...myself at things...according to...her...

MARCH

Tyler did nothing to defend my honour. But what should I expect from a pop star with a career to protect and a girlfriend to please?

My editor went home that night and asked him if I had thrown myself at him. All he said was that he had had a lot of people approach him that evening, that it was dark in the venue, and he couldn't remember one face from the next.

He didn't say I did it. But he might as well have done.

I cannot help thinking that other colleagues have started to respond in kind since all of this. Gleam has a close-knit team who do a lot together outside of work – long lunches on a Friday afternoon, piling into the pub after work, and random weekend trips to theme parks to ride rollercoasters. Since the party, the invitations I have had to those have dried up.

It seems unfair, given I am not the only member of staff who has ever been caught out.

Queen Bee for example is being a massive hypocrite, by taking the moral high ground. It's well known that she often takes men home from the parties she gets invited to – in some cases sparing no detail in what they get up to once they are alone together. Her best friend is even worse, covering events solely to hunt down available young men, keeping a tally of her conquests as she does. And nobody says a thing.

I felt I had for a while, and began leaning on him more, sharing my problems and issues.

He was initially sympathetic. Like everybody else there, his attitude soon changed, and he became dismissive of me, saying nobody cared, and I should move on and stop moaning. I was mortified. Has she got to him too?

I wouldn't be surprised.

ELENA

I can't look Nathan in the eye.

I spent the rest of the morning considering my options, and I couldn't end things without giving him the chance to explain his situation. For all I know, he could be in trouble and is protecting me by shielding me from the truth. I love him way too much to let him go without a fight. Even if I haven't been able to tell him how I feel.

I can only give him a few more days with the awards looming. If he won't open up to me after that, then I'll have no choice but to call time on our affair and resign myself to a future with Daniel. Either that or spend the rest of my life alone, Bridget Jones-style, with no Colin Firth-alike and nothing to cuddle at night except the row of plush bunnies on my pillow.

Neither bears thinking about.

It's not only the Nathan situation that makes me feel uneasy when I log in.

Paula is still mad at me after the Weird Nina incident, while Nina herself has ignored me ever since. This might be a good thing, except she blabbed to the rest of the family about how I treated her and now they're barely speaking to me. Hearing Dad say he was 'very disappointed' in my behaviour broke my heart. Especially as he doesn't know the half of what's been going on at work. He thinks Katja's a lovely person. Like everybody else does.

Tonight, I aim to prove otherwise.

The first few hours of my shift are uneventful, but I struggle to concentrate on my work. Instead, I focus on a little Squawk chat with Nathan:

Nathan
Hey! Guess what I'm up to tonight?

He's avoiding any mention of earlier. Maybe I should too.

Elena
Go on...

Nathan
Got invited to this big record company party. My mate's head of press, so he's sneaking me in. Can't wait

Elena
Oh wow! On a school night. Jealous!

Nathan
Yeah. But I won't make it to work tomorrow. I'll be way too hungover. I'll need to stay in bed. Yours, perhaps?

Elena
I'm not sure that's a good idea. I think I'm about to get my period. I'd rather not leave the bedroom looking like the ice-pick scene in *Basic Instinct*

I'm not, as it happens – but if it's over between us, it's over, and if I give into that temptation, how will I ever manage to quit him?

Everyone drifts away between five and six with talk of meeting in the pub. For once I don't feel left out. I have more important things on my mind. I need to put my plan into action. I'm hoping I'll find some answers on Katja's desk. I need to wait until the coast is definitely clear.

The hours tick by:

7.12 p.m.
Biding my time.

8.00 p.m.
Focus on the story list.

9.24 p.m.
Pick at a microwave pasta bake which features twenty-seven mystery additives and is about as tasty as the wooden fork I use to eat it with. My mind is not on either.

10.37 p.m.
Everybody else on the floor has gone home. I am finally alone. At least, I think I am.

I wait. The late shift slump hits. I stick on a 90s playlist and make short work of a bag of Maltesers, half-melted and merged into one giant chocolate globe after sitting on my desk all day.

11.00 p.m.
The 'surviving on sugar' phase of the late shift hits. Except in this case, it's joined by its good friends, adrenaline and anxiety.

11.29 p.m.
OK. I think it's safe now.

Where to start? I am not even going to attempt to guess her computer login details. I can barely remember my own password, never mind decrypting somebody else's.

Instead, I rifle through the piles of paper and notes on her desk. Nothing out of the ordinary there. Just a load of old copies of *Heat* magazine, a few random sheets of interview questions, a discarded Starbucks cup, and assorted biros. For such an organised person, Katja sure loves clutter. Oh, this is hopeless. What was I thinking? There's no way she's going to leave anything incriminating plonked in the middle of the office for me to find.

Disappointed my plan has not worked out, I walk away – but before I can even consider my next move I knock a black notebook off her desk. "Damn it!" I say to no one in particular, bending down to retrieve it.

That's when the newspaper cutting flutters to the floor. I notice the headline:

Tragic Death of Promising Young Journalist

What is Katja doing with that? I read on:

A young journalist tipped as one of the industry's rising stars has died unexpectedly in East London. Laura Lucas, who was 22, suffered devastating injuries after a fall from a window during a music event hosted by the website Gleam, where she was a junior reporter. She was rushed to hospital, but doctors were unable to save her, with the family switching off her life support machine a few days later. Laura's family have said in a statement they are 'devastated and grief-stricken at the loss of their misunderstood angel'. While it's thought to be a tragic accident, the exact circumstances of how it happened remain unclear at this time. Police are continuing to investigate.

Laura Lucas! I stare at the paper in shock, the name brings up all those long-buried memories.

Laura was the young, ambitious girl who worked with Lindsey and me back at Gleam, and it was well-known she died horribly during a work event. What does this have to do with Katja? I notice there is one more item of hers I have yet to check. Earlier today she picked up her outfit for the Publishers' Awards – but she didn't shut up about it for the entire afternoon. The dress is hanging up in a suit bag close to her desk, and I cannot resist a peek.

I move to the coat stand and slowly unzip the garment bag. I am stunned by what I see.

Because inside it is a pale pink dress shimmering with sequins – identical to mine. It can't be a coincidence. This is horrendous. Pale pink isn't even her colour.

Will somebody please tell me what the hell is going on.

KATJA

How did I end up spending all evening in the pub?

This isn't like me at all. I had planned to head home after my usual single-glass-of-Chablis act. It's awards week, and Paula insisted on buying everyone the Prosecco she can't drink because of that brat she's preparing to ping out. Then we discussed our favourite childhood sweets – some crap about Trebor Fruit Salads getting stuck to everyone's gums. I pretended to join in, projecting ahead to a time in the not-too-distant future when I'll be free of these tedious fuckers.

Closing time and I need to pick up my dress from the office before the cleaner arrives. I don't trust them for a second. They'll probably end up using it as a tea towel. I give everybody meaningless good-night kisses (except Nina because her halitosis is so bad it could condemn whole species into extinction) and trot back across the road.

Elena's on the late shift tonight. But I'm in a good mood, so I'll leave her alone. Well, maybe I'll add a couple of breaking stories to the list so she's there until two. A little sweetener for my amusement. Nothing too extreme. It's freaky being in the office at this time of night, with all the floors in darkness. I wouldn't know because I'm too senior and important to do late shifts. Leave those to the lackeys.

I reach for the door handle and...WHAT the bloody hell?

ELENA

I have to know if Katja's dress is the same as mine.

There's only one way to find out. With trembling fingers, I slide the frock from its cover and fumble around for the label as if finding that she has bought the same outfit would be validation of how she has been treating me. I'm aware of how ridiculous this sounds, but I need to know. It takes me just a few seconds to find what I'm looking for – the label, the little white tag of evidence which confirms it.

It's the same dress.

I don't know what to think. I hear the door handle creak. Oh, God, no. Someone is coming into the Showbiz Shack. At this time of night? I need to quickly hide – before anyone sees what I'm up to. Without a second thought I dive behind the dress bag, still hanging from the coat rack. It's the worst hiding place ever. You can see my feet sticking out, and I'm wearing silver cowboy boots, which are visible from the office across the road. I might as well have drawn a giant arrow on a piece of paper and stuck it up on the adjacent wall.

I had no alternative and stay as still as a sentry, hardly daring to breathe, hoping the mystery arrival doesn't stick around. I hear footsteps, papers rustling, and a bag zipping open. It better not be the cleaner who's just walked in because she'll be here bloody ages scrubbing all those tea-stained mugs in the sink.

No. It can't be. Whoever it is they'll be gone in a minute. With that the bag is lifted away from the coat rack – to reveal me standing behind it.

"What the *hell* are you doing?"

I jump back in fright. It's Katja and her face is contorted with wrath.

BREAKING NEWS

Robins rumbled! Crazed glam journo defiles Deputy Editor's dress

Katja Lake reportedly furious: She's gone too far this time!

ELENA

Caught red-handed. There is no explanation for my current position; standing in the office holding Katja's party dress. She looks enraged. Steam pours out of her ears and her face is as crimson as my favourite boots.

"Well?!" she bellows, at such a high volume that the office mice scuttle into dark corners.

"Do you normally snoop around people's desks and go through their stuff on the late shift? Explain why I shouldn't have you fired right now!"

That's when it hits me. I'll never get another chance like this to confront her. I hold the dress out in front of me like a protest banner. "I'm not explaining a damn thing to you, Katja! What the hell are you doing with this dress?!"

"I don't know what you're talking about!"

"Oh, bullshit!" My pent-up anger bubbles to the surface as though my head is full of boiling water. "None of your little acolytes are here now, so stop trying to talk your way out of this! Why did you buy the same dress as me for the awards? Is this another way of tormenting me, like you've been ever since you got here?"

I'm ranting out of control, but all she does is stare at me as though I'm disturbed. As though I've imagined all the hell she's put me through.

"This crap again?!" she eventually says. "Elena, how many more times do you have to be told I haven't done anything to you?! Why are you so paranoid?!"

"So that's why you messed up my work, gatecrashed my family dinner, gave my fucking cousin a job? What about the Freddy Taylor interview? Was that coincidence too…?"

"Stop being ridiculous! Why would I put my career at risk by being unprofessional towards a colleague? Elena, I have bent over backwards to be decent to you – and all you've done is badmouth me and gossip behind my back!" She walks right up to me and sticks her perfectly powdered face in mine, "Admit it! You're jealous of the fact I came in and took your precious job! You can't stand it, so you're setting out to make trouble for me! Well, I've got news for you, you little madam – it's backfired!"

I'm bewildered. "How do you mean?"

"You're the only person who believes your pathetic lies! "If you hate it here that much, why don't you leave?"

"It's not like that! I was popular! I was doing well here! And then you showed up and next thing I know, I'm making mistakes, having work piled on me which I didn't deserve!"

"Don't give me that crap! You're the one who keeps going on about how brilliant and talented you are! Why would a little extra work bother you so much?"

"Because I worked all hours! I missed out on office events! I never saw my boyfriend! Do you know how that *feels?*"

Katja snaps back. "You're attacking me for doing my job? You know what? Maybe I'm not messing with you at all! Perhaps you've been *allowed* to get away with sloppiness for too long!"

"How dare you!" I notice I am still clinging to her dress but less dramatically now. Like a flag of surrender. She will have a hard time ironing out the creases before the big night, I think to myself with the smallest hint of satisfaction. I snap back to reality at her next words.

"I'll say what I damn well like," she hisses, jabbing me in the shoulder. "I've put up with so much shit from you! Well, you've gone too far this time."

"What – what do you mean?"

"There's no coming back from this Elena." Her voice drips with twisted satisfaction.

"You're finished at Spark."

For a few seconds, all I can hear is my panicked breathing. "You wouldn't!"

Oh God. No. Please don't let her tell Paula.

"I would. And I'm going to." Katja is mocking me. "What are you going to do – get your dad to call up and get you out of trouble like he did at Gleam?"

At those words, something snaps inside me. There is no way Katja can have known about what happened at Gleam unless she worked there too – or knew someone who worked there. It becomes clear. She must have some connection to Laura Lucas. Is that why she's here? Does she think I had something to do with her death?

She won't get away with this.

"Well," I say, in triumph, "If I'm going to be fired anyway, it won't matter if I do this!" And I tear through the chiffon of her pink dress, sequins scattering across the carpet with the impact.

The effect is alarming.

"You BITCH!" Katja roars, flying at me in a frenzy. My anger surges, and since I'm not sure she isn't going to punch me square in the face, I react in the only way I can think – I push her back with every bit of strength I have. Katja – who is a lot smaller and slighter than I am – screams as she flies backwards and stumbles on the castors of my office chair.

She smashes her head on the edge of the nearest filing cabinet and slumps to the floor.

LAURA'S DIARY
APRIL

*"If you hate it here so much, why don't you leave?" one of my colleagues
snapped at me today.*

*They are right – nothing would give me greater happiness than to tell
them where to stick their job, given how miserable life is for me there now.
Would any of them care? It is not as if I'm irreplaceable – if I go they will
fill the post with some other desperate lackey. And I doubt my successor
would complain so much about the opportunity they've been given.*

*Besides, if I did flounce, where do I go from here? This is my first job,
and if it isn't working out so well there is little chance of getting a good
reference from my editor, which will hamper my chances of going anywhere else. This is not a huge industry, and everybody seems to know everybody else – which won't help me in the long run.*

*I'm stuck, in other words. Put up with things, or quit and still be living
in my parents' attic when I'm 40, jobless and hopeless. If I could at least
think straight, I could plan a way out of this situation, but I'm so tired.
It's all those late nights I've had in the office in recent weeks. I don't know
what's going on, but aside from being assigned way too much work, I've
been plagued with technical difficulties. My computer keeps going into
meltdown taking all my work with it, so I keep having to stay and write
it all up again. This has happened a couple of times in the past fortnight,
right before the end of the day.*

*I don't get it. The blue screen of death happens sometimes, but twice
like that? It seems too much like coincidence, and yet my editor didn't care.
"Fix it!" she snapped like some kind of B-grade dictator. Last night, I was*

in the office until ten o'clock sorting it out, meaning I missed out on a rare invite, a birthday night out with the team, which we had all been looking forward to for weeks. By the time I finished I was so tired and despondent I wanted to go straight home.

If I didn't know better, I would think that my colleagues had some-thing to do with it – that someone had been tinkering with my machine. The way Queen Bee looked at me when it happened, her expression drip-ping satisfaction, raised a red flag with me that she might have been re-sponsible. "Oh, I'm sorry to hear that, Laura," she said when I explained I would have to stay late. "We were all SO looking forward to your com-pany, weren't we?"

I'd had enough of her attitude this time. I challenged her over it, ac-cusing her of sabotaging my PC. "Oh, for fuck's sake Laura," she snapped. "What are you accusing me of?

You think I've got nothing else to do but start messing with your stuff?" I regretted the accusation, but she wouldn't let it lie. "I haven't touched your things," she insisted. "It's not my problem if you don't know how to use your computer properly, is it?"

I need to be practical about this. At least I have a reason to get up in the morning; at least I am earning enough to pay my way. I should con-tinue to remind myself there are so many others out there doing awful, mundane jobs just to pay the bills, who would kill for the chance to do what I'm doing.

Besides, things can't get any worse.

ELENA

What the fuck just happened?

Katja is lying on the floor by my desk, unmoving, a trickle of blood dripping onto the remains of her dress, staining the pink fabric dark red. I must have dropped it when I pushed her back. She'll be furious when she finds out I have ruined it.

Except…no. No! I think I just killed my arch nemesis.

This wasn't meant to happen. I know I despised Katja, and I'm now sure she has an agenda against me. That doesn't mean I wanted her to die. What do I do now? Panic mode sets in. My deputy editor is lying dead on the floor of the office. And it's my fault. All of those story errors, the late working and the botched interview – it pales in comparison with this. Now I am definitely going to get fired, and maybe even go to prison. Except I didn't mean to kill her. Do people still get locked up for manslaughter?

Maybe it's not as bad as it looks. Perhaps she is just unconscious. "Katja…?" I say in a timid voice. No response. "KATJA!" I try shouting, to no effect, moving closer to her unmoving body. Is she breathing? I cannot tell. My breath comes in rapid staccato gasps, my anxiety levels rocket, and a waterfall of acid pools in my throat. I rush to the adjacent bathroom, reaching the toilet just in time for the plastic ready meal I ate earlier to make an unwelcome return.

Better, I think, leaning against the stall wall, sweat beading my upper lip. Must stay calm and stop the panic rushing in. That's the only thing that is going to get me through this. But what to do? I cannot leave Katja lying there to be found by the morning team, dead and bleeding. I'm not sure I can move her myself. There is only one thing for it.

I dial Nathan.

His phone rings several times before I hear him, shouting against a barrage of noise: "Elena?"

"Nathan!" I croak, my throat still sore from vomiting. "It's me."

"What's up? Are you OK? Hold on..." The background sound fades. "I'm here...what's going on?"

"I need help! I'm in the office, and Katja's here. She's dead, and I killed her..." My words tumble over each other, and before I know it, I am sobbing. "Please...help me Nathan...I don't know what to do...I didn't know who to call..."

There is a silence of several seconds. "Jesus. Elena...what have you done?"

"I don't know, I don't know," I say, almost hysterical. "Nathan, please, I'm scared!"

"All right. Stay there. I'm on my way. I'll call you when I'm nearby." The line goes dead.

I am reluctant to go back outside, petrified of what I might see. I take some deep breaths to stem my tears, splash water on my face and rinse my mouth out to rid myself of the lingering taste of sick. The sight of myself in the mirror is unnerving. I look as pale as a ghost, albeit one with unkempt hair and eyes rimmed black with mascara from crying. I cannot deal with this. I need a few more minutes before I steel myself and go back out there, to sit with Katja's cooling corpse until Nathan arrives.

He'll know what to do.

Those few minutes turn into forty as I cower in the bathroom stall, staring at my phone over and over again as I wait for Nathan to call. I am too terrified to move.

Whatever happens, this is a grim situation. If Katja is dead, we will have to go to some serious lengths to cover up the fact. And I will have it on my conscience for the rest of my life – if I don't snap and confess, that is. On the other hand, if she is not dead, she will point the finger at me for the events of tonight. This means that even if I don't end up behind bars, my career at Spark is finished. Either way, this is not going to end well.

I'm contemplating my fate when my phone springs noisily to life, shearing through the silence, and I jump back in fright. Who the hell changed my ringtone to JAJA DING DONG?

Is that James' idea of a joke? How hilarious. Not.

It's Nathan. "I'm on my way up," he says.

Fine. Time to go outside and face what I have done – the blood, the torn dress, the mayhem. I tease the bathroom door open with a creak and tiptoe out. But I am not prepared for what I see.

WTF!

The torn dress is gone. The blood has disappeared. Katja's body is nowhere to be seen. I am gaping at nothing in utter horror, when Nathan walks in.

NATHAN

Well, this is weird.

Elena stands next to her desk, eyes red and puffy from crying, hair all over the place. Is that vomit on her shirt? She's staring at the floor as though expecting to see Katja's body.

Only there is nobody there. What is she playing at? Anger rises in me, but I push it back down.

Not now.

"Elena…what is this all about? You call me after midnight to say you've killed Katja in the office, I rush halfway across London – and she isn't even here? Is this some kind of joke?"

She's speechless. There's nothing there. No body, no blood, nothing but carpet. Maybe a sequin or two from that stupid dress she didn't shut up about.

"I – Nathan, she was lying here, I swear!" She points feebly at the ground before her legs give way from under her. Shit, is she going to faint? Luckily, I catch her in time, guiding her onto the sofa.

"There's nothing here now," I point out as I sit beside her. No shit Sherlock. The place is deserted. "Elena, I don't get this. What happened here? Are you sure you're not imagining things?" I've never seen her this pale, almost deathly. "You look like shite," I tell her in a gentle voice I don't recognise. "Have you been throwing up?"

It's no good. I can't be annoyed with her. But she's scaring me. Is this what a breakdown looks like? Is she having one? Fuck, what do I do?

"Katja was here, she caught me looking through her things, and we had an argument. I pushed her backwards, and she slipped and fell and smashed her head on the filing cabinet. I didn't mean to hurt her, but that's what happened, and she was lying there and now she isn't. I don't know what's going on. I don't know what to do!" She dissolves into tears, crying so loudly that I start to feel upset. Christ. She believes this. I wish I hadn't been so short with her.

"Hey...hey, it's OK. Don't worry." I pull her into a tight hug, stroking her hair and shushing her lightly. It's a crap attempt to comfort her, because I don't think anything will at the moment. "What's happening to me?" she wails as she melts into my arms, her whole body shaking with fear. Her skin is like ice. This is horrendous. I don't want to do this here. I want to scoop her up, take her back to mine and tuck her up in bed, cradling her and telling her everything is OK, until she feels better.

Then I remember I can't do that. Shit. Oh God, what have I done? It's several minutes before she's calm enough for me to speak again. I can't bear the look of distress on her face. My heart races. I need to keep it together. Please don't let her notice my hands are shaking.

"Look, I know you've had a bad time with Katja, but the things you're saying – I can't get my head around them," I say to her. "Are you sure you're not just sick, and you fell asleep in the bathroom and dreamed it?"

"I didn't. She was threatening to fire me and I..."

"If Katja is dead, and you killed her, then where's the body?"

She shakes her head in resignation.

"Right. I think you need help, Elena, this – this isn't normal behaviour. This – counsellor, they've got you seeing, was she any good?"

"I – I don't know," she mutters, "I only just started seeing her." I hope she doesn't think I'm angry with her. I only want to help.

"Well, you need to get your head sorted if you're seeing things. This is beyond the realms of what I can deal with, what any of us can deal with, if you believe you killed someone tonight."

I want to say more but my phone is buzzing, and insistent, lighting up in my pocket, and it's showing the last name I needed to see. A stab of fear shoots through me. This isn't good.

Elena doesn't need to see this. She stares uncomprehendingly. I jab the mute button before I turn back. I'll have to deal with that later.

"What do you think I should do?"

"Go home," I tell her. "Please. You look shattered. It's almost one. Write your handover, then get out of here and get some sleep. Get in touch with the counsellor again tomorrow and see if you can see her as soon as possible. Maybe give your doctor a call, too. Whatever it is that's going on in your head, you need to get it sorted, because I'm worried about you."

She nods miserably, firing a quick message to Paula, while I order an Uber. No way am I letting her walk home in such a state. I hate the thought of Daniel, who has been sending nosy messages every few minutes asking her why she isn't back yet being the one to look after her when I could care for her so much better.

What else can I do? I'm in enough trouble as it is.

"Get some rest," I tell her ten minutes later through the open window of the taxi before it speeds off into the night. "You'll feel much better in the morning." I don't know about that. Not when she still looks so weak.

I walk back towards the glass front of the building and the panic starts to properly set in as I read the messages which have been setting my phone alight.

Where are you?

Why aren't you replying?

How the hell do I get out of this? *Thank fuck I still have a joint left.* I need something to calm me down. I smoke it quickly before I return to the reception area – empty except for a lone security guard more interested in watching some crappy cop show on his iPad than paying any attention to me. I ignore the squealing tyres and tinny gunshots, flop down on one of the sofas and make the call I've been dreading.

"Hi," I say seconds later. "It's me. Look – I'm sorry, but I can't do this any more."

ELENA

Daniel is still awake when I get home, wondering why I'm back late.

I'm afraid it will lead to another conversation about my future at Spark – although his demeanour changes when he sees what a state I am in. I am too bewildered by the evening's events to tell him the truth, instead mumbling something about having eaten a dodgy chicken tikka in the canteen. "I thought I was going to throw up in the cab," I tell him. "Had to wait until I felt better before I could leave."

I push past him, not wanting to talk more. He shows me sympathy for once, running me a bath and tucking me into bed once I've cleaned up, sticking his arm around my waist in a vice-like grip. It's like being pinioned by an arcade machine grab claw.

I don't want his form of dutiful kindness. I want Nathan. I want him so badly, but it's adding to my misery. My thoughts are more chaotic than a Primark sale as I lie in bed, unable to sleep a wink. Why am I such a despicable person? Why have I been doubting someone like Nathan, who was so caring tonight? Daniel would have frog-marched me to the police station if he'd heard what I'd done, and he wouldn't stop to question whether I'd done it.

I dread to think what he'd say if he knew about Laura. After seeing that cutting, I can't stop thinking about her, and everything that happened to her.

Laura Lucas joined Gleam seven years ago when I was working there as a senior reporter. So talented. So precocious. You feel as if you know it all when you're twenty-two, don't you? Well, that was Laura all over. I took an instant dislike to her. We all did. Nobody at Gleam went out of their way to be mean to anyone. But Laura was different. She took criticism much too personally, and did not take kindly to being teased. On the occasions when we did venture out as a team she made everything about her. I sensed she was nervous and eager to make a good impression in her first job, but she went about it the wrong way.

When we were tasked with keeping an eye on her at a party for Tyler Bard, the pop star who was dating my boss, we knew it would be tricky. Laura was obsessed with Tyler, which made her impossible to keep tabs on that night. She had interviewed him the week before and genuinely seemed to think he had shown an interest in her – which of course, he hadn't. He flirted massively with everyone, and we all knew it. It meant he paid her no attention at all when he arrived, leaving Laura frustrated and drowning her sorrows in free alcohol. Given how sweary and rude she became after that, I don't think she was used to drinking. I would have kept a better eye on her if I'd known since she ended up angering several important people we were trying to charm into giving us some exclusives for the site. In the end, I took her home and handed her over to her concerned-looking parents – lovely people who even gave me a lift home despite having never met me. If they were shocked by their daughter rocking up semi-conscious at one in the morning, they didn't show it. But it was awkward as hell.

The following day, the PR Laura had insulted that night complained to our boss. When I was asked about my side of the story I didn't hesitate to drop Laura in it. Why wouldn't I? I had my job to think of, and covering her back would have done me no favours, especially if my boss had found out the truth.

I'm not proud of what I did next, though, claiming that she had made a drunken pass at Tyler and proved difficult to shake off – knowing she had done no such thing. You can imagine how that went down. The consequences were far-reaching. I got off scot-free, but Laura had a rough ride. The PR refused to allow her anywhere near any clients, limiting the assignments we could give her. And my editor didn't trust her with many others. Laura became sullen, uncooperative and difficult to work with, but she was convinced we were all out to get her.

Instead of putting it down to experience and moving on, trying to do better, she complained constantly, throwing out accusations of sexism and double standards, convinced others wouldn't have been treated so harshly. The office became toxic in her presence.

It wasn't helped by a massive dose of bad luck at this stage – work full of typos and factual inaccuracies, followed by Laura kicking up a hissy fit because she claimed we were making her stay late on purpose. I hate to admit I put the boot in further when a rare interview she got to do ended in disaster – because of me.

It was rumoured she was on the verge of being asked to leave before she died, but what happened remains a mystery. Gleam was holding a big event for its readers, packed with pop stars, and midway through, Laura was found critically injured outside the venue. She was rushed to intensive care, where they tried in vain to patch her up. The next thing we knew, inquiries were being made of her colleagues. Accusations of work bullying flew. We wanted to tell them our side of the story.

Then she died, and nobody wanted to hear our version of events.

It was a bad time all around. None of us were allowed near the funeral, while the police had their suspicions that someone had pushed Laura from an upstairs window. We were all questioned, but nothing was ever proven. For a while, there was talk of closing the site, tainted as it was, but they would never do that. It was popular as hell.

So, we kept it going, our editor saying it's what Laura would have wanted (what she would have wanted was not to have fallen out of a window to her death, but that's by the by).

Once the dust had settled, life went on. I was convinced I could never work anywhere else because of what happened.

But incidents are forgotten, and when Paula offered me the job at Spark a few years later – knowing nothing of my past – it felt like a second chance. That I was redeemable for that one huge mistake. The way I treated Laura.

I've never stopped feeling bad about it, mind. All this time, I've used my exuberance and ambition to paper over my guilt and push down my grief, never telling a soul how her death affected me or confessing what I did. The thought of anyone at Spark finding out about it fills me with fear. And I don't even want to contemplate telling Nathan. He'd hate me.

There was something about Laura that brought out the worst in me. I've never behaved like that towards anyone else in my career. I have always feared rivals and I saw a massive rival in Laura Lucas.

She was a *troublemaker*.

That doesn't mean I killed her though.

I message Nathan around two as I struggle to sleep. I'm desperate to talk to someone:

Thanks for being so sweet to me tonight. God, I feel like shit

He doesn't reply. Of all the nights I could have done with him being up late. It's after five before I finally nod off, only to be interrupted two hours later by Daniel banging around the bathroom. I am still unsure whether I feel well enough to face tonight's late shift. I know that Daniel, who sometimes has difficulty sleeping, has a stash of pills by his bed, so while he is in the shower, I grab two. Perhaps when I wake up this nightmare will be over.

I'm so exhausted. I mutter something about staying in bed when Daniel emerges. So much for the care he showed me last night.

"I hope this has made you reassess your position," he says, slipping into his favourite Dolce and Gabbana suit. "Spark is impacting your health; I think we all saw that last night. Maybe now you'll see sense and make the right decision about your future because I'm not picking you up off the bathroom floor next time it happens." He sprays himself in Tom Ford and the heady aroma makes me feel sick to my stomach. "Let this be a lesson to you, Elena," he says and sweeps out of the bedroom.

I lie in bed, shell-shocked. How can he be so cruel? How can I even think about dropping Nathan for someone like Daniel, whose true colours are coming out so vividly? I don't think I can take much more of his behaviour. Yet, after the way I behaved towards Laura, I'm beginning to think I don't deserve anyone better.

Nathan hasn't responded to my message – only a blue tick confirming he's read it.

That's odd. He'll surely be on his way to work. It's not like him not to reply. I'm too drowsy to message him again. All I can think about is whether or not Katja is at work. I try to reassure myself that she will be. Of course, she will. By 8.05 a.m. she'll be giggling about some trifle with James, who'll be fawning over her footwear, and everything will be back to normal. And from now on, I will try so hard to get on with her, and push those evil thoughts about her to the back of my brain.

An hour goes by, and nobody calls. I breathe easier, assuming that Katja has arrived at Spark HQ, and all is well. I finally fall into a deep, medicated slumber. Only to be roused out of it by my phone splutter-ing into life right before noon. It's Paula.

"Elena? Sorry to bother you at home, but wondering if you've heard from Katja this morning?"

"No, I haven't…why?"

"Because she's not shown up for work."

BREAKING NEWS

Popular showbiz journo reported missing: We want our Katja back say 'heartbroken' colleagues.

THE PRESENT

It might be May but there's no sign of summer in London, with unseasonal rain lashing the windows of a faceless office block across town, Inside, it isn't even lunchtime yet and Detective Bonnie Pace is exhausted.

She's always tired these days. Life balancing a career with a toddler is taxing, to say the least, especially when teething and broken nights are involved. Her desk is as cluttered as her brain right now, crammed so full of loose papers, coffee cups and half-open packets of biscuits that there's barely room for her laptop. But she wouldn't have it any other way. While her son is her world, she's grateful for the return to work after a long spell of maternity leave; to have something to talk about other than mother and baby groups and bloody *Paw Patrol* reruns.

She wishes they'd give her something more interesting to do though. Gone are the days when she was off investigating intriguing, juicy cases. These days, it is largely desk jobs as though Eric Lord, her supervisor, doesn't want her doing anything which might overtax her motherhood-addled brain. The most challenging thing she's done since she got back involved a chain of illegal sweet shops selling knock-off wine gums, and even that was pretty low-rent.

Who wants to base their entire career around dodgy confectionery?

Eric saunters in and helps himself to a Hobnob without being offered. Too bad for him they've been sitting there since last Friday and they're stale as hell.

"Something's come in this morning," he says through a mouthful of crumbs. "Revolves around some showbiz website or other – Spark, I think it's called."

He lost her at the word 'showbiz'. Bonnie couldn't care less about the lives of celebrities.

"What's happened?" she asks, expecting to hear about a couple of airhead losers scrapping on a red carpet over a jar of Freddy Taylor's breath. But even she is mildly intrigued by what she hears.

Missing?

ELENA

It's been nearly forty-eight hours since anybody saw Katja. Forty-eight agonising hours. Jesus wept. With every passing minute, her reappearance seems less likely.

Team Spark is horrified by this turn of events. The last they heard from her was on Monday night, when she left the pub. Before she came to the office to collect her dress. Before we had that fight. It did happen then. I didn't imagine it and I'm paralysed with fear.

Where has she gone? Is she lying, anonymous, in a hospital somewhere? Or did she succumb to her wounds, collapsing dead in a side street or at the bottom of a filthy ravine, her body yet to be discovered? Oh, stop it. How many ravines are there in London? My mind is running away with me. None of this bears thinking about, but it's all I can think about.

I try to carry on as normal to avoid suspicion. Only I haven't slept more than a few hours since it happened, stone-cold dread keeping me awake until dawn until I pass out from sheer exhaustion. I can't eat. I can't focus on my work. I break out in a sweat every time I clap eyes on the spot where Katja fell. Paula asked Nina to put some papers in the filing cabinet yesterday, and I swear my heart rate ramped up about 100 beats in a second, like that time I couldn't turn the treadmill off at the gym.

The worst part of all this is I can't tell anyone. Only Nathan knows what happened that night, and I am counting on him to keep quiet.

He is trying so hard to look after me while all this is happening. I came in today to find a cup of tea on my desk. I appreciated the gesture, but I am so strung out I could only manage a few sips. It tasted like pond-water.

"Now, do you believe me?" I ask him for the twentieth time while alone in the kitchen as I surreptitiously pour the tea down the sink.

"Elena – I don't know what to think any more," Nathan says abruptly. Wow. I didn't expect him to snap at me like that. He doesn't think I killed her, does he? He softens when he sees how taken aback I am.

"Look, I'm sorry, OK?" His brow furrows as his phone lights up in his pocket. It's been doing that a lot lately. "I – I have a lot going on this week. It's complicated," and makes a rapid exit. He's worrying about something, I can tell. Neither of us has suggested a lunchtime get-together since Katja went missing. Getting jiggy is the last thing on my mind.

Who knows if we ever will again? I might have to stay with Daniel if it turns out Katja is dead. As a lawyer he'd be my best hope of not spending the next twenty years staring at the walls of a prison cell, thinking about how it's nothing like *Orange is the New Black*.

I am contemplating the grimness of my future when Paula calls an urgent meeting. Oh crap. What now?

Paula has managed to pour her curves into a stylish camel-coloured jumper dress today. Why is this springing into my head? There are times when thinking like a showbiz journalist is inappropriate. The severe look on her face suggests this is one of them.

"Hi everyone," she says, looking at the row of subdued faces around the table. "It's not great news, I'm afraid – Katja's boyfriend has reported her missing, and the police are trying to locate her." I hear James give a little gasp. This is not good. "If you know anything at all which might lead to her being found, come and talk to me, and I can put you in touch with the detective leading the case. Anything at all," she concludes, firing me a knowing look.

I hide my quaking hands in my lap. Why is Paula assuming I know something about all of this? Who knew that Katja had a boyfriend? I spent so much time being destroyed by her in the office I never gave much thought to her having a personal life outside of work.

What next? Will we be seeing her parents on TV, looking teary-eyed and desperate, pleading for her safe return? An even bigger worry worms its way into my mind. The possibility that my colleagues might tell the police everything I've said about Katja.

Oh. Hell. No.

NATHAN

"I don't know what to think any more," I snap when Elena asks me for the twentieth time if I believe her. I immediately feel like shit for doing so. How can I be such a dick to someone who's scared out of her mind? Especially not someone like Elena. I can't bear the thought of upsetting her.

I feel the familiar buzz of my phone. The one that is making me want to throw my handset from a great height right now. "I – I have a lot going on this week. It's complicated," I tell her as I race from the kitchen. I hear Paula, calling us all into a meeting, but I have to take this.

I'm so knackered. I've barely slept these past few days from worrying about Elena – and everything else. About fourteen hours of shut-eye, waking up to all this being over, would be perfect. Not going to happen though. Definitely not, if the latest message is anything to go by:

Next time I ask you to do something bloody well do it – you know what'll happen if you don't

Seven Years Ago

LAURA

Somebody get me out of this…

…Seriously…

Put a mattress down…A safety net…

…Anything!

Like it'll help…I'm doomed…

…Exactly as I was back then.

MAY

My editor decided she trusted me again this week and sent me to interview the star of a new Disney Channel show. It's been a while since the Tyler Bard disaster, so I suppose she thought I couldn't get into much trouble with malleable teen stars who would answer anything you put to them.

How wrong she was.

In some ways, it was my editor's fault, given she made Queen Bee sit down with me to go through the questions pre-interview. I tried to protest, saying I didn't need help but she insisted. Despite my reservations, my nemesis was unexpectedly pleasant, saying she would do her best to ensure things went smoothly for me. I relaxed. I cracked a few jokes with her.

I let down my guard. Bad move. Queen Bee knew something about the Disney Channel star that I didn't – namely, that he had been dealing with a difficult family bereavement that he did not want to talk about. She didn't bother telling me this or that we had been specifically warned not to mention it. Instead, she slipped in a question about it, saying it would give me an amazing exclusive, which she couldn't wait to read. And boy, did I fall for it.

To say the assignment was a disaster is an understatement. I asked the question, and the response I got was alarming – the actor shouted and screamed and accused me of trying to dish the dirt. Chairs were kicked over. Lamps were thrown. At one point he tried to tear the TV off the wall and smash it over my head. I tried to apologise, but he was having none of it. Within minutes, security had marched me out of the interview suite, off the floor and out through the hotel foyer in front of dozens of waiting journalists, all preparing their sheets of acceptable questions that hadn't been sabotaged by a bitter rival.

When I got back to the office. My editor, who had spent the past hour trying to placate the PR, was raging – yet when I told her that Queen Bee suggested that question, she denied all knowledge – showing up with an emailed list which didn't include it. "For God's sake, Laura," she snapped, sounding impatient. "Everybody knows you don't ask about that. Why would you do it?"

I knew the answer I wanted to give – "because you told me to", but I also knew it was no good, that my editor would never believe me – and the one piece of evidence showing that she did, the question sheet had been removed from me at the hotel and was probably sitting in a bin somewhere.

The small triumphant smile she gave me as we left the office and returned to our desks sent chills through me. I know this was my one chance to win back the respect of my editor, and thanks to her, I have blown it. Although she said nothing more to me, I couldn't help but notice.

The surrounding hostility, the giggles and the whispers as she told everybody in hushed tones what I'd done.

ELENA

I'm minding my own business, trying to focus on a story about *Married at First Sight* when I hear the police cars.

A fleet of them. Screeching to a halt outside the Spark building. Before I know it, two grizzled detectives who wouldn't be out of place in *Line of Duty* have swept in and felled me to the ground with their tasers before strapping the cuffs on me for something I didn't do. The eyes of the entire team bore into me like screwdrivers as I'm marched out of the office to my inevitable fate. I can hear the words of people I once regarded as friends, muttering: 'I always knew she was no good'.

The image fades. I snap back to reality. I haven't been arrested, but how long before that happens? It's been nearly four days since my altercation with Katja, and with every passing day the chances of her showing up again are looking less likely.

My racing thoughts are being made worse by the fact that the police did turn up at the office this morning. A couple of bored-looking constables, sniffing around for clues. I said a silent prayer of thanks I wasn't here at the time, arriving for my late shift after they left. Things have been strained here since. James, Molly and Nina are giving me a wide berth. It's as if they told the cops I murdered Katja and left her dismembered remains in Hyde Park to be pecked at by a curious murder of crows.

Nathan snaps me out of my fugue. "Everything OK?" he says, perching on the corner of my desk. He holds out one of his infamous mugs of tea to me and my stomach rolls. I'd rather drink from a puddle.

"Everything is not OK, Nathan! James and Molly and – my cousin! I think they told the police I've hurt Katja!! Can you go and talk to them, tell them I don't have anything to do with it? Please! I've never been so scared…"

Nathan looks panicked at the suggestion. He is about to reply when Paula sweeps through the office, reminding us that we have another meeting. This time, it's to decide what we will do about attending the Publishers' Awards tomorrow night in the wake of Katja's disappearance.

I'm not interested in what Paula will say about the awards now that my relationship with my colleagues has plummeted to an all-time low. Even if by some miracle Katja shows up in the next 24 hours, the poisonous atmosphere that's infected the desk will prevent it from being the fun celebration it should be. Maybe I'll give it a miss this year.

Chances are I may have been arrested by then anyway.

It's obvious everyone is avoiding me from the way they crowd onto the opposite side of the meeting-room table. Only Nathan takes my side, sitting next to me and giving my arm a reassuring squeeze as he does, and Paula remains as impartial as ever. I wonder what she is thinking.

"Right, everybody, thanks for taking time out for this. The awards are tomorrow night. I wanted to ask you all, with Katja still missing, whether you think it would be appropriate for us to attend." She looks at the silent, earnest faces of her team. "I suppose we should think about what Katja would want us to do, if she were here with us."

I feel my phone vibrate. What timing, I think, pulling out my handset in case it is something urgent. Has Katja been found? But I am not prepared for what I see. The message, accompanied by an attachment, comes from Daniel – and reads simply:

How could you?

It's a video of Nathan and I kissing passionately, that first day outside the building.

And my boyfriend has seen every damn second of it.

LAURA'S DIARY
MAY

I doubt my editor will even consider me for another interview now, and my reputation as a troublemaker has spread – effectively blacklisting me at all the major film and TV companies.

After the Tyler Bard party and this new incident, nobody will let me anywhere near their talent – and who can blame them after what I am perceived to have done?

We have a big Gleam event in a few weeks' time – our first-ever readers concert, one we have been preparing for ages. The show will bring boy bands and pop stars to the stage for the thousand or so adoring teenage fans lucky enough to secure tickets – and we are expected to be on our best behaviour. I've got more chance of marrying some minor royal than I have of being allowed anywhere near the talent. Instead, I'll be consigned to the menial tasks that nobody else wants, while Queen Bee and her acolytes swan around with the pop stars like they're all best buddies. The day I found this out was the worst, and I took it upon myself to tell her how furious I was, laying the blame for it at her Zara shod-feet.

"Nothing to do with me," she snapped. "And we're all sick of your moaning. This is how the industry is sometimes, and if you don't like it then fucking well go and do something else because your attitude sucks." She said it in front of the entire office and I swear her captive audience looked as if they were about to applaud.

Why is she being so vicious...

Seven Years Ago
LAURA

No! I can't think about this any more! There's no time! I need help! NOW!

…Except nobody can hear me screaming…

…Why don't you kids just shut the fuck up already?

…Stop it! Stop screaming at the band! Help me! This is all your fault!

…Oh, what's the fucking point?

ELENA

"Elena!"

Paula was furious at having her meeting interrupted. It's not only her – everybody's head swivels in my direction. I'm mute, my mouth agape at such a private moment being filmed.

At being caught out, like some forgotten *Strictly* reject snogging their dance partner in the studio car park.

But how? I cannot give Paula an answer. What the hell is Daniel going to say to me?

"I…" I begin, reddening under the gaze of so many pairs of eyes – but it is too much.

I run from the room, the door slamming in my wake. I have to get out of the office.

In the distance, Paula shouts. "Elena…wait!" I don't want to and race back to my desk to pack my bag. Seconds later, the door slams again, and Nathan runs up.

"Elena, where are you going? What's going on?"

"This!" I tell him, pushing the screen in his face, watching his expression darken as he views the clip. "It was sent to Daniel! Who sent it to him? Was it you, Nathan?" I fling items into my bag at a rate of knots, not caring if it's a mess, not wanting to do anything except try and explain things at home.

Nathan looks appalled. "No!" he insists. "How could you think that, Elena? Why would I do that?"

"Well, someone has! Someone knows about us! They were recording us! I have to get out of here! Tell Paula I've gone home sick or something!" I zip my bag and make for the door before he stops me. "Oh, and Nathan – why so taken aback? You didn't seem to care about Daniel when you were fucking me, so why does it bother you so much now what he thinks?"

He has no answer. I leave him standing, bewildered, in the middle of the office.

I'm back at the flat in minutes, knowing Daniel has a half-day today. There's no point pretending it was a one-off mistake. Perhaps he'll let me explain how I've been feeling. When I walk in he's sitting at the kitchen island, tears shining on his cheeks, I know that is not going to happen.

"I am so sorry I never meant you to find out like this…"

He turns, his face twisted with fury. "How could you do this to me Elena?"

"Daniel, I tried…!" I am suddenly desperate to smooth things over, but as the words leave my mouth my phone buzzes – Nathan:

Everything OK? Call me!

Daniel grabs at it and as I dodge him, the phone falls to the floor. He gets to it before I do.

"Oh, did you now?" He opens up WhatsApp with slow, careful precision. My heart plummets as he sees all of my correspondence with Nathan. The explicit attachments, the filthy messages. I know I wanted out of the relationship but this wasn't how I had planned it.

"You little skank," he says, voice almost primal. "You evil fucking bitch!" For a heart-stopping moment, I think he's going to hit me, but I'm not sure even Daniel would stoop to that. "That wasn't Lindsey's earring, was it? And what's this? '*Hope that fuckwit boyfriend of yours didn't see it?*' What, not content with cheating on me you're laughing at me behind my back?" I've never seen him like this; he's like a cornered animal. "How can you be so ungrateful?" he bellows, throwing the phone at me in a fit of anger. It misses my cheek by inches and smashes into the kitchen island.

I lose it. "Enough!! No, I shouldn't have done it! It was wrong of me! But have you stopped to ask why I did it? Has it occurred to you it's because of how you've treated me? Using your amazing wealth to keep me sweet while making everything about YOU! Why would you make me leave my job if you really love me? Why force me to have children with you when you never even asked me if I wanted them?! Threatening to make me homeless if I don't fall in line? How is that love, Daniel? No wonder none of your other girlfriends stuck around!"

"I *never* forced you to stay with me," he snarls. "If you were that unhappy, why didn't you end it?!"

"I wanted to! I tried so many times to end it."

"You didn't, did you? I mean, why bother? You were having a bloody great life at my expense while all the time you're sneaking off – with that – that bastard? Nathan Flynn, of all people?!" He grabs my arm roughly and pulls me towards the bedroom.

"What, Nathan hasn't had enough conquests already in that office? Are you that naïve that you don't know he's slept with half the girls on your floor, probably still is?" My face contorts with alarm. Is this what Nathan's been keeping from me? "You know he fucked my ex, right? How is it supposed to make me feel he's done it with you, too?" He is deafening me.

"You think a guy like that cares about you, someone who's just out to get it wherever he can? Flynn doesn't care about anything except himself and his own ends! How dumb can you get!"

"No! That's not true!" He's not listening and practically throws me into the bedroom.

"Where did you and Nathan do it, Elena?" he asks, sounding almost threatening. "Did he fuck you in this room, in our bed? What, better than me, is he?"

"Yes! He is! A *million* times better! And you know why? Because he listens to me! And he respects women! Maybe if you did, this wouldn't keep happening to you!"

"Oh, that's what this is all about, some cheap thrill! I should've known you'd spread your legs for anyone, you filthy whore!" I am shocked to hear such a slur coming from him. He flings open the wardrobe and begins throwing my precious outfits across the floor.

"Daniel – what are you doing?" I shout as the extent of the damage I have done starts to sink in. "Where did you even get the video, who sent it to you!"

"Who cares! Daniel snaps. "I don't know who sent it to me, but whoever it was, they've done me a favour! And I want you out of my apartment NOW!" He drags piles of clothes and shoes to the window. "I'm just giving you a helping hand since you care about this lot more than you ever cared about me!!"

With that, he flings the pile outside. My favourite outfits fly into the air and I start screaming.

"What have you done!"

"What I should have done a long time ago," Daniel shrieks at an ear-splitting volume.

"Want your clothes? Go and get them! And don't bother coming back!! I don't ever want to see you again!!"

It's useless trying to argue. He collapses to the bedroom floor, sobs ringing in my ears as I race for the door, desperate to salvage my clothes. The sound is heart-rending, echoing across the entire flat, and yet I feel nothing for him. Not after the names he called me, the way he twisted my arm as if he was pulling it out of its socket. He didn't listen when I tried to point out why this happened. He'll wallow in self-pity for a bit, then move on to the next poor sod who's taken in by his charms and his bank balance while failing to see what he's really like. And the same thing will happen all over again.

I know I should've ended it sooner. I know cheating on him was wrong. But how could something that wrong feel so right? All I care about is getting as far away from here as possible, and retrieving my stuff which is lying on the lawn in the rain – a soggy mess of fabric. My pink frilly shirt is ruined, and one of my favourite boots is sitting on one of the spikes of a nearby fence. The other is nowhere to be seen. The dress I bought for the awards sits in its bag, the damp threatening to seep through, while my sparkly heels are caked in mud.

I stagger around the street, tears streaking my cheeks as the cold reality dawns. Where will I go now that Daniel has thrown me out? What about the rest of my stuff? I left my plush bunnies upstairs, all at his mercy. I may never see them again. There's an even bigger question preying on my mind. Who filmed that video?

And who sent it?

NATHAN

We're all going to the awards. Because it's what Katja would have wanted.

Like it matters. I don't even want to. I'm sick with worry about Elena. I've messaged her to find out what's going on with Daniel but she hasn't replied. I'm assuming the bastard won't be happy, though.

Maybe it's for the best. I'm not sure he's fit to be around women. What the hell's going to happen next? I need a drink. A whisky would take the edge off, but I'll settle for a strong tea if it'll calm my nerves. I need to think straight about planning my next move.

I'm outside the kitchen when I hear James and Molly.

"More attention seeking from Elena. Wonder what's up with her now?" Molly says.

I was surprised to hear her talk; she normally says even less than I do.

"Who knows?" says James. Nothing she does makes sense any more. Not since Katja arrived. She's jealous. And you know what else I don't get? This – thing she's got with Nathan all of a sudden."

Sorry, what? I was going to go into the kitchen, but now I'm thinking I'll hang back and listen to this.

"What do you mean?" Molly says.

"You must have noticed! They're always hanging out, talking shit together…did you see how he squeezed her arm in the meeting? She never used to be like this with him…maybe they're sleeping together!"

"They can't be! She has a boyfriend, doesn't she?"

"Yeah. That guy from legal. He adores her. Why would she go off with someone like Nathan? I can't stand the guy, acting like this job's beneath him. He isn't even a trained journalist, just a chancer who thinks he can write. Massive cokehead too—"

Fuck me sideways. Saying those things about me in front of junior staff? I mean he has a point. But still.

"You're joking! I had no idea," says Molly

"Yeah! After the Christmas party one year he got caught in bed with one of our lawyers. Both off their faces, at least that's what I heard. Doubt it was the first time he'd done that either. He's *very* popular with the girls on the ad team if you get my drift. Be careful around him darling, he's repellent and probably riddled with God knows what."

I've had enough of this and walk into the kitchen, with James in full flow. He stops abruptly when he sees me. I hear a sharp intake of breath from Molly.

"Hi," I say, "I hope I'm not interrupting." I calmly flick the kettle on as though the last two minutes hadn't happened.

Their silence is awkward, to say the least.

"Er, Nathan…you didn't…hear our conversation?" James panics. Time to have some fun.

"Conversation? I ask casually, filling my mug to the brim. "Oh, you mean the one about the 'untrained journalist' who got so pissed off with colleagues bitching behind his back that he made a formal complaint to HR and had them both fired? No, I didn't hear a word."

They look gobsmacked. "Oh, and by the way, James," I add as I make for the exit. "I'd stay away from the kettle if I were you.

Wouldn't want you catching my ultra-contagious super-herpes, now would I?"

And with that, I leave them. Stunned. Exactly as they deserve. They're subdued when they return to their desks. Molly keeps her distance. As if she's worried I will have my wicked way with her against the photocopier.

"There is one thing that still bothers me, though," I hear her say to James. "People are pointing fingers at Elena but do we have any evidence she hurt Katja?"

"I guess not," he says, glaring at me. "Maybe I should try and patch things up with her when she's back."

Elena doesn't need your fickle version of friendship, James. I pretend to ignore them.

I'm quietly assessing my future at Spark, and it's not looking good. Perhaps it's time to leave and go back to Dublin, give myself some time and space to think clearly. I could camp out at my folks' place. Or stay in my sister's spare room and annoy the shit out of her.

Except I can't bear the thought of being without Elena.

James shrieks. What the bloody hell's happened now? Did someone watch more than four and a half seconds of his YouTube crap or something? Apparently not. I glance over to see Molly and Paula racing to James' side. He's looking all wide-eyed like a smacked-out meerkat.

"I – found this under Elena's desk…it has to be Katja's." He holds it out – a piece of fabric, covered in blood.

Shit. She didn't. She can't have done. As chaos erupts, I feel the buzz of my phone. I read the message and nausea swirls:

I need your help tomorrow – don't try anything stupid

Oh no. I have to find Elena because I think things just got a million times worse.

THE PRESENT

The investigation into Katja Lake's disappearance has ramped up a notch.

Bonnie had been unsure what to make of it at first. It was totally out of character for her, she'd been told. Katja is a much-loved member of the Spark team, they'd said. She wasn't in any trouble. Something hideous must have happened to her. Yet they have no evidence of foul play at this stage. It's baffling.

Bonnie didn't like to contemplate Katja meeting some dreadful fate. Maybe there was nothing sinister afoot. Who's to say she hadn't been swept off her feet by one of those non-entities she's always interviewing, and was right now sailing around the Galapagos Islands on his yacht, unaware of the chaos she'd caused back home while everyone looked for her? Stranger things have happened.

For her own sanity, she'd kept an open mind until now. One name seems to be cropping up in this inquiry – Elena Robins, a senior reporter. Based on what her colleagues have said, she has quite the grudge against Katja.

Elena hadn't been in the office when the cops showed up. Bonnie browses Spark, shuddering with distaste as she comes across one of Elena's exclusives about a supermodel producing her own range of breastmilk perfume. She looks fresh-faced and wholesome in her by-line photo, a soft wave of blonde hair obscuring her left cheek as she beams out from the screen.

She doesn't give off the vibe of a potential killer. But she's hardly going to leer demonically while wielding a bloodstained power tool in her profile pic, is she? That snap tells us nothing of what she's like. Her co-workers, on the other hand, had plenty to contribute on that front:

James Meadows: Fellow senior reporter – told the police how resentful Elena was when Katja arrived in the office, stealing the job she thought was rightfully hers.

Molly Bates: Office junior – revealed how Elena smacked Katja in the eye during a badminton match, landing her in hospital.

Nina Lister: General dogsbody and tea maker – said her cousin Elena was so angry with Katja for giving her a job that she tried to rip the printer out of the wall and hurl it through the window.

Nina said a lot of things based on the notes. 'Complains Elena always ignores her and never invites her to anything even though she calls her all the time', it reads, droning on for several more lines as her resentment towards her becomes clear.

None of this, of course, immediately condemns her, especially not with a lack of physical evidence. She was bound to be upset by not getting a promotion, and accidents did happen in competitive sports. Bonnie once got so fraught during a tennis match at school that her racket flew out of her hand, smashed through a nearby window and knocked the headteacher unconscious. As for Nina – well, looking at the endless ramble of notes about how much the world is against her, she'd probably ghost her, too. She sounds unhinged.

However, further research reveals that Elena used to work for Gleam, a frothy website for tweens, which became briefly notorious after a staff member, Laura Lucas, died in suspicious circumstances seven years ago. She's been browsing some old news stories on the case, which ended in a verdict of misadventure after nobody could prove foul play.

As a side note, it seems Laura was not popular with the Gleam staff, according to the old case notes she's dredged up. And wouldn't you know it, Elena was working there at the time.

This is starting to look too much like coincidence. Maybe it's time they had a little chat with Elena.

ELENA

Lindsey is bewildered when I turn up on the doorstep of the flat, bundles of soaked clothing in my arms, my cheeks damp with rain and tears.

"Elena? What the hell…?" She ushers me into the hallway.

I hadn't intended to bring Lindsey into all this, but I am out of options. My colleagues are not speaking to me, my family is annoyed over the way I treated Nina, and I am unsure how to feel about Nathan, after what Daniel said about his body count. I don't want to believe it. But it explains all those furtive phone calls and why he never wanted me to be around at his place.

Suddenly, the possibility that I was one of many seems all too real. No wonder he wouldn't commit.

Thank God, then, for Lindsey. I grabbed my phone and my bag as I fled Daniel's flat, and called a cab. I threw all my ruined clothes into the back as the driver watched in bemusement, and headed to my former home.

I almost collapse once I am inside. Lindsey guides me to the sofa, which I fall into, dropping all the outfits into a heap on the floor. In an instant she is hugging me so tightly I might burst. I cannot stop shaking.

"I'm sorry," I stammer, "I didn't know where else to go…"

"No need to apologise! We're friends, remember?" She turns down the pop-rock racket pouring out of her soundbar, crosses to the kitchen and returns with a bottle of vodka, a cheap-looking lemonade bottle, and two tumblers. "I think you need some of this, and then you need to tell me what's going on."

Lindsey looks appalled when I finally finish speaking.

"Bloody hell, Elena! Why didn't you tell me about this sooner?

"She's messed with my head!" Nobody believes a word I've said about her! She's turned so many people against me I've got no-one left!"

Lindsey takes a big, ungainly gulp of vodka. "You've still got me," she says pragmatically.

I am so grateful for her comment I start crying again.

"I'm going to help you. There has to be a way out of this."

"I don't see how though."

My phone bursts into song: Nathan. We need to talk, but I cannot speak to him right now, and I press the reject button. I do the same when he calls back less than a minute later.

"That was Nathan," I explain. "I don't want to talk to him – he's a serial shagger. Daniel says he's slept with half the girls on our floor at work, that he probably still is, and for some reason, I think it's true."

"Woah. Well, that makes sense. Would explain why he jumped up and left that time."

"I know! I shouldn't have gone so far with Nathan, but Daniel was forcing me to give up work and have his kids, literally threatening to throw me out on the street if I didn't. Lindsey, he was so awful, and Nathan was the exact opposite! I felt we were meant to be together! I hoped he might feel the same way. I guess I was wrong. I am so through with men!" I hold my glass out for a top-up. "I'll deal with all of that later. What am I going to do about Katja?"

"We'll think of something. There must be a way to prove that she did all those things deliberately." Lindsey crosses to the kitchen again, returning with two bags of crisps. Her snacking habit hasn't diminished while I have been away, but tonight, I am past caring. Instead, I am relieved that there is still one person in the world who has my back.

Although I haven't a clue how she can help me.

I take a shower. The steaming water washes away the rain, the tears, the mud and the sweat which has been a near-constant presence on my forehead in the past few hours. My poor clothes are in the washing machine, and I'm curled up on the sofa in a dressing-down I swiped from Lindsey – a fluffy white number with 'INTERCONTINENTAL' stitched on the breast pocket, leading me to suspect it may have 'accidentally' fallen into her suitcase on a press trip.

Nathan has attempted to call me twice more, but I cannot face speaking to him. I put the phone on silent and leave it face down on the coffee table. Why is he still calling? He must have realised I'm not going to answer.

"Right then," Lindsey says, tearing open the second bag of crisps, the scent of artificial cheese and onion filling the living room. "Where did we get to?"

"We've been through it all! I cannot think of a single way of proving that Katja did all of those things on purpose but I want to know why she did them." I grab a handful of crisps and shovel them down. I'm not sure they've been within sniffing distance of a block of cheddar. I should sue.

Lindsey looks serious. "Is there anything you've noticed about her that might offer a clue?"

It hits me. The one thing I forgot to tell Lindsey. "I don't know if it has any significance, but she keeps a cutting about Laura Lucas in her notebook."

Lindsey shrinks back, alarmed. "Laura Lucas? You're joking. What does she have to do with anything?"

"I don't know. Perhaps she has some connection to Laura – but why would she keep a cutting like that? Laura's been dead for six years already. It's ancient history."

Lindsey stuffs away another paw full of crisps. "All I can think is…Elena, what does Katja look like?"

"Why is that relevant?"

"Just curious."

I'm confused, but I tell her anyway: "She's very pretty, small, dark brown hair, dark eyes – wait a minute, I've got a photo." I pick up my phone. Four more missed calls from Nathan. What is going on? I fire off a quick WhatsApp:

> Daniel called me a filthy whore and threw my clothes out of the window, it was awful. I am at my old flat with my friend Lindsey. Please stop calling

Having dealt with him, I flip open my camera, scrolling until I come to the snap Molly took of us all on the day of the badminton match. How different we all look there. James and I throwing dazzling grins at the camera, and Nathan looking embarrassed to have his picture taken. To the right of us all is Katja, luminous in her sports bra and cycle shorts, hoisting her badminton racket into the air.

"Look at us all," I tell Lindsey. "This was taken right before the badminton match when I hit her in the eye. We all look so happy, don't we? How can so much have changed since then?"

Lindsey isn't listening to my lament.

"Oh shit," she whispers, almost inaudible.

"Lindsey?"

"Can you close in on Katja?" she asks me. I oblige and Lindsey's eyes grow saucer-wide.

"Oh, Elena," she says, fearful.

"What – what is it?" My voice is hoarse with panic.

"That tattoo round her wrist," Lindsey says. "It's Laura's."

LAURA'S DIARY
JUNE

I had a rotten shock when I came into work this morning. I have always kept a framed photo of my family on my desk – the four of us out in the garden during a family barbecue, my parents smiling in the background of the shot, my sister and I front and centre, arm in arm. Looking at the photo has always helped me to get through the day.

Not any more. When I arrived today, I found shattered glass around my desk, the frame broken, and the photo mangled on the floor. To say I was upset was an understatement, but I didn't want anyone to know that. I refused to believe this was something the cleaner did by mistake.

There was only one person who could be responsible for this. Queen Bee must have done it, another petty act to try and drive me out of the office. She wasn't going to get away with it. I marched up to her desk and asked her what the hell she was doing breaking my things. It didn't go well.

"What are you accusing me of now?" she asked. "Don't be so fucking dumb, Laura. Why would I smash your photo? What would I have to gain from doing that? How dare you!"

I didn't believe a word of it. I stood my ground, but she refused to own up, and I'm afraid to say things got heated. "You have to stop this, Laura," she shouted. "I'm not touching your stuff! Why do you keep suggesting I am?!" She was so loud that our editor ran into the main office to see what all the fuss was about. A few seconds later, and I swear things would have got physical. We were hauled off to explain ourselves – where I insisted she had deliberately broken my photo. She swore blind she hadn't been near it, and the bickering kicked off again until she shouted at us to pipe down.

"She's accused me of all sorts!" Queen Bee bleated. "Says I've been messing with her computer, making her lose work and now she's saying I broke her precious photo! Why would I do something like that? When have you ever known me damage someone else's things?"

My editor sided with her, as predicted. She asked me why I kept making such wild claims. She asked Queen Bee to leave, so she could talk to me alone. That's when it all came out.

The deterioration of my work, the fact that she could no longer send me on even the simplest of assignments. The complaints others had made to her about my attitude. That was the biggest sticking point.

"People will forget the mistakes you made in interviews," she said. "We've all been there. But I have a duty of care to my staff, and I can't have one person making everyone else feel uncomfortable. I'm – I'm sorry, Laura, I don't know if you have a future at Gleam after everything that's happened."

The look on my face said it all. The career I had yearned for was already in tatters. All because of one person. My boss fell silent while she contemplated her next move.

"Look, I get this isn't working out as I hoped. But – I like you, I wouldn't have given you a job otherwise," she concluded. "So, I'm going to give you one more chance. I want you at the concert this weekend. If all goes well, I'll do my best to help you get back on track here. If I have any complaints about you on Sunday then don't bother coming in on Monday – because you won't have a job."

I was outraged it had come to this, and I opened my mouth to protest, but she pre-empted me. "If you prefer, you can leave now, of course."

For a moment, I considered the brief satisfaction of telling everybody where they could stick their job and flouncing out. I knew that wouldn't be a good idea. None of them would care, and I'd be unemployable in the industry – every bridge burned.

I had no choice. "OK," I said, defeated. "Let's give your suggestion a go."

I returned to my desk, head spinning, and spotted Queen Bee glaring at me. Except this time she looked sad rather than spiteful, as if she was about to cry.

Everybody was rallying around to offer support. "Don't let her get to you," I heard her best friend say in a low voice. "I know you didn't do it."

Nobody rushed to do the same to me. I still cannot work out what she has against me, but I can only assume there is some jealousy at play. Or she regards me as a threat to her position.

That's fine with me. There is nothing wrong with healthy rivalry. What I can't deal with is the way she looks at me with such hate in her eyes.

It's almost as if she wishes I was dead.

THE PRESENT

Bonnie hasn't stopped thinking about Elena and whether she might be behind Katja Lake's disappearance.

There's no denying she's got the motive.

What Bonnie didn't have – up to now at least – was any real evidence against her. That may have changed. A bloodstained piece of pale pink fabric, evidently from the dress Katja had been going to collect from the office before she disappeared, has been found under Elena's desk.

It was discovered by her colleague James, who sounded hysterical when he spoke to Bonnie.

She's still waiting for the DNA results to come back from the lab – which could still take a couple of days. Who knows what fate might have befallen Katja by then?

It's been nearly four days since she was last seen. Bonnie knows that most missing people return, safe and well, within a few days of disappearing. Right now, that's looking less and less likely.

There's a whiff of foul play and she's involved – it's only a matter of time before the press come sniffing. With one of their number missing, she won't be able to keep them at bay forever. Yet the person she's most keen to speak to has proven elusive. Bonnie had stopped by the office late yesterday afternoon only to be told Elena had left early. She went to her home address, but nobody answered the door.

She's back there this morning, determined to get answers.

Daniel comes to on top of the covers in the guest bedroom, having passed out in the early hours in a haze of alcohol. He couldn't bring himself to sleep in his bed, thinking about what Elena and that awful Nathan had been doing there – although he is unaware they avoided it all along, instead favouring the bed in which he just spent the night.

He winces at the stabbing hangover between his eyebrows and glances at the bedside table. The congealed remains of a sweet and sour Pot Noodle sit next to a half-chewed box of chicken nuggets and an empty bottle of Lambrusco. Last night is a blur. All Daniel can remember is going on a rampage across his pristine flat, destroying everything in sight as his emotions took over, downing half a £200 bottle of brandy and calling Uber Eats for a McDelivery before making a desperate midnight run to the foetid local corner shop. He hates himself for bingeing on such crap. But his life has been shattered. He wasn't exactly in the mood to prepare a charcuterie plate.

What's the point of having the best of everything if you have nobody to share it with?

It occurs to him, albeit fleetingly that he might have put too much pressure on Elena to give everything up for his sake. She wouldn't have been the first to baulk at his demands. That still doesn't give her the right to destroy everything they had. She'd better not come crawling back today begging for forgiveness.

As that thought crosses his mind, the door buzzer goes, grating on Daniel's pained brain.

What the hell? He lurches off the bed to answer it. Who can that be at nine in the morning unless it's Elena begging for another chance. She isn't going to get it.

"I thought I told you never to…" he says, flinging the door open and stopping short when he sees a woman who is not his ex-girlfriend.

Daniel is startled. The woman is around his age, with a kind face, ash-blonde hair swept up into a bun and holding an ID badge.

"Good morning," she says. "Sorry to bother you so early, my name is Detective Bonnie Pace."

"Gosh – I'm so sorry for how I answered the door," Daniel tells her before she can say another word. "How can I help?"

"That's OK. I'm looking for Elena Robins, I was told by her office that she lives here. I wondered whether she might be home, as I need to ask her a few questions?" She takes in the man standing in front of her and cannot help but notice how attractive he is – but also senses there is something wrong. His black hair is unkempt, stubble crowds his chin, he wears a white T-shirt covered in luminous orange food stains, and grey jogging bottoms that look like they've been slept in. Bonnie notes dark shadows under his eyes. Has he been crying?

Daniel's mind flips. What has that dumb bitch done that the police are now after her?

"I'm sorry, she's not here."

"Do you know when she might be home?"

"I'm afraid not. I – well – it's a bit complicated. You'd better come in and tell me what this is all about."

"Thank you. And you are…"

"Daniel Carrington, Elena's boyfriend." His face falls. "Or at least I was."

Bonnie is astonished when she sees the state the place is in. The flat is beautiful, but someone has ripped right through it, leaving torn clothes and broken furniture everywhere. Particularly unnerving is the floor by the sofa, where a row of plush bunnies lie with their heads snipped clean off. One of them has a vegetable knife protruding from its pink fluffy torso. Her toddler would be hysterical if he saw such a senseless crime. Bonnie tiptoes gingerly through the mayhem and perches on a kitchen stool, its seat damp and sticky and reeking of booze.

Daniel stumbles past, picking at the remains of a Pot Noodle and fires up the coffee machine. What on earth has she walked into? Is Daniel Carrington safe? She knows she can call Eric for assistance if her host turns out to have Patrick Bateman tendencies, but he might not be quick enough to save her. She could have been slaughtered like one of those plush bunnies by the time he gets here.

"Mr Carrington…Daniel…is everything OK?"

"Not really." He places a steaming mug in front of the detective. "Why do you need to speak to Elena?"

Bonnie takes a much-needed sip of coffee. "We're investigating the disappearance of one of Elena's colleagues, a Ms. Katja Lake, who vanished a couple of days ago."

"I see." Daniel is curious.

"I was hoping I might find her here."

"I'm sorry. Elena and I – broke up last night, so I threw her out along with her clothes."

So that explains it. "I see," Bonnie says. "I'm sorry to hear that. So, you have no idea where she might have gone."

"I don't," Daniel replies, his voice unsteady. "She may have gone to stay with a friend, or family, but I couldn't say – I told her I never wanted to see her again. She was – she was cheating on me with a colleague, you see." His shoulders shake, and he begins to cry again, but Bonnie wants to know more.

"I know this is upsetting for you. But if you have any information that you think may help us – could she have gone to this colleague's house? Do you have any idea who they are, where they might live?"

Daniel rubs his eyes with his hands like a preschooler who's missed nap time.

"OK. I'm not sure it'll help you, but I'll tell you what happened."

Bonnie can't believe what she hears next.

ELENA

I come to on Lindsey's sofa after two hours of fitful sleep. The first thing I do is check my phone. It's nine o'clock and I have twelve missed calls from Nathan. Why is he so desperate to talk? A WhatsApp message provides little insight:

> I'm sorry about Daniel. Are you OK? I have to talk to you.
> Please call me back – it's urgent

I stopped checking the phone after his fifth attempt. I was way more concerned about Katja and her flower tattoo. What had been staring me in the face for months took her mere seconds to realise – she had the same curling garland of purple flowers round her wrist as Laura Lucas.

I knew something about her looked familiar, but I had been unable to put my finger on it – until Lindsey pointed it out.

Katja's behaviour over the past few months has now made sense to me. Everything that's happened to me at her hands also happened to Laura. Except Laura died. Am I facing the same fate?

I am still bleary-eyed, and sleep deprived as Lindsey slopes in with two mugs of coffee and a plate of toast and Marmite. "I called in sick," she says. "I think you need me here today."

She nudges the toast in my direction, but the bread tastes dry and unappealing. It sticks to the roof of my mouth when I take a bite.

"You've got to eat," she tells me. I shove the plate aside and reach for one of the mugs, scalding my tongue on the hot liquid.

"You can't survive on coffee."

Evidently, she's never seen me when I have a deadline.

"Did you sleep at all?" Lindsey asks. I haven't looked in a mirror this morning and I'm not sure I would like what I see.

"A couple of hours. I can't stop thinking about what you told me. Lindsey, surely Katja can't be Laura, she's dead! Do you think this is a revenge thing for – what happened?"

"It sounds like it." Lindsey remembers all those incidents at Gleam – the lie I told after the party to save my own skin, the interview disaster. I know all that happened. I've beaten myself up over it time and time again.

If she's after me because I think she killed Laura, then she's misguided and she needs to realise that before she does something awful.

Four hours later – after I force down the remains of the toast to shut my best friend up – we're still no closer to figuring out who Katja is and what she wants. The fact she's still missing hasn't helped. I'm certain she's not dead.

"I can't stay here forever, Lindsey. Sooner or later, someone is going to find out where I'm hiding, and whether it's Katja or the cops, this isn't going to end well." I flop back into the sofa cushions, weak with frustration.

My phone rings. Nathan. Why is he so obsessed? I press the reject button, wanting to throw the infernal handset across the room and vanish. From all of this.

I know I cannot do that. "I think it's time to give up," I say. I am so worn out by the events of the past few weeks that I don't want to fight any more.

"You can't! That bitch is trying to ruin your life for something you didn't do! There must be a way you can prove what she's done?"

"Only if I can prove she's still alive. And there's no way of knowing when she will show up." I need to face facts. It's over. Every option I have looks bleak.

Until something on my phone catches Lindsey's eye. "Oh, I think you do." She passes me the handset. My hands are shaking so much that I almost drop it – but the message is plain to see. It's from an unknown number:

Let's end this tonight

The Publishers' Awards. Of course.

KATJA

DEAD?

MOI?

Fuck that for a game of soldiers. I doubt Elena's figured it out. She couldn't find her own brain if you gave her a magnifying glass and directions. I'll be honest. The possibility that she might try to kill me didn't feature in my original scheme. I should have been prepared for it.

We all know about her horrific temper.

And I am all too familiar with her habit of pushing innocent people through windows.

But this wasn't something I saw coming. I guess even the best laid plans can be blown off course. I hadn't intended to do anything devious that night. Not with the grand finale of my scheme just days away. I was saving myself.

The last thing I expected to see when I went to fetch my dress was Elena buzzing round my desk like an out-of-control vibrator. The events that followed were unprecedented. I hit my head quite hard on the filing cabinet, enough to feel my brain rattle in my skull. I could have staggered to my feet, but when I heard Elena's reaction, thinking she'd killed me, I decided to play along. The panic in her voice was delicious. Holding my breath so it looked like I'd died – not so much. Then she disappeared. It wasn't until I realised she wasn't coming back that I had that other bright idea – to vanish completely and make her think she'd imagined it all.

I'd love to know how she reacted. I bet it wasn't pretty.

Besides, I was injured at this point. My hair was matted with blood, and I had a lump the size of a melon forming on my head. The nurse at the hospital I checked into was lovely when I rocked up in such a distressed state at one in the morning. She stitched me up and reassured me that I wasn't concussed or badly injured.

I was so grateful for her care. I always am when someone shows me such kindness.

My wrath is for people like Elena Robins.

She may have figured out my connection to Laura Lucas. The tattoo around my wrist is a dead giveaway. Laura was so proud of her tattoo when she got it on her eighteenth birthday.

She'd been waiting to have that done for years. Her death was devastating. That a healthy young woman with so much going for her should be taken so cruelly. They said there was no proof she was murdered – but I know that's not true. The things she was saying about Elena, the fact she died at a work event – consider those a giveaway. We all know Elena wanted her gone.

This must have been much more convenient than complaining to HR.

I knew none of this until I found Laura's hidden diary a few years later. By that time, the case was closed, and nobody cared any more. There were very few people left to care.

Laura's dad died a couple of years later, while her mother unable to cope with so much heartbreak disappeared a few months after that. Is she still alive? Who knows?

Which leaves me. It's taken its toll, that's for sure. My adult life has been a succession of one-night stands, partying hard, way too much coke – anything to blot out the pain of what I lost.

I even got married at one point, but that didn't last. Poor Mr Lake couldn't cope with my tantrums, my drinking, those nights when I'd stay out until dawn with random men and not tell him where I was. He wasn't a bad guy, but it had to end, it wasn't fair on him. Especially not when one of those strangers left me needing a little dose of, well, antibiotics, and before I knew it, my hapless husband did too. 'The couple that shares everything stays together, right.' Nope.

Nothing like a dose of the clap to bring your marriage to a crashing halt.

It did shock me into doing better, though, and since I met my current boyfriend, I've behaved – or at least tried to (what he doesn't know about those occasional slip-ups won't hurt him). He's loyal, and gets it, more than anybody I've ever been with. I do regret that part of my past. If you'd had everything taken from you, can you honestly say you wouldn't do the same? I've tried to convince my psychiatrist that I am moving on with my life. That isn't easy when all you can think about is revenge. People say I'm not well and I'm inclined to believe them.

But I'm beyond grateful for that journalism qualification, which eventually led me to Spark – and right to Elena Robins' desk. It's been fun watching her squirm over the past few months. I've had to employ a few sneaky tactics, mind. Sticking those spelling errors into Elena's stories, claiming she made them herself. Messing with her computer when she wasn't there. Sabotaging her Freddy Taylor interview. Oh, and sending a certain video to her boyfriend to split them up. That was a piece of luck, and I knew it was only a matter of time before she gave in to her desires for Nathan. I felt bad about making Molly ill that time – I had to keep that one quiet as harming innocents is not in my beloved's remit. But sprinkling an overdose of laxative on her pain au chocolat worked wonders when it came to overloading Elena with extra work. Besides, Molly's a pointless airhead. A reality show contestant waiting to happen. Like, I care if she wound up on a drip.

Everyone in that office has played their part – without even realising. Who knew, though, that Elena would eventually end up as a suspected murderer? That development will make the final, greatest part of my plan so much easier to pull off. After all, people in the depths of despair are sometimes driven to take drastic action, aren't they? For somebody whose state of mind is as troubled as Elena's, it wouldn't be a surprise if she did.

All I need is for her to know I'm waiting for her. And I'm hoping the message I've just sent will do the trick. Given that she has an ego the size of Saturn there's no way she'll skip the awards. Anything for the chance to prance around in her new frock like an over-excited teenager on prom night, driving everybody to the cocktail table with her constant showing off.

Never mind the fact that the dress looked a lot better on me than it ever would on her.

I'm all set and fizzing with excitement. I've got the champagne in, an expensive bottle of Cristal chilling in the fridge – I consider pouring a glass. No, I'll have plenty of time to celebrate later. I need a clear head for the long night ahead.

The night when Elena finally finds out who I am.

ELENA

I wasn't going to go to the Publishers' Awards. Not after everything that's happened and with every instinct in my head is telling me I shouldn't. Katja is dangerous. If being there will bring all of this to a head, then the only chance I have of saving myself is to give her what she wants.

Unfortunately, I'm not sure I still have anything nice to wear.

We have a plan. Assuming I win the Exclusive of the Year award – and if Ladbrokes were taking bets, they'd have me down as their hot favourite – I will accept my prize and instead of a speech, will tell the entire room everything Katja has done to try and discredit me – right down to faking her own death to make me look like a killer. I get that it isn't foolproof, but there will be over a thousand people there tonight. Someone has to believe me.

It's my only option.

Since I have been unable to attend my planned hair, make-up and nail appointments Lindsey has stepped in as my stylist for the night. This means my hair is blow-dried into a bouffant helmet the 1980s will be wanting back at some point. My nails, painted a dark burgundy, are covered in chips and smudges and the polish creeps over my fingers staining them deep red.

My dress could have been worse. The suit bag it was in saved it from the muddy puddle of doom outside Daniel's flat although there is one suspicious dirty mark on the waistband.

Lindsey came to the rescue with a dab of pink nail paint. My shoes were beyond repair, so I borrowed a pair of shiny nude heels from Lindsey's wardrobe. They're about half a size too small for me, but since my only other option is the Doc Marten boots I arrived in, they'll have to do.

The overall effect is not quite drop-dead stunning. All I see when I look in the mirror, is big hair, overly bright lipstick and shoes that don't fit. They push me forwards and make me look like a Barbie doll who's overdosed on pina coladas.

Whatever. It will have to do.

I hastily throw some essentials – phone, keys, power bank – into a sequinned clutch bag, and am assessing my mediocre appearance when there's a buzz at the door. We look at each other in alarm. Nobody knows I am here.

"Are you expecting anybody?"

Lindsey shakes her head. "Not that I know of."

The door buzzes again, louder and more insistent. I screw up my last remaining ounce of courage and venture onto the balcony. To my amazement, Nathan stands on the lawn, looking frantic. He catches sight of me staring down – a twisted Romeo and Juliet scenario.

"Elena! Let me in! I have to talk to you!"

"What are you doing here?! How did you find me?!"

"You told me you were at Lindsey's place! Let me in. I'm not leaving until you do!"

No. Nathan is the last person I want to see. I can't deal with the thought of being a notch on his overworked bedpost right now. That's for once this is all over. Something about the tone of his voice concerns me though, an urgency which suggests he will stay there yelling if I leave him outside. With some reluctance, I cross to the entry phone and let him in.

Nathan is at the door seconds later, pushing his way inside before I can speak. "Elena, thank God I found you," he says. Then he sees my outfit.

"You're not going to the awards, are you? Please say you're not going to the awards."

"That's exactly where I'm going! What business is it of yours anyway?"

Nathan puts his hands on my shoulders, and my spine starts to tingle. Even knowing where those hands have been. Something's not right. He looks wide-eyed and freaked out.

"Please listen to me. You mustn't go, it's not safe, Katja's going to do something terrible if you do..."

"What the actual hell? Katja is going to the awards? How do you know that? We don't even know if she's alive..." I say, not wanting to share my suspicions.

"Trust me. She's alive, she faked it! And she's furious. Elena, please."

"How do you know she faked it? I thought her boyfriend had reported her missing?"

The expression on his face is chilling. No. Surely, he can't mean...? He drops his bombshell.

"I reported her missing," he admits, guilt clouding his voice to a whisper. "It was me."

NATHAN

I wish it wasn't true. But it is. I'm Katja's boyfriend and have been for about eighteen months.

I can't pretend any of this comes as a surprise because I knew exactly what she was up to. I'm the mysterious lover who reported her missing, after all. I didn't want to. I've been begging her to stop all this for weeks. But she'll go to any lengths to get her way. The thought of what she did to me makes me shudder. It's irrelevant, though. I'm complicit. I don't deserve anyone's sympathy.

Elena's backing away from me, her face a mask of confusion and hurt. Gorgeous, sweet, perfect Elena. The woman I never imagined I'd fall for when all of this started. How could I do this to her? "No!" She's screaming over and over again. "Please, no! You can't be...!"

Tears spring to my eyes, but I bat them away. Like she's going to give a shit if I start blubbing. "I'm sorry...I'm so sorry! I never thought Katja would take it this far. I told her to stop. I told her I don't want anything more to do with it, but she won't listen! You need to keep away from her. She's out of control!"

"How COULD YOU!? What the hell are you playing at?"

Before I can reply she's flying at me and knocking me back against the door. I feel the latch digging into the back of my head. Fuck, that's going to be bruised tomorrow. But it's nothing compared to the volley of slaps and punches she's throwing. One blow connects with my left shoulder, and I wince. She's got a mean right hook on her. Even Tyson Fury might be rattled with this.

"Stop! Please!" I grab her wrists, trying to calm her down. It's now or never. "You don't get it! I don't want anything to happen to you…because…because I'm in love with you!"

There. I've said it. For all the good it'll do. She shakes herself free of my grip as though I'm contaminated. Her voice is a low growl. "Get out." She loses it. "GET – OUT!"

"Please, Elena…!" I've resorted to begging. Pathetic. She's having none of it.

"I mean it! I don't want you anywhere near me. How could I have been so stupid as to fall for it? And now you say you love me?" She's puce with rage. "Daniel was right. You don't love anyone except yourself! You've only made me more determined to go to the awards tonight because I think you're lying about Katja, to get yourself out of trouble! Now leave before I call the police."

"I'm not! I swear! You don't know what she did to me…" I see Lindsey behind her, mouth in a grim line, looking as if she's about to ask me what I want written on my headstone.

Shit. I can't handle her as well. She's terrifying.

"I think you'd better leave," is all she says.

It's no use. I can't stop this trail of destruction I've caused, and I've lost the true love of my life.

I throw up for real this time the second I'm outside in the garden. At least I would do if I had anything to bring up since I've barely eaten all day. Instead, I heave a string of bile into one of the ornamental rose bushes surrounding the block. Destroying lives and natural beauty. I'm the worst kind of human. I can't stay here now. I've broken Elena's heart. I know I've lost my final chance to talk her round when

I see her emerge from the side entrance seconds later and climb into a white car. It drives off before I can reach her.

"Shit!" I shout, loud enough to have the blinds twitching in the neighbouring blocks.

Seconds later my phone buzzes. It's Katja:

Where are you, idiot?
You'd better show up later, or you're as dead as Elena

No! She really is going to do it. The urge to puke overtakes me again. Elena's going to die tonight, and it's all my…

"Hey! Dickhead!"

The shout shakes me out of my stupor. It's Lindsey. She's glaring at me from the balcony. Like I'm not in enough trouble already.

"Are – are you talking to me?"

"I am. Get your arse back up here if you want me to help."

Is she serious? I must be the last person she wants to help. It's a trap. She's probably going to throw me over the railings and tell my grieving parents I mistook them for the front door. What if she means it? I decide to take the risk.

Because on balance, she's still less likely to murder me than Katja.

Seven Years Ago

LAURA

The Gleam concert should have been the most exciting day of the year.

Not for me, it wasn't. I woke up with an overriding sense of dread. Knowing that my career was hanging in the balance. Terrified that Queen Bee would try and make trouble. I was determined not to let that happen. I decided to remain as inoffensive as possible. Even down to my outfit, a simple white T-shirt, dark blue jeans, and a black cardigan thrown over the top although it was a warm day. I knew I'd fade into the background against her fantastic get-up – she'd been talking up designer jeans and expensive pink trainers all week – but today was not the day for anything more flamboyant. I had my oldest and most battered trainers on, the designer imitations I picked up on a market stall for a fiver. They've got a huge hole in the sole where the water seeps through when it's raining but they're comfy as hell, and I can't bear to part with them.

Besides, if I lost my job today, I wouldn't be able to afford new ones.

I was grateful I decided to wear them as it turned out the venue was in a remote corner of East London, several hundred yards away from the nearest road, and a good twenty-minute walk from the Tube. I wasn't splashing out on a taxi when I didn't know if I'd have a wage slip next month. The building itself was circular and looked almost derelict from the outside, although the noise I could hear left me in no doubt that I had come to the right place. Tyler Bard's ear-assaulting soundtrack with the strains of 'Out Here by Myself' was audible even from outside. If I ever heard that song again after today, it would be about twenty million years too soon.

I decided the best way forward was to keep quiet, speak only when spoken to and then only give short answers. If I didn't say anything, I couldn't get into trouble, could I? As it happened, there was no need for me to consider that. My editor decided I wasn't fit to go anywhere near the acts, leaving the job of looking after them to the staff members who could be trusted. I tried not to feel bitter – but I bit my tongue, reminding myself of her promise that things might improve for me at work. Instead, I smiled, remained diplomatic and picked up all the menial jobs without complaining.

For the first half of the show, things went smoothly. Until the fateful moment I was asked to fetch some water for the crew. I was directed to a small storeroom towards the back of the venue, up several flights of rickety stairs. It was as tired looking as the rest of the place. I had no intention of hanging around.

I wasn't prepared for what I saw when I opened the door.

A certain colleague of mine – I think you know who I mean – was in the room with Tyler Bard himself. And they certainly weren't discussing the weather. Tyler's trousers were round his ankles as he went hammer and tongs into my colleague, half-naked and clinging to the stacks of bottles.

I was rooted to the spot. The scene was curiously unsexy, and I knew I should fetch my editor and show her what was going on in that room – with her boyfriend. But I was too thunderstruck to move.

It was those split seconds which cost me dear. They saw me and abruptly sprang apart. Tyler brazened it out, pulling his trousers up as he transformed into his usual cocky self. "Hey, how are you doing!" he said, lurching forward to fold me into a hug. I'd had quite enough of those today from excited staffers pretending they gave a damn about me and dodged his clumsy pawing.

As for my colleague, her look was harder to read. Somewhere between fury and blind fear. My own expression was more triumphant.

It was the one which said: "Well now, how's that for turning the tables?"

ELENA

The Publishers' Awards is always the best night of the year. In the wake of everything that's happened, it's turned into the worst. All because of the massive, sprawling mess my life has become. I've lost my boyfriend. My job is hanging by a thread. My family has practically disowned me. I've got nowhere to live. My best sparkly heels are caked in mud and most of my clothes are ruined. Everybody thinks I'm a murderer.

Nathan is not the man I thought he was.

That's the one which hurts most of all. I could get another job, talk my folks around, and replace my beloved outfits. I'd sleep in a discarded Amazon box on the street if I had to. At least if I end up in prison, I won't have to worry about the housing situation. But losing Nathan?

There's no solution to that.

I'm struggling to process the betrayal. The haunting thought of him getting out of my bed, going home and getting into bed with Katja. The fact he knew all along what she was doing and allowed her to get away with what she's done to me. That's why he kept making excuses about his place. It was nothing to do with notches on the bedpost at all.

It was because Katja was there.

My head is in turmoil. I'm still too stunned for an emotional response, but I know it will hit me sooner or later. I'll refuse to get out of bed, weep rivers into my pillow and forsake all men, while Lindsey tries to persuade me to eat something other than that dusty two-year-old tub of *Celebrations* from the bottom of the cupboard. I know I'll never meet anyone else. I'll die alone, unloved, and surrounded by Persian cats. When the police eventually break down my door because nobody's heard from me in weeks, they'll find me crushed to death under all the freebies I've nabbed from press conferences, which I've been hoarding because I have nothing and no one else. Other people get buried alongside the love of their life. I'll be buried alongside my promotional *Ex on the Beach* tote bag.

Slow down. My mind is firing a million thoughts at once. There are too many questions that need answering here. I need a distraction. I don't have time for heartbreak tonight. I have to think about how to deal with Katja and how to salvage my reputation. The radio's on in the cab – some Easy Listening FM nonsense. I'll focus on that for a bit to calm myself down.

"Here's another classic from our Power Ballad hour," the presenter says, "From 1980, it's the beautiful track, 'All out of Love', by Air Supply."

All out of love? Why don't you just turn around and stab me in the heart, Mr Uber Driver? It's no good. However hard I try to think about something else, my mind keeps returning to Nathan. Whether everything between us was a set-up. He could've been reporting back to Katja, for all I know.

Yet he seemed genuine enough. The conversations we had, those days he cheered me up when all seemed crap at work. That time, he brought me homemade chilli for lunch because I told him it was my favourite. The way he shouted my name out in bed. Maybe he was telling the truth. Maybe Nathan really is in love with me.

He should've thought about that beforehand.

THE PRESENT

Could this case get any more insane?

Bonnie didn't see how. A woman disappears without trace. On top of that we have office politics, badminton injuries, and rivalry over a pair of boots. Staying at home looking after a small person who couldn't talk, scribbled on her Farrow and Ball painted walls and covered everything she owned in mashed carrot was a breeze by comparison. Add to that the complication of chief suspect Elena Robins having an affair with the missing woman's boyfriend.

Nathan had seemed nervous and skittish. Now she knew why. Could he be in on it, conspiring with Elena to get Katja out of the way so they could be together? There is no evidence at this stage that he was involved, and his alibi checks out. But it wouldn't be beyond the realms of possibility. And she could see what Elena sees in him, how working together all that time must have proven too tempting in the end. It wouldn't be hard to fall for someone like Nathan, who might not be as classically good-looking as Daniel but has an animal magnetism about him, which even Bonnie couldn't ignore. If Eric looked like that, she'd never get a scrap of work done.

Daniel though. What has Bonnie done to deserve him? Nobody has tried her patience as much as Daniel. Not even that nutty Nina woman. And that was saying something. She was forced to sit in his wrecked flat for what felt like hours, acting more like a therapist than a police officer as he rambled on about how Elena had betrayed his trust. He told her how the same thing had happened time and time again. "There's been so many like her," he said, oblivious to the fact that wasn't why Bonnie was there. "I offer my girlfriends the world and all they do is throw it back in my face. They're so ungrateful."

She had nodded and clucked sympathetically and taken notes while being driven to distraction by his poor-little-me act. Bonnie isn't much of a drinker but by the end she was wondering if ten o'clock on a Friday morning was too early for wine. She was far too professional to say what she was thinking: *Maybe you're the problem, you misogynist shit-for-brains.*

Bonnie feels done in. She's grateful her husband isn't like that, even if he had once suggested maternity leave was just an excuse to sit around in her PJs with her feet up, in a way that had made her want to thump him with a truncheon.

As soon as this case is wrapped up, she will be through with Spark. She never wants to look at another showbiz website again. Not if this is how the people on it behave. Maybe if there are no further developments tonight, she can get home in time to do the toddler's bath and bedtime. A light reading of *The Very Hungry Caterpillar* will soothe her frayed nerves.

She climbs into her car and her phone lights up with Daniel's number. Her heart sinks.

This time, it's the news she's been wanting to hear.

"Detective Pace?" he says. "It's Daniel Carrington. I know where you can find Elena."

ELENA

Lindsey's shoes are biting when my driver pulls up to the Publishers' Awards venue – a rusty old warehouse in East London where Gleam used to hold some of their events. It looks better on the inside than it does on the outside. As I make my way around the building to the front entrance a gust of wind blows my hair sideways; the cheap spray doing nothing to protect it from the elements. My make-up has also run slightly after half an hour in a stifling car. That would never have happened if I'd had a professional job done.

I will have to weather it all as best I can.

Inside, I'm surrounded by champagne cocktails and shiny pink drinks with flowers floating in the top. I know I need to act normal to avoid any further suspicion from my already hostile colleagues. I push through the noisy crowd mingling in the foyer, and grab a Peach Bellini. Anything to muster up some courage, although I've eaten so little in the past forty-eight hours that one mouthful goes straight to my head.

I'm half a glass down when I clap eyes on James and Molly, dressed in sober dark clothing. They look more dressed for a funeral than a party.

"Elena!" James pipes up. "We didn't know you were coming! And you look – er…"

He appears lost for words.

"Of course!" I say. "I wouldn't miss it, would I?" Oh God. Katja's still missing. Maybe that was a little tactless. "Excuse me a minute." I totter off, claiming I need the bathroom. I hear James saying "Drunk already…" to Molly. I shut myself off from his words and focus on the task at hand.

When I see myself in the toilets, I understand why they were eyeing me with such confusion. My hair is windblown, falling to my shoulders in matted clumps, and Lindsey's blow dry is doing little to keep it neat. Mascara has pooled around my eyes in dark smudges, and a line of lipstick extends up to my cheek instead of on my lips. My dress is creased, and the nail paint is flaking off, revealing the dirt mark below. I look like I got ready in the dark and fell into a wheelie bin on my way here.

It can't be helped. I'm here now. I doubt I'll be winning any best dressed awards tonight.

I return to the foyer to see Paula marching up to me, looking formal in a black velvet gown, curls piled on top of her head.

"Elena, what are you playing at?" she asks.

Time to stand my ground. "I have every right to be here," I tell her, swaying slightly in my too-tight shoes. "I have been nominated for a major award."

"And that's the most important thing right now? Katja is missing, and this is how you behave?" I can feel James and Molly's gazes burning into me. I'd love to walk away, head held high, while telling them they can choke on their award nominations.

As if. I can barely move. I have no choice but to brazen this out.

"I was invited. I'm staying, and I don't care what you think." I deposit my empty champagne glass on the side and stumble off, head held high. I can hear the hushed whispers of my colleagues.

"Unbelievable."

"She'll get what's coming to her."

"If she keeps this up, she'll be behind bars before we know it."

I feel a surge of annoyance. Their opinion of me is that low. To think there was a time when I got on well with these people. They'll be regretting those carefully chosen words later when I expose Katja for what she really is.

All she has to do is show up.

KATJA

Where are you, idiot?

I'm en route to the awards to confirm I'm not dead and have sent
Nathan another message. That makes five in the past two hours. I
can't believe he's let me down like this. He's been so aloof lately. Questioning my motives. Becoming distant. Turning away from me in bed.
I've been the one making all the moves on that front lately. He usually
can't get enough of me.

Maybe he's got a bit on the side? No, that's not possible. He
stopped all that when we got together. Has been quite the model boyfriend since then. Why didn't I lock him in the bathroom and go it
alone while I had the chance? Why did I let him carry on going to
work as normal? Nobody there knows about us, and I didn't want to
arouse suspicion, that's why.

Besides, it never occurred to me he'd do a runner.

Not after the threats I made to keep him in line.

Nathan couldn't have shown up in my life at a better time. We met
while I was trying to move on from my cowpat of a marriage. I didn't
want to feel sad or bad about it, so I'd gone to a press screening that
night, some shit reality show about divorcing couples competing in a
string of challenges to see who got to keep the sofa. I was sitting alone
at the launch with a glass of unremarkable white wine when Nathan

appeared at my side. Blue-eyed. Well-toned. At least a foot taller than me. Kind of edgy-looking.

One thousand per cent my type.

"Is it me or is this show a pile of crap?" was his opening line. His accent turned my insides to liquid.

"You're so right," I said.

That was that. We bonded over our mutual dislike of the programme we'd been sent to see and continued the chat over drinks. Then dinner. Then bed. After that, we never looked back. I couldn't believe my luck at landing a boyfriend like Nathan. I never considered it possible given my path of self-destruction. Who knew I could land someone so sweet, gentle, and eager to please, who listens to me and looks after me? And who's an absolute demon in the sack?

Talk about having all your birthdays come at once.

I didn't know Elena was a colleague of his when we first met. I knew he worked for Spark, where he had the worst reputation for his former bedhopping antics, but that was all. Until one night, I was idly browsing the site and saw her byline winking out at me. What an unexpected gift. I knew then I had her exactly where I wanted her. All I had to do was unveil my sob story to Nathan, get him on side and find some way to get into that office.

The first part was easy. He can't bear to see anyone cry, especially not when he's smitten with them. He was so shocked to hear about Laura that he didn't stop to question my desire for revenge. Of course, I had to feign surprise when he told me Elena worked with him.

But honestly, it was an Oscar-worthy performance.

Getting close to Elena was another matter. I had to wait for the right job to come along, and that took months. When it did, Nathan was right on board with my plans. The poor boy is so easily led. That floozie he claims 'fucked his brains out' at the Christmas party that time didn't leave him with a single pair to rub together.

Which is why I didn't give him anything too taxing to do: Get close to Elena, pretend to be her friend, report back to me everything she's saying to you. Then, kiss her in an alley so I can film it and find a way to use it against her. It's foolproof.

So why is he getting cold feet all of a sudden? I've told him time and time again not to worry, that he won't get in any trouble. Once I've done what I have to do, we can go anywhere, do anything, go find ourselves in Goa on the money my dad left me if that's what we both want. Nobody will suspect a thing.

But no. All I've heard for the past few weeks is that it's wrong. That we've taken it too far. That we should stop. As if that's going to happen. Now he's gone AWOL when I need him most.

I can see the venue in the distance. It looks as decrepit as it did on the day Laura died.

How coincidental that the same thing will soon happen to Elena. I've dressed up for the occasion, even though that bitch ripped up my outfit. Although we all know she's got form when it comes to destroying things.

So instead, I've opted for a glittery purple gown, stilettoes you could poke someone's eye out with and the pièce de résistance – my lilac evening gloves. The ones designed to cover any unfortunate fingerprints I might leave. All I need now is for Nathan to be there, waiting for me.

I'd hate for him to meet the same fate that I have in mind for Elena.

NATHAN

I knew I shouldn't have trusted Lindsey. She slaps me in the face the second I'm back in the flat.

"Jesus! What the...!" I shout as the force knocks me sideways. Where the hell did she learn to do that? I think my left eyeball has exploded.

"That's for being a two-faced sack of shit!"

There's no answer to that. She's raging. The silence between us seems to last decades.

"Right then. Now we've got that out of the way, I suppose you'd better come in."

Do I have to? Yes. I do. This is for Elena. But I'm bricking it.

My nerves are shot to hell as I stand in Lindsey's living room taking in the surroundings. It's hard to believe Elena used to live here, with its cluttered shelves, chaotic spider plants and dark wooden floors like the ones at school. The *Friends* cast stare down from a crooked poster on the opposite wall, like they're taunting me. Lindsey is moving around in the kitchen, probably looking for a sharp object so she can cut me into strips and bury me under the rose bush I just threw up in.

She's got a bottle of vodka. Is she going to poison me instead? She pours shots into two glasses and slides one to me. I down it in a single gulp. I don't die. Maybe it's not a trap.

"I asked for that slap, didn't I?" I say, holding a hand to my smarting cheek.

"Too right you did. Is that how you always treat women?"

Oh, for fuck's sake. "Of course not! Is that why you got me back up here, to have a pop at me?"

Lindsey knocks back her shot like she's trying to drink me under the table.

"I am furious with you for what you've done to my best friend, and right now, I do want to chop your balls off and post them to your mother in a Jiffy bag. Since Elena's life might be in danger, I'm prepared to give you an olive branch. So, grab a seat and tell me how the hell you got into this mess."

So she's not going to castrate me. At least, not yet. "All right," I say, parking myself on an ancient-looking sofa, that creaks under my weight. "I'd always found Elena a bit full-on. I used to call her Little Miss Flawless behind her back because she'd arrive at work looking so perfect and I'd show up as if I'd chased a tornado on the way in. She was always trying to flirt with me. I ignored it, though. I know I've got a bad reputation but that doesn't mean I sleep with anything that moves."

"I find that hard to believe!"

"I haven't tried it on with you yet, have I? Look, do you want me to tell you what happened or not?"

"Calm down! Elena's boyfriend told her you'd slept with half the girls on your floor at work."

This is worse than I thought. "Oh, you don't believe him, do you? That arrogant cunt's bound to spread shit like that! I haven't!"

"How many was it then?"

That bluff didn't work. "I don't know...three or four maybe?" She's not buying it.

"Six…eight…ten…maybe twenty…then those two others at the same time…I get it, I'm a horrible person, OK? Is that important right now?"

"All right! Tell me what happened with Katja."

"Fine. I met Katja about eighteen months ago at this press launch for some shitty TV show. We hit it off, and we went for dinner afterwards, and then she came home with me that night…"

"Oh, quelle surprise!"

"At first, everything was great," I say, ignoring Lindsey's jibe. "Then one day I come home and she's crying, and she tells me about Laura, who died, and how badly her colleagues treated her. I couldn't stand to see her upset, so I was getting angry on her behalf, and she started talking about someone called Elena—"

"I see. And it went from there."

"Yeah. When she got the job at Spark, she asked me to get to know Elena better, so I could report back what she was thinking. It helped her – plan what she was going to do to her. Except I liked her. She wasn't cold towards me like everybody else at work. And she didn't seem like the sort of person to have done the things Katja was accusing her of. That's when I started to have doubts about what we were doing. When I tried to make Katja stop."

"Should've tried a bit harder then, shouldn't you?

"What are you talking about? I did! I begged her to call it quits the night she faked her death. Elena couldn't stop crying; she thought she'd killed her. I was frantic."

"Yet you still reported her missing. For God's sake, Nathan what were you thinking?"

This is the worst possible thing she could have said. "Stop it! You don't get it, do you Lindsey!"

"What do you mean? You couldn't have said no?"

I turn to face her and realise my eyes are wet with tears.

"No," I say in a shaky voice. "Not after what she did to me."

KATJA

Of course I'm not proud of how I treated Nathan. But he left me no choice. I can't bear disloyalty. He looked like shit when I finally returned from the hospital at around four o'clock in the morning after my fight with Elena. I mean, I didn't look so hot myself. Stitches and bruising and a Belgium-sized bandage will do that to a girl.

This was different. He clearly hadn't slept, and there was a haunted look in his eyes, as though he was terrified of me. He had every reason to be after the way he'd spoken to me earlier. I tried to keep it light, but he wouldn't look me in the eye, instead focusing on that damp patch on the bedroom wall.

"Look, Katja…" he began, but I chipped in before he could continue.

"Nathan, she's overstepped the mark this time. Look what she did to me!"

"You said it was an accident, that you fell…"

"Only because she pushed me. And don't give me any of that self-defence crap, I should have the little harridan arrested for assault. Watch as her sorry arse is carted off to prison. I paused for dramatic effect. "But how boring would that be?"

"Please, can we just talk about this?"

"The time for talking is past, my love. We're going to have so much fun with this next bit, you and me. Now, here's what I need you to do."

"Katja, please! You've gone too far now! You can't go on treating Elena like this, it's not right!"

He was pleading. It was pitiful. Nice try, bozo, I thought as I circled him, as menacingly as a shoal of starving piranha round a lifeboat full of passengers. I could feel him flinch as I edged closer.

"I'll decide when we're finished, Nathan." I snapped. "What's wrong with you? Why do you care about Elena so much all of a sudden? I thought we were in this together!"

"I can't do this any more Katja. Can't you see how fucked up this is?"

"What, you don't love me? You don't want to help me? Of course, you do." It was time to bring out the big guns. I ran a light finger under his beltline, always guaranteed to get him hot under the collar, but he shrank back as though he didn't want me touching him. His attitude was really pissing me off. "Here's what we're going to do...I'm going to book myself into a lovely hotel for a few days, order a load of room service and watch crap daytime TV. And you are going to report me missing to the police. Let's see how Miss Elena Robins gets out of that one then..."

"No, Katja! Enough now! I won't do it! You can't make me!"

How disappointing.

"I know I can't *make* you," I said in my most persuasive voice. "But tell me Nathan, do you know what it's like to lose a loved one? You'd be devastated, wouldn't you?

"What are you saying?"

"I mean, I know where your sister Vicky lives. You took me to hers last Christmas. I remember the address even now from the car sat nav." Actually, I hadn't a clue, but what he didn't know won't kill him. On the other hand, I might if he didn't stop his pathetic whining.

"Lovely house, huge windows and a concrete patio right below? Be a shame if something happened to her like it did to Laura."

"You wouldn't...!" He looked so distraught it snapped my heart-strings. I came this close to giving in.

But no.

"Why wouldn't I? I could do with a break. Dublin is lovely at this time of year. Let's be honest Nathan, Vicky and I didn't exactly get along. Talk about shrill and annoying, with that yappy little mutt of hers trying to hump my leg. And her Christmas pudding had the texture of a Brillo pad. Seriously, if you're going to subject me to your hideous relatives, at least give me one who can cook."

"Please, Katja...please don't do this."

"I'm not sure anyone would miss her much...oh no wait, you would. Maybe your mum and dad. Probably more so, if it turned out you were responsible." I moved closer until we were inches apart, my hand resting on his hip. "Put it this way Nathan – I'm very good at fudging evidence. Especially when I live in a flat full of someone else's DNA."

He was silent. I could feel him trembling beneath my touch. I knew I'd stunned him into submission.

NATHAN

Lindsey doesn't believe me. It's obvious. She probably thinks a guy like me will make up any old story to get out of trouble.

"I had no choice," I tell her. "She wouldn't listen! She *threatened* me, my *family*!

What else was I supposed to do?"

I'm trying not to cry in front of Lindsey. Like the woman who wants my head mounted on the toilet wall would be sympathetic. That's when I felt her hand on my shoulder.

"Wow, Nathan, you really have got yourself in deep, haven't you? And you love this woman?"

I'm taken aback.

"No," I tell her. "I don't. I mean, I did, back when she was sweet and vulnerable and didn't want to kill anyone. Lindsey, you have no idea how good she is at winning people over. Everyone at work behaves like she's some kind of saint. Why do you think they've all turned against Elena?"

"All of them except you."

"Yeah. The one thing Katja didn't count on. That I'd end up falling for Elena."

"You think you're in love with her?"

"I know I am. See, we'd been getting closer, but it was that first kiss that made it happen. It was a set-up, Katja filmed it and sent it to Daniel."

Lindsey's horrified. "Seriously? It was her?"

"Yep. I'll never forgive myself for that. I was so nervous that I over-did the weed in my lunch break! But even then, that kiss – it sparked something in me – the stronger feelings I had for Elena. It didn't feel fake. It felt like the most natural thing in the world. And the rest you can figure out for yourself."

"OK, I don't need details! God, Katja is twisted!"

"Yeah. I know. She is. And I realised afterwards if I'd truly been in love with her, with what she was doing, I'd never have cheated on her like that." The memory of that first afternoon floods me with warmth. "Honestly, *nobody* has ever made me want to be a better person like Elena does! She's smart, beautiful and funny. I miss her so much when I'm not with her! I've felt like I could tell her anything when we've been together! Apart from the fact that I'm Katja's boyfriend."

Lindsey's silent. The uncertainty returns, the full scale of how much I have screwed up reveals itself.

"I wouldn't blame Elena if she never wanted to see you again," she eventually says. "She's crazy about you – the way her face lights up when your name's mentioned, it's adorable. She was devastated when she left here earlier. She feels like she's lost everything."

Lindsey pours us both another shot. Fuck me, I need it.

"You're not a bad guy, Nathan. It's obvious you adore Elena. But you're not the sharpest tool in the shed are you, getting yourself in-volved in all this? The question is how to get out."

"I know. I've been trying to work that out all week. I was going to leave tonight, go back to Dublin and stay at my parents' place for a bit. Katja doesn't know where they live and even if she did, their grumpy bastard cat would probably savage her," I say with a wry smile.

"I wanted to persuade Elena to come with me. Not much chance of that now, I guess."

"Well, there might be. I think you need to get yourself to the awards. Katja's already on her way there, right? Go home now, pack up your stuff, and leave it here, you can pick it up afterwards. Better bring a change of clothes too – you'll never get in dressed like that." She has a point. My jeans are covered in mud, and there's a gaping rip in the left knee.

"You need to get to Elena before Katja does."

"And if I don't?"

"Leave that with me. I have a plan. Now go." She's practically pushing me out the door. I've survived. I live to fight another day.

"By the way…" she asks me when I'm back in the hallway, "you never said why it is Katja cares so much about what happened to Laura. I mean I know it was tragic but still…"

"After all that, you still don't understand?"

"Understand what?"

"I thought it was obvious," Nathan says. Lindsey shakes her head. So he tells her.

To say she's surprised is the understatement of the decade.

Seven Years Ago

LAURA

Tyler had made himself scarce like the coward he was, leaving me to face my colleague head-on.

Although she had guessed how much trouble she was in.

"It isn't what it looks like," she pleaded. Tyler and I – well, we're only friends – it got a bit out of control." She tried to laugh it off. "You'd do the same. We all know you'd shag him senseless if you could."

I wouldn't, though. That ship has long since sailed, and even if it hadn't, I would never touch someone else's man. I held my nerve. She looked frightful – hair in disarray, clothes askew, smelling of alcohol, and wild-eyed, like she was under the influence of some substance. I had no proof she and Tyler had taken anything, but I could hazard a guess. We all know music industry types like their coke. And I'm not talking about a soft drink here.

"He's not yours," I told her. "You know he's with our boss, you know how much trouble you'd be in if she found out, don't you?"

"But Laura, how's she going to find out? It's your word against mine, and who's going to believe a pathetic creature like you, who everyone hates anyway?" She started to laugh, almost hysterical.

That was it. She'd been vile to me once too often. Except this time, I had a trump card.

"It might be my word against yours," I said, "but I'm not sure how she will react when she sees this."

I held up my phone and played the video. The one I took before she'd realised I'd walked in. The one of her and Tyler going at it like badgers.

The laughter stopped. "You wouldn't," she said in alarm.

"Oh, I would. In fact, shall we go and see her right now, show her what you've done?"

She stumbled towards me. "No – no – you can't! I'll lose my job! I'm sorry…we're friends, right? All that stuff I did – that's what happens when you work in an office, isn't it?"

I was staggered. All that 'stuff she did'. She'd just convicted herself. What a piece of work she was. Perhaps she now realised the eggshells I had been walking on at work all this time, terrified of saying or doing the wrong thing in case I was fired, nervous that the others were deconstructing me, turning my every move into a funny anecdote to be laughed about in the pub later when I wasn't there.

I moved towards the window, circling the room to free myself of my guilty-as-hell colleague as I attempted to stand my ground. "That's not my problem," I said. "Besides why should I care if you lose your job? You've worked so hard to ensure I lose mine!"

"What are you talking about?" She moved towards me, backing me into the wall, blocking off the door. I couldn't escape.

"Face it – you're jealous of me!" I snapped. "Enjoy making my life hell, did you? Well, I've got the upper hand now. How does that feel, huh?" She was shook her head in furious denial as I waved the phone. "I'm taking this to our editor to show her what you've been doing behind her back. Let's see who she believes then, shall we?" All my fear had subsided. "Let's face it," I hissed. "You're finished at Gleam!"

Everything happened at once. She flew at me, screaming – cries which would have been drowned out by the ones at the show below us – as she attempted to grab the phone from my hand.

I scrambled onto the windowsill, holding the handset out of reach. She wrenched it painfully from my hand, crushing my fingers in her grasp. I tried to fight back, kicking out at her. That's when she pushed me right into the window. The cracked window.

Which splintered into thousands of sparkling shards, taking me with it.

ELENA

"And for their tie-in with *Pet Food Central*, the award for best promotional campaign of the year goes to – *Cat's Life*!"

They haven't won again have they? By now, the *Cat's Life* crew's
table must be groaning under the weight of all those trophies. It's an
awards ceremony triumph on a par with *Titanic* winning all those Os-
cars. I've sat through over two hours of this crap so far, and there's still
no sign of Katja. I've drunk champagne cocktails. I've nibbled on a
couple of miniature fish and chip cones in an attempt to appear normal. I've braved the withering stares of my colleagues, who genuinely
think I am celebrating her absence.

But she's not here.

I'm wondering whether Nathan was lying. If he was pretending to
save me from danger in the hope I'd forgive him. What if it was him
who sent me that mysterious message earlier?

'*Let's end this tonight*'. The only person I've ended anything with
was him. It won't help my cause if Katja's not here. Because my award
– the final one of the night – is next.

The host – a second-tier comedian whose main claim to fame is
guest turns on *8 Out of 10 Cats* – ushers the *Cat's Life* folk from the
stage. "There's a few people who must be feline good right now!" he
quips to a trickle of laughter. "You guys deserve a bonus – hope your
editor has enough money in the kitty!" The trickle pipes down to one
awkward laugh. He looks panicked. "Actually, I heard they only won

that one by a whisker!" Not even a chuckle. The guests are getting restless, murmurs of chatter erupting from all around. Just get to it, I think to myself, desperate for it to be over.

"And now – you'll be delighted to know, for those of you who are just here for the free disco, we come to the final award of the night – best exclusive!" he announces.

Finally. The idiot reads the nominations – the first four being people I have never heard of. Surely, my name must be coming up soon, I think, lifting a freshly filled glass of champagne to my lips.

Then I hear it.

"The next nominee is Katja Lake, from Spark Showbiz – for her exclusive on the *Big Brother* housemate who turned out to be fake."

The blood rushes from my head. The room tilts. The glass drops from my hand, scattering fizz across the tablecloth. I was so wrapped up in my own nomination that it never occurred to me to see who my contenders were. As a final zinger, Katja is one of them. I struggle to breathe as the applause, punctuated by a few drunken whoops and whistles, ripples around the room. "Some great stories there," I hear the comedian say. He reaches for the envelope.

I know what he is going to say before he opens it.

"And the award goes to – Katja Lake from Spark Showbiz!"

The entire venue erupts in applause. Molly and Nina are on their feet cheering, while James and Paula hug each other in triumph as he heads for the stage to collect the award on Katja's behalf. I am numb with disbelief. James takes to the podium as everybody pipes down, clutching the award as though it's a precious jewel.

"Thank you, thank you so much," he begins. "As you might have heard, Katja has been missing for several days, and as of this evening, we have no further clue on what might have happened to her." His voice is trembling with emotion. "Although she hasn't been with us for long, Katja has become a much-loved member of our team at Spark Showbiz."

He is tearful. "We had to think long and hard about whether to attend tonight – but we knew that Katja would have loved this evening, and she would have wanted us to collect this award on her behalf if she were to win it. It's an honour for me to do that for her, wherever she might be – and even though she might not be with us…"

"That's where you're wrong!" shouts a voice from the back of the auditorium.

There's a collective gasp as the house lights swivel around. And there she is. Katja, standing by the entrance, in a glittering dark purple dress. Missing no longer.

"What?" she says, as the fear vaults into my mouth. "Did you all think I was dead?"

KATJA

I've got a headline for you:

MISSING JOURNO KATJA LAKE RETURNS FROM THE DEAD TO CONFRONT MURDERING *WITCH!*

THE PRESENT

Daniel is champing at the bit to see Elena's comeuppance. Except he can't get into the awards.

As big an event as it is, it's also only for editorial staff and senior management. The budget doesn't stretch to ad teams and legal departments. And even wearing his one undamaged D&G suit and shouting, 'don't you know who I am?' at the sour-faced girl on the door did nothing to help.

"No, I don't," she snapped. "Piss off before I call the police."

They're already on their way. Bonnie will be here any minute, and he intends to lead her right to Elena. The ultimate payback for what she did to him. She needs to hurry up.

Daniel skulks around the side of the building as the rain falls in sheets, drops spattering onto his glasses, blinding him. He's just finished his fourth cigarette in an hour – the old habit returning in the wake of Elena's betrayal – when he sees a flash of blond hair race past. Bonnie? No. That person is way too tall. Oh hell. It's Nathan Flynn of all people.

"You!" Nathan stops in his tracks as Daniel emerges from behind the wall with a look of pure wrath. The one which says he is about to employ all those fighting skills he learned in those two judo classes he took aged eleven. "You life-ruining *bastard*!"

Nathan shrinks back, hands in the air. "Hey, I don't want any trouble," he insists. "I need to get inside." Daniel bristles with anger, his fists clenched. Even drawn up to his full height, he is several inches shorter than his arch nemesis, but he still intends to knock him for six. "Had fun with my girlfriends, did you?" he starts. "Elena and I were happy until you came along and fucked it all up! How's this for a punchline?!"

He flies at Nathan, determined to have his revenge, but Nathan merely watches with a bemused expression on his face before he moves sideways, sending Daniel flying. Unable to stop, he trips on the uneven ground and lands face first in a huge puddle.

"No, *that's* a punchline!" Nathan roars as Daniel slips around in the sludge, coughing and spluttering from a mouthful of filthy water. Great. Not only is his favourite suit streaked with mud, but he's also probably contracted cholera. He doesn't know which is worse. "I'll – I'll have you arrested," he wheezes.

"For what? I didn't lay a finger on you! How about you stop treating your girlfriends like crap in future? Elena doesn't want to give up everything to have your kids Daniel – and nor did any of the others!"

With that, Nathan runs off in the direction of the venue, leaving Daniel dirt-caked and speechless. Bonnie walks up seconds later as he scrambles to his feet, cursing and swearing loudly.

"Er…Mr Carrington, is everything OK?" she asks, raising an eyebrow at his appearance.

Daniel instantly straightens up and calms down. "Yes, I…slipped…"

"Only I couldn't help hearing a commotion. Something about you treating your girlfriends like – crap…?"

Shit. She heard it. "Honestly, it's fine, it's nothing," he blusters, "a misunderstanding. I wanted Elena to prove how much she loved me by giving up her job and having my child, but it all went – a – bit wrong…" He tails off when he notices the look Bonnie is giving him – something between pity and contempt.

"I see," she says. "Mr Carrington – has anyone ever told you you're a bit of a dick?"

ELENA

Katja is bathed in light like an angel, beaming at the room of stunned faces. Of course, she is.

She knows how much mayhem she is about to cause.

"Don't look so surprised," she announces. "I wasn't going to miss the biggest night of my career, was I?"

My colleagues are struck dumb. I glance round at their wide-eyed faces and feel a torrent of emotions. One minute, I'm triumphant. They know I'm not a killer. Seconds later it's replaced by sheer blind hatred towards them. For thinking I was capable of killing. Terror slices through me. She's here. She looks stunning. I wonder where she got that dress? Oh, stop, now is not the time. Not when she's won the award that should have been mine. What now? I feel sick. This is the last thing I was expecting. I should get out while I can, but where would I go?

Before I can move, James screams Katja's name.

"KATJA! Where have you been?" She makes her way around the tables, onto the stage, and they're hugging as if they haven't seen each other in years.

"Look who's back!" James shouts, overcome with emotion. "We don't need to look for Katja any more – because she's here, with us, alive and well!" He turns to her, handing her the award, an ugly square of clear Perspex with her name scrawled on it. Hers. Not mine.

"Katja, congratulations on your Exclusive of the Year award. And I'm sure you'd like to say a few words." He steps aside and the room bursts into applause. Katja looks as humble as any award winner might pretend to do when they knew the prize was theirs.

She's a bloody fantastic actress and has been all along.

"Thank you so much! My fellow award-winners," she says, as if she's giving the King's speech on Christmas Day. "It's such an honour to receive this prize so soon after I joined the company. In all the places I've ever worked, I've never felt more like I belonged. It's like a family here. You should all be very proud of yourselves."

A murmur of approval runs through the room. The charm snaps off. Exactly as it did on that first day when I asked her if we'd met before.

"You know, it hasn't been easy for me the past few years. I owe my colleagues an apology. I hope I didn't upset anybody with my absence." At this point, she glances over at James; looking emotional once again. "I needed some time alone, you see. The thing is, none of my lovely Spark colleagues know this, but I had a sister. She was a journalist like all of you. Her name was Laura. And it's almost seven years since she died."

I jump so abruptly that my knee bangs the underside of the table. This time, Molly's fizz goes flying, soaking the tablecloth I drenched moments earlier. She scowls. I couldn't care less.

It all comes back to me in a rush. Throughout her time at Gleam, Laura never shut up about her wonderful sister and how close they were, and it was tedious as hell. If she'd spent her life raising awareness of the Polar ice caps melting or saving lost kittens from peril that would have been one thing. But all Laura's sister ever seemed to do was sit around her student digs watching *Big Bang Theory* re-runs and drinking mojitos with her dull flatmates. We didn't care because none of us knew her – or ever thought we would meet her.

Until now, that is.

So that's why Katja was so familiar. I remember her now from the family photo Laura kept on her desk. Her real name is Katherine Lucas. She's the elusive student sister of the tragic Laura. And she's out to avenge her death. Because she's decided I killed her. The only problem for her is I didn't. But judging from Katja's laser-eyed glare, eyes pivoting in my general direction like an out-of-control robot in a horror movie, I'm not sure she'll believe me.

I was wrong to come here. I need to get out. I push my chair back noisily and totter to my feet on my painful shoes. Everybody stares. It's too late. Because Katja produced a photo of Laura from her evening bag.

"Everybody – this is Laura," she tells the room in an impassioned voice. "She was beloved by everyone who met her. She was my world, and when she left it, that world collapsed."

Team Spark are tutting now as I creep towards the door as quietly as possible except a security guard in an ill-fitting blue uniform blocks it. She's the most disagreeable woman I have ever seen – the type who deadlifts 1000 kg before settling down to an entire cow for breakfast.

"I – I don't suppose I could..." I hear Katja's voice ring through the silence.

"I don't know what happened to Laura on that day of...but there is somebody in this room who does!" She rises to her full height and says the words I've been dreading: "My colleague Elena Robins. It's *her* fault that Laura died!"

Gasps and squeals echo across the room. But she is not done.

"I know you're here, Elena," she snaps, now hard and unyielding. "Why don't you show yourself and tell everyone what YOU DID!"

She points to where I'm standing, and the spotlights which illuminated her glorious return are on me.

Along with the eyes of a thousand horrified colleagues.

Seven Years Ago
LAURA'S KILLER

Laura falls out of the window as I fall to the floor. That bloody push. It knocked me backwards, and I went flying into the stacks of water bottles before I hit the ground.

I can already feel my arms turning purple with bruises as I pull myself to my feet. But that's nothing compared to what's happened. Shit. No. This can't be my fault! How was I meant to know the window was broken? I can hear Laura's desperate screams pierce the air, the sound fading further away as she plummets down. It seems to last for an eternity.

I swear this is the longest fatal fall in history.

Until a grim thud stops the screaming in its tracks. My pulse pounds, and sweat beads on my forehead as I edge towards what was once the window and peer out, dreading what I might see.

She's still alive. I don't believe it. Something broke her fall.

Oh. That's not good. The something was a set of sharp railings, and she's been impaled on them. The scene is grim. At least two inches of fence spike is poking up through her white T-shirt, the area around the wound rapidly blooming scarlet. She's writhing around in a fruitless attempt to free herself, pinned helplessly. Like a butterfly being tortured by a child.

Wow. That must sting a bit.

Wait. She's saying something. A faint croak: "Help me."

Laura's body convulses and she vomits up a sticky mass of blood. Shit. Shit. *Shit.* What do I do? They can't pin this on me. It was self-defence. She was trying to ruin me. What was I supposed to do? I don't think she has long. Maybe if I fetch help, they can still save her and save me in the process. I hate Laura. We all do. She was fucking impossible to work with at times.

We all treated her like crap, but that doesn't mean I want her to die.

Hang on a second. People don't just fly out of windows onto railings at random. There'll be an investigation into this. The police will be involved. Fingers pointed. Laura's phone scrutinised for evidence. My infidelity with my boss's boyfriend revealed. And if by some miracle that spike has somehow missed Laura's vital organs, and she survives, she'll tell everybody what happened. What will that mean for me? A life behind bars. The destruction of my reputation. Career death. 'Attempted murder' doesn't look good on a CV unless you're applying for a job as a hitman. Forget Gleam. If this gets out, I won't even get a job editing the prison newsletter.

Laura's face is pallid when I stare down again. Her eyelids flicker and her body jerks as though she's trying to escape. Dipping in and out of consciousness. I know what I have to do.

I grab her phone from where it dropped. There's a photo of her and her sister smiling from the home screen. Cute. Thank God it isn't password-protected. I open up the camera to where Laura has taken several photos and the video of me and Tyler bumping uglies. Within seconds, I've wiped the lot before I close the camera and fling the phone out of the window, where it smashes on the ground, as broken as Laura's now unmoving body.

The evidence is gone. I leave the scene of the crime and go back downstairs to join the hysterical crowd screaming marriage proposals at the boy band.

Like none of it ever happened.

ELENA

I have never wanted to leave a room more than I want to leave this one. Not even when Freddy Taylor turned on me. Not when Daniel found out about Nathan. Both of those pale in comparison with this. I've been denounced as a murderer. I don't know whether to be outraged, ashamed or fearful. All I can think about is how Nathan was right all along. How, despite everything he did, he tried to save me from a fate worse than Katja. Maybe I should have listened to him. But it's too late now.

The shock resonates across the Spark table. Paula wears an expression that tells me I am getting fired on Monday. Molly stares in disapproval. Nina looks as though a sea sponge has replaced her brain. She's probably more worried about how this will affect her ability to use me as a meal ticket.

Maybe I should fight back.

I lurch forward as best I can, although by now, my toes feel as though they're about to develop gangrene and drop off. Damn you, cheap plastic Louboutin knock-offs. "Katja – you know that's not true. I didn't have anything to do with your sister's death." I sound hoarse and uncertain, my voice unlike my own. I struggle to keep my balance in my heels amidst the whirlwind in my head.

To my surprise, it works – at least momentarily. Katja is stunned into silence and I feel emboldened. I move towards the centre of the room. "How about we talk about some of the stuff you've done to me in the past few months – your little revenge plot?"

She stares me down like a vulture regarding its next meal.

"People – Elena has no idea what she is talking about," Katja says. She is trying to sound confident, but I can detect a faint note of uncertainty in her voice.

I'll never get another chance like this.

"Go on, Katja! Tell them everything you've done to me! Ruining my career, my personal life, all over something I didn't even do?!" I am practically at the stage by this point. The comedian is standing in the wings foot drumming against the floor. Surely one of his cat jokes would break the tension, but they've dried up.

"Ladies and gentlemen, I can assure you Elena is lying," Katya tells them.

"Oh, is that so? Because Katja, I know something you don't. I know all about your little boyfriend. And he told me the truth. You have to end this campaign against me Katja – because your sister's death has NOTHING to do with me."

At the mention of Nathan, Katja looks appalled. James stares at her, unsure who to side with. You could cut the tension with a scythe, and for a few brief seconds, I feel as if people believe me. Until a jowly staff member from *Cat's Life's* trophy-laden front table stands up and points in my direction.

"Don't listen to her Katja!" he shouts. "Look at her, she's drunk!"

The shock ricochets off the walls. "Hey, she is drunk! Look how she's stumbling around!" "Someone get her away from Katja!" I'm not. It's those goddamned shoes, those size five instruments of torture on my feet. There's no way the mob will believe that.

"You don't get it, she's nuts…!" I insist, but the shouts continue. "Get her out of here!" shrieks a red-haired woman in an ill-fitting forest-green jumpsuit. It's like being chastised by a walking tomato plant.

There's a more decisive cry: "Call the police!" That's when I see her. A blonde stranger, in the far corner of the room. Dressed in a grey suit like a detective in a TV cop show, flashing her badge at the door security. She looks like she's in the mood to arrest someone. Is that Daniel with her? Why is he covered in mud? What the hell's been going on while I've been holed up at Lindsey's? There is no way I am surrendering to the cops, not now Katja has shown up alive and well.

But what to do?

Quick as a flash, I turn to the table on my right and, in one sweeping motion, push everything off it with my arm. The crash is unholy. Plates, platters of sliders, programmes, glasses and two half-full bottles of Cristal slide to the floor, shattering and soaking several people nearby in fizz. What a waste of good champagne.

Hysteria descends as guests rush to assess the damage, a babble of shouts and chatter rising into the air. One woman sobs over-dramatically and is being led away by a waitress dabbing at her wet finery with a napkin.

In the distance, I can just about make out Katja's shouts of 'Stop her...!"

Nobody pays attention to either of us any more and that's when I make my move. There's a narrow beam of light shining in from the corridor outside. An open door. I kick off my uncomfortable shoes, tiptoeing carefully through the mayhem to the exit.

And...RUN.

KATJA

Damn it. That bitch has given me the slip. One minute I was exposing Elena Robins for the murderer she is. The next, mayhem. My big moment ruined. My favourite champagne wasted.

She did that on purpose.

"Stop her!" I yell. It falls on deaf ears. People are so busy flocking to the scene of Elena's latest crime, or being taken away to dry off, or picking bits of flying burger from out of their ears that nobody is listening.

I need the evening to resume so I can get on with finding Elena. I notice the host watching from the wings. I've seen him on TV. He's about as funny as gallstones. But I need him and his humourless material right now. I wave my arms frantically in an attempt to get him back onstage and calm things down. He stands there, impassive. We're paying him a huge sum of money for tonight. Why is he doing fuck all? I strut over.

"What are you doing? Get back onstage now!" I shout through gritted teeth. He looks alarmed. Shit. Why am I showing him that side of me? Everybody expects sweet Katja. The grief-stricken sister. The one who doesn't have a jewel-encrusted knife in her evening bag.

"Sorry." I offer him a fake apologetic smile and he relaxes. "I don't want the evening ruined. Can you help me?"

Finally, he gets it. He walks back to the podium and speaks.

"How are you all doing out there? I hope everybody's having a *smashing* time!" He wants shooting for that joke alone. "If we could all pipe down and let our fabulous staff clear up this mess. Katja has something she'd like to say to you all."

It works. Everybody shuts up. I return to the podium and switch on that glowing smile. I stare out at the assembled faces. What a bunch of saddos. Half of them can't dress properly.

What are all these websites we run? *Tractor Gazette? Amazing Allotments?* Who the fuck reads that crap?

It doesn't matter. They're nothing to me. I don't want to harm any of these people.

Well, maybe for wearing chinos to a lounge suit event. I push back my feelings and speak.

"Thank you again. I want to apologise for what happened back then. I'm sure Elena Robins will be found and dealt with by the relevant authorities. In the meantime, please enjoy this amazing party. If my sister was with us tonight, she would have wanted everyone to celebrate their outstanding success. Let's do it – for Laura!"

The room erupts in cheers, and I signal to the DJ to crank up the music. Like I give a shit if the party continues or not. I've got more important things to do.

Part one of my plan for tonight worked. I knew I'd win. Having a friend in the awards planning department certainly helped. Although I now owe her a bucket of wine.

The next part? That's more of a challenge.

One thing I didn't mention in my speech is that Laura died in this very building. I never saw her body after the accident, but I can imagine what happened. My sister, screaming for help, bloodied and broken, and Elena doing nothing to save her. Walking away. Laughing as she did. I've played the scenario on a loop in my head and woken up screaming from nightmares of Laura's lifeless eyes. So many times.

She has to pay for what she's done.

What a pity I can't throw Elena onto those railings myself. I'd love her to feel how Laura must have felt in those last moments, but the venue removed the fence after the accident. Screw you health and safety. But it's OK, as I have something better in mind. Cutting those pretty wrists of hers. Watching her bleed to death in agony. Telling everybody she did it to herself. That the shame of being outed as a killer became too much for her to bear. As for that boyfriend of mine, the little snake – I'll deal with him later. Not sure that face of his will look so desirable once I'm done carving it up.

Where is she? Where is she? I'm roaming the dancefloor, but the disco is loud and pumping, and people keep getting in my way. I don't want another bloody bellini. I don't want a mini éclair from a giant silver platter. Oh God, they're playing the *Macarena*. There's a guy on the dancefloor who knows all the moves. He's standing in front of me, gyrating furiously, trying to get me to join in. *Oh, just fuck off already.* I have a murder to commit. Do I look like I want to swing my hips to the Macarena? I'm desperate to set fire to that disgusting Hawaiian shirt he's got on. Preferably while he's still wearing it.

No. I said I wouldn't hurt anyone else tonight. Let the proles and halfwits enjoy their corporate event. They'll have enough to worry about later when Elena's body is found.

I know she can't have gone far.

ELENA

I'm lost. Help me. Please, someone, get me out of this and I'll behave. I swear. I won't be a *troublemaker* any more.

That's what I am if you think about it. All that trouble I made for Laura. For Daniel.

For so many others. Think of all the lies I've told, the lives I've ruined. What I did to my boyfriend's expensive rug. Why did Nathan ever say he was in love with me? Who could love someone like me after all that?

I've never felt so alone. I have no idea where I am in this rabbit warren of a building.

My phone reception is non-existent. Nor can I ask anyone for help. They'd only deliver me straight to Katja. My plan could not have gone more wrong. Of all the things that have happened to me in the past couple of months, can any be more humiliating than being publicly denounced by someone from *Amazing Allotments*?

I hear the vague pounding of the music from inside the venue. The smell of grilled meat suggests I'm near the kitchen, but I have no idea where the hell I've run to. This place is circular. It has several floors. I ran out of the event space in a blind panic without thinking to look for an exit.

Even if I had found it, where could I go? This is the only venue for miles around and there's nothing outside except waste ground – an empty stretch of land reserved for yet more high-rise luxury flats. If I could get to the car park around the back, I might have a chance of reaching the road we came in on. But how? I'm surrounded by stairs and walls. Right now, I feel as if they're closing in. My escape options aren't looking good right now.

I can't run any more. I'm purple with exertion. There's a reason why I was never picked for the cross-country team at school. I have to stop. If Katja doesn't get me, the cardiac arrest will. I hear a sound. The light scuffle of feet. Breathing behind me. My heart sinks into my gusset.

I'm being followed.

KATJA

I'm out of there. Probably just as well. Another two minutes, and I swear the editor of that goddamned tractor website would have been on his way to hospital to have his award surgically removed from his bellend.

What sort of place is this, with its ropey-looking stairs and ancient corridors, all falling to bits? Who the fuck has an event at such a decrepit old dump when the Dorchester exists? The cost-cutting bastards. On the plus side, we're nowhere near the exit. Which means Elena's probably still here, somewhere. After all, she only had a head start of about one song chorus. I don't care what it takes.

I'm going to find her.

ELENA

More footsteps. More breathing. I daren't look around. It's her, for sure. All I can think about is getting away. But where? There are no doors. No windows. Nothing. It's like trying to fight my way out of a shoebox.

There's an old metal staircase in the distance. The sort that looks unable to withstand anything heavier than a wafer-thin mint. Whatever. It's still lower risk than being found by Katja. I inhale a lungful of air and take the stairs two at a time. At the top I find more narrow corridors. More walls and no exit at this height unless I fancied taking the long way down, and there's another staircase to my right. How many floors are there in this place?

More footsteps. Coming closer! The breathing heavier, more pronounced, as though they've been running. My panic levels spike. A slight squeal escapes my mouth. I race for the other staircase and scramble up it as fast as I can, but I miss my footing and half-fall, half-slide down several steps, landing in a heap on the floor below.

"Shit!" I shout, remembering I shouldn't make any noise. Did Katja hear that? Did she see me falling? I pick myself up as fast as I can, although it's tricky now because I caught my right knee on the edge of one of the steps. It's pink and inflamed. There's a small trickle of blood snaking down towards my calf. Not enough to kill. But God, it's sore! How can something so small hurt so much?

I limp to the top step as fast as I can, even though every movement sends fresh pain shooting through me. No more stairs above, only a small, narrow passageway and two doors to my left. I practically weep with relief. Surely one of them will be unlocked. Perhaps I've found myself a hiding place. Before I can investigate, someone grabs me from behind. I don't have time to react before they open the first door and shove me inside, slamming it with a resounding clang.

Inside, it's pitch black. I can't even see the sequins on my dress. My reaction is one of utter terror. It's Katja. She's here with me!

I don't want to die!!

I'm hysterical and lash out, my handbag connecting with something hard. A body part. I hear the other person gasp.

"Jesus! For fuck's sake, Elena…!"

Hang on. That's not Katja! I fumble along the wall for a light switch and find one within seconds. I'm in a storeroom, one half piled from floor to ceiling with stacks of water bottles and drink cans. Nathan is in front of me, reeling from where I just whacked him around the head.

NATHAN

Christ on a bike. How many more people are going to thump me today? Elena. Lindsey. Elena again. At least she didn't get me in the balls. But that hurt like a bitch. I guess I'm getting what I deserve.

"Elena, I…" I'm so winded the words won't come. Her dress is filthy and torn. She's bleeding. And where are her shoes? I hate seeing her like this. For a minute, I think she's going to lamp me again, but she edges back, eyeing me with suspicion. As though I'm doing Katja's bidding.

"Nathan, you scared the crap out of me! Why did you follow me?!"

"Why didn't *you* stay away? I warned you not to come here!"

"Oh! Oh, you mean earlier when you confessed that you've helped ruin my life!"

I reach for her hand, but she jerks away.

"Don't touch me! You show up here in your best suit thinking you'll win me back? What bargain bin did you fish that out of?"

Harsh. It's from Reiss. I can make an effort when the mood takes me. I say nothing and let her rant.

"Everything about this is – wrong! Sneaking off with me at lunchtime for sex, knowing all along what you were up to behind my back. Why should I listen to a word you say any more?! Daniel told me about all those other women you're probably fucking on rotation! There I was thinking I meant something to you."

"You do."

"What?"

It's now or never. The throbbing in my head has faded. I feel sick with nerves. Help me. I can't start throwing up again. I'd have to do it out of the window, and it would probably land on a partygoer's head.

"It's true," I tell her. "I don't deserve to be forgiven. I meant it when I said I'm in love with you. I have been since that first kiss – OK, I admit that was a set-up, and I hate myself for that. But everything else? That happened because I wanted it to, and it was fantastic. You're fantastic. It was when I realised that I started doubting what Katja was doing to you. And when she faked her death, I knew it had to stop."

"Oh, how kind of you. I suppose that's why you dropped me right in it by reporting her missing."

"She blackmailed me!"

She's stunned into silence at that last remark, staring at me wide-eyed. I place a tentative hand on her shoulder. She doesn't shake it off.

"Just listen! Katja forced me to do a lot of bad things this week, and right now I'm in as much trouble as you are! If she finds us – all I do know is if anything happens to you, I'm not sure I could live with myself. So now you know why I followed you here."

Her face softens. She knows I'm on her side. "We don't have much time," I tell her. "I'm getting out of town, going back to Ireland, and I'm leaving tonight. The thing is – I know you probably want nothing to do with me – but is there any chance you'd come with me?"

She's about to tell me where I can stick that idea. I can feel it. I've lost her. Not sure it would've worked anyway. Imagine what we'd tell people when they asked how we met. *Well, it's a funny story. I had this psychotic girlfriend and she thought Elena had killed her sister.*

She doesn't kick me to the kerb. Instead, she asks: "Nathan, are you serious?

"Why wouldn't I be?"

"Because – because I'm not a good person…"

My voice drops to a whisper. "Nor am I."

Before I can catch my breath, we're in each other's arms and kissing, passionately. As if we're the only people in the world and we're not about to be murdered. It's like I'm back in the alley, stoned and confused, with all those feelings clouding my brain. Only more so. It might be the most meaningful kiss I've ever had. Does this mean we're back together? We pull apart and she looks at me with such sadness it nearly breaks me. Confession time.

"I mean it, Nathan. I'm not a good person. I was awful to Katja's sister, and I am so ashamed. You're the first person I've ever admitted that to. My stupid insecurities got the better of me, and I've felt bad about it for years. But I didn't kill her – I couldn't have done. You have to believe me." A single tear rolls down her cheek. Oh God, please don't cry. You'll set me off.

"I do." I gently wipe the tears away. "There's no way you would have freaked like you did when you thought you'd killed Katja. Not if you'd done it before. You can't change the past. Nor can I. All those dumb mistakes we've made, it's learning from them that matters. Reckon you can behave yourself if we move on together?"

"Reckon you can stop thinking with your dick?"

Ouch. That's a low blow. "You seriously think I'd cheat on you? OK, I admit it. I'm as awful as everyone says. But I wouldn't do something like that. Not to someone I'm in love with. Not to you."

She nods slightly. "We've both done terrible things, haven't we?"

"We have. But I know we can help each other do better. Come with me. Please. I swear I'll take care of you if you'll give me a chance."

She doesn't hesitate.

"Yes, Nathan. I'll come with you. We make sense together and it's not as if I have anything left to lose."

I'm thrilled. I can't believe it. She said yes. But we don't have time to celebrate.

"Now," she adds, "how do we get out of here?"

"The window. There's a fire escape outside."

"You're kidding! We're four storeys up."

"You can think of a better way? There are hundreds of people out there, you'd be spotted in a second!" I race to the window and unclip the latch. A rush of chilly night air whooshes in. Elena joins me, nervously peering to the ground.

"Go! I'll be right behind you. We can get to the road from here, get a cab back to Lindsey's and take it from there."

"Lindsey?"

"Yes. It's complicated. I'll tell you later. And Elena – thank you for agreeing to this.

I'll make it up to you, I promise."

"You'd better." Before I know it, she's shoved me back against the stacks of bottles and we're kissing again. It's fierce. It's intense. I hear the bang of the door opening. Someone is watching us and I draw back.

It's Katja. Standing like a statue, clutching that jewelled antique knife of hers. Looking horrified.

ELENA

The silence in the room is lethal.

Because Katja's here. She's armed. She's dangerous, and she's just caught me in Nathan's arms.

"No!" she gasps. "You can't be...!"

Katja appears genuinely shocked, having stumbled across the one situation she cannot charm or lie her way out – that her beloved Nathan has fallen for somebody else. Of all the people he could be in love with, it's her sworn enemy. The person she wants dead. She stands rigid, a chunk of her perfect updo freeing itself from its bonds and falling to her shoulders. She looks deranged.

So, what happens now? Nathan breaks the deadlock.

"I'm sorry, Katja," he says. "It's true! Elena and I, we..."

Her expression clouds over with fury. "You calculating prick," she snarls. "Her, of all people? How long has this been going on?" Neither of us answers, but the looks on our faces, the way he has a protective arm around me, tells her everything she needs to know. "You betrayed me! She killed my sister, and this is how you..."

That's it. I've had it with her.

"I didn't kill your sister. I'm sorry about Laura. I know I should have treated her better.

We all should. But you think she was so damn perfect herself? I've got news for you – she wasn't! Always boasting about how brilliant she

310

was, complaining about us, accusing me of stuff I didn't do! And here you are idolising her like she's the only person that matters!"

Katja shakes her head. "No! Laura was an angel – and you, all of you, how you behaved – she wrote it all down in her diary!" She tips the contents of her jewelled bag onto the floor, a disorganised heap of tissues, tampons and coins landing at our feet, alongside several packs of prescription medication. However much she's on, it's not working. There, in the middle of it all, is a small white book decorated with hand-drawn purple flowers. Katja grabs it. "It's here, it's all here," she says, breathless. "I found it after she died. Pages and pages of everything she said, all about you!"

I am struck dumb.

"How could you? To another human being! The inquest said it was an accident, but I know you killed her!"

No. She's got it all wrong. "All right!" I snap. "You think I killed your sister? Where's your evidence?"

Suddenly, it's Katja who can't speak.

"Seriously? Show me where you have evidence that I had *anything* to do with Laura's death."

"I…" Katja is floundering, and I know I have her on the ropes.

"You see? You don't have any," I say. "You're so obsessed with this idea I must have had something to do with it because Laura wrote in some stupid diary that you've twisted the truth! But you don't have any concrete proof – and you never will. Because, Katja…" I pause dramatically, like in the closing scene of a soap opera. "I wasn't even there."

"Stop lying!"

"I'm not! I wasn't there the day Laura died. There's no way I could have been involved! I can prove it to you! Why won't you listen to me?"

"Katja – you know this isn't the answer." Nathan steps forward, speaking in a cautious tone. "You're not well. You need help if you believe Elena was responsible for Laura's death.

Does she look like a killer to you? I mean, look at her."

"She's taken everything from me," Katja says in a low growl. "Look at my life since Laura died! Parents dead and gone, marriage a disaster, and now she's taken you from me too? You were all I had left, and now I don't even have that any more."

"I know things seem bad," Nathan cuts in, "but you know you can get the help you need, move on from all of this, start again…"

How is he staying so calm? Katja wields a knife, looking like she wants to turn me into an attractive table decoration – and Nathan isn't even breaking a sweat? My legs are trembling so much I'm struggling to stand, and he's acting like this happens all the time.

"I know you think Elena killed Laura," he continues. "But I believe her, and she's right. You don't have any proof she had anything to do with it. Why don't you give me the knife, and we can all sit down and discuss this?"

Yep. Obviously, she's in the mood to go downstairs and laugh about her dead sister over a Kir Royale. Katja shakes her head, her eyes wild with emotion. Nathan steps forward, to try and disarm her. He is inches away.

"Why don't you hand the knife over? Come on, Katja, you know there's no need to…"

She darts behind him, grabs hold of me roughly, pushes me to the floor and forces me down.

"NATHAN! Help me!" I wriggle frantically beneath Katja, dodging the knife on several occasions as she tries to embed it in whatever soft body part she can find. One of her stilettos has fallen off. If only I could reach it, I could use it against her, anything to get her off me.

This is it. I'm going to die. Tears spring from my eyes as I squeeze them shut, bracing myself for the impact of the knife.

Except it never comes.

Because Nathan is there within seconds, pushing her away from me. Katja tumbles on to her back with a cry of frustration. The knife flies from her hand. He pulls me to my feet, throwing me out of harm's way as she recovers herself and drags him to the floor.

"Go!" he yells, gesturing to the window just inches away.

"NO! I'm not leaving you!" I wish I was as brave as I sound because the wind is blasting into the room with a horrible wailing noise, and Katja crawls back towards me like a crazed tarantula. Nathan grabs her ankle to keep her away from me. Before either of us can react she grabs her stray stiletto and slashes him in the side of the neck right above his collarbone.

Everyone goes deathly quiet. Nathan gasps. His hands rush to his neck. The spiked shoe drops beside him with an eerie clatter. Blood soaks rapidly into his shirt collar, and before I can help him, he thuds to the floor. There's another horrible wailing noise in the room. It's coming from me. Katja is rooted to the spot, open-mouthed at the sight of Nathan's unmoving body, his white shirt saturated with blood. Her breathing is loud and guttural and I know I'm next.

Except, to my amazement, she doesn't kill me. Instead, she turns and races from the room. I dash to Nathan's side, dread catapulting into my throat, but I am already afraid there is nothing I can do to save him. "Nathan – please…*please* wake up – I love you, I love you so much…please – please don't leave me…!" I squeak. I can't bear it. The only man I've ever truly loved. Sacrificing his own life to save mine. I'm numb with grief, too traumatised to cry or call for help. My legs won't work.

When the shrieks rise from downstairs, followed by a hysterical voice which can only be Katja's, I know there's no hope left.

"HELP! SOMEBODY!" she shouts as the music grinds to an abrupt halt. "SHE'S KILLED MY BOYFRIEND!!

It's over.

KATJA

Wow. It looks like this party really died. All those half-wits, showing off their best dad dancing to 'Blame It On The Boogie'. Jumping around like idiots as a net of balloons is released across the dancefloor. Acting as though it's the highlight of their year.

Then I show up and ruin it. Screaming, crying, telling them Elena Robins has murdered my boyfriend. Like I give a shit if Nathan's dead. I loved him. Honestly, I did. But he deserved to die. He betrayed me. Like I'd even want to be in the same universe as him after he's been fucking Miss Yo-Yo Knickers. I might have guessed she was a total tramp on top of everything and most likely everyone else.

Now she'll get what's coming to her.

James is at my side within seconds, arm around my shoulders as I push out yet more crocodile tears. "Darling, what's happened?! Tell me!" God I'm good at this.

"My boyfriend...Nathan...Elena...dead...she killed him...up there!"

"Katja, slow down. I don't understand! What's happened to Nathan and Elena?" Other people are gathering. A blonde woman pushes through the crowd, flashing an ID badge. Is this the detective Nathan reported my disappearance to? What's she doing here? And is that Elena's rich wanker boyfriend? For fuck's sake, is there anything he doesn't show up at?

How convenient that the cops are here. Let's give her something to do other than hog the free bar. I dial up the volume of my sobs.

"Katja," she says. "I'm Detective Bonnie Pace. Take a deep breath and tell us what's happened."

"Nathan." I almost choke on my words. "Elena's killed him – she's stabbed him with a shoe! Upstairs!" The boyfriend looks alarmed. He probably thinks she'll be going after him with a pair of testicle-removing pliers. "You have to come with me right now. He's dead, he's bleeding—"

"Katja – you're not making any sense." This is from Paula. Calm down, lady. You don't want to pop that sprog out in the foyer. "Elena stabbed Nathan with a shoe? Are you sure that's what happened?"

"A stiletto! I swear, I'm not making it up! She was having an affair with him! I caught them, and she was jealous of us being together, so she stabbed him! Help me! Please!"

"OK…OK." Bonnie's voice is like a balm. Finally, someone in this sorry saga I don't loathe on sight. "Katja is clearly distressed. I think we need to go and check out what's happened up there."

Bingo.

I lead the way to the fourth floor, pretending to be in a blind panic. Bonnie follows and James and Paula join me for support. The wanker boyfriend, whose name turns out to be Daniel, insists on coming too, keeping up a patter which is meant to calm me down. Only it doesn't because he smells like he's been rolling in horseshit.

"This doesn't surprise me," he says. "I thought Elena was so sweet. I wanted her to have my children. Can't believe how naïve I was." I want to tell him that nobody would ever have his kids even if the continuation of the species depended on it. I'll give him the benefit of the doubt. "Look, if you need to talk about anything why don't you take my number?" he adds.

Seriously? You dumped Elena yesterday and you're already trying to pick me up? Don't even think about it, twatface. I have a cupboard full of stilettos, and I'm not afraid to use them.

All I care about is getting Elena Robins behind bars where she belongs, and I'm about to achieve my aim. My excitement levels surge as the room looms before me. I practically break into a run, dragging James along.

"In here!" I shout. I reach for the handle. "See what—"

My words are cut off when the door swings open because Elena and Nathan are nowhere to be seen. Have I got the right room? I walk in, slowly. Ignoring the confused row of faces behind me. It is the right room. There's the pile of water bottles. The contents of my bag – the tissues, my meds – are exactly where I dropped them.

Not a trace of my dead boyfriend. Or his blood. What the actual fuck?

"I don't understand. They were here, I saw them, I saw it happen—"

"Katja, are you feeling OK?" This from James, concern crossing his face. "I mean, the last few days must have been very upsetting with you, with your sister, and everything – are you sure you didn't imagine it, are you sure you didn't…"

"Oh, shut up, James." You have no idea how long I've been waiting to do that. He looks utterly crestfallen. It's awkward as hell. Now, what do I do? But then I spot it.

A piece of pale pink chiffon stained with blood, trapped between one of the floorboards.

"They were here! Look!" I make a beeline for the shred of pink material, which is the only evidence that the last few minutes happened. "She must have got away – we have to find her!" Before they can stop me, I'm out of the room and tearing down the stairs towards the exit.

Whatever she's done, she won't get away with it.

The others talk about me in their indoor voices, hoping I won't hear. "Poor Katja…must have been so difficult…she can't be well, poor thing…" Fuck them. Fuck the lot of them. They don't give a shit about me. All they care about is pretending to care, to make themselves look good.

I have to get Elena back.

The foyer is crammed with overdressed people, and I push my way through swathes of taffeta and velvet and ignore all the tuts and huffing before bursting outside into the cool night air. It's windy and that bit of chiffon, the one piece of evidence I had that Elena was up to no good, is whipped out of my hands, and soars out of reach.

"SHIT!" I start screaming and crying again, only this time my tears are for real as the others catch up with me.

"Katja…?" James says as I throw myself to the ground.

Bonnie crouches down beside me and asks if I'm OK. I have no answer as I beat the tarmac like a two-year-old having a supermarket tantrum and asking myself the same question over and over again.

How the fuck did she do this?

My phone buzzes in my handbag. I slowly retrieve it, dreading what I will see, and open up *WhatsApp*. When I see what it says, I shriek in pure primal rage.

Ten Minutes Earlier
ELENA

The love of my life is dead. I collapse on him and await my fate. Except...is that his heartbeat? It's pumping through the tacky mass of claret coating his shirt. And as strong as I've ever felt it when he's been pressed against me in the flare of passion. It wouldn't sound like that if he were on the verge of death. I've seen *Casualty*. I know these things.

What the hell's going on? I feel him shifting beneath me.

"Fuck me, that was close," he utters, pushing himself up. "I thought she'd slashed my throat for a minute. Good job I moved when I did. You OK?"

What the hell? How is he sounding this laid-back when I was this close to choosing his cremation urn? He's damn lucky I haven't thumped him again. I'm unable to form words. He says nothing but opens his hand. He's holding a scattering of fake blood capsules, staining his palm red.

"Lindsey," he explains. "She called me back to the flat after you left and told me to go after you. She had these left over from a Halloween photo shoot – thought they might come in handy. You know, in case Katja tried anything."

"She could have killed you."

"I know. It was a risk, but I had to take it. I couldn't let you die."

It's not all fake. He winces with discomfort, drags himself to his feet and I notice a garish wound just above his shirt collar, a line of actual blood trickling down his neck. Another few inches to the left and there would have been no coming back.

"You're hurt."

"This? Just a scratch. We'll sort it out later."

It's more than a scratch. He needs a hospital. We also need to get out of here before Katja returns. I can hear a tangle of panicked voices coming nearer. How can we escape? There's no other way out from this height.

Nathan nods towards the open window, and my heart sinks. It's the only chance we've got. I grab a bottle of water, splashing its contents over the spots of blood on the floor. Luckily, most of it has soaked into Nathan's shirt, and it cleans up quickly. I rip two swathes of fabric from my dress, the one that cost me six months' worth of Pret baguettes. I'll never be able to afford something like this again.

But needs must. With one piece, I dry the floorboards as best I can. The other I use to bandage his neck, padding my makeshift tourniquet with a couple of Katja's tampons.

He looks ridiculous, but at least it stems the bleeding. The whole thing takes less than a minute, and the shouts are getting louder. I can hear Daniel's voice offering Katja support. Now, there's a gruesome twosome in the making.

"Let's get out of here!" Nathan hisses. Seconds later, I'm climbing out of the window.

The night is breezy, and the wind rattles the fire escape when I reach the top step. Nathan catches me, sliding his arms around my waist.

"Don't worry, I'm here. Besides, what's the worst that can happen if you fall?"

Put it this way: I doubt my funeral would be an open coffin affair. We're on the same floor where Laura met her terrible fate, and it occurs to me she must have fallen from this height – maybe even in the room we were in. What went through her mind as she tumbled through the air to her doom? Thoughts of her final moments torment me as I tiptoe onto the staircase.

We're already on the first platform when I hear Katja's voice as the door opens. We both freeze. Oh God. The window is still open. What if she looks outside? My throat constricts.

There's air all around me, yet I'm suffocating. Nathan, sensing my anxiety, pulls me into a tight hug, smearing real and fake blood all over my dress. He must be in so much pain, yet he's shrugged it off as though it's a paper cut. How on earth? I'd be demanding an ambulance, preferably one with fluffy pillows and a duvet.

"What if she...?" I whisper, but he puts a finger on my lips.

"Shhhh." He crouches, stealthy as a cat burglar, taking me with him. We can hear voices – Katja's confusion and James asking if she's all right. The staircase wobbles in the wind again, making an eerie creaking sound. It is as though Laura's ghost is trying to give away our hiding place.

Katja peers out of the window, so close I could touch her. Part of me is suffused with rage. I should be celebrating with colleagues who care about me, not barefoot, grubby and terrified for my life on a rickety fire escape, hated by everyone. I want to rip the hairpins from her now imperfect bun, pull the rhinestones off her gown one by one and have a full-on 80s soap opera style girl fight. Payback for all the damage and misery she's caused.

Instead, I keep as still and silent as I can, pushing myself further into Nathan, who's rubbing my back to keep me calm. Please don't let me sneeze right now.

And then she's gone. She didn't see us. I feel as if I've aged twenty years.

Katja doesn't stop there. She finds a scrap of my dress, which sends shudders shooting through me. What if Nathan's blood is on it? It's the others murmuring about how she can't be well, which talks me down from that ledge. No one's ever going to believe a word she says now.

The voices fade, and the door slams. A weight rolls away from my stomach. Nathan says the words I've wanted to hear.

"Let's go!"

We take the remaining flights as quietly and quickly as we can until my senses sharpen at the feel of solid ground underneath my feet. "We need – to go that way," I gasp. People appear on the other side of the car park alongside coaches taking them back to civilisation. We can't let them see us. We creep along the ranks of vehicles, keeping our heads low and concealed by the cars. No sign of Katja. Relief as we reach the road. Please let there be a cab.

I can't run any more. I can't do this. Yet, as the comforting orange glow of a taxi light looms in the distance, one last burst of energy overtakes me. Nathan is frantically typing something on his phone. "What the hell are you doing?" I yell, but he ignores me. I'll have to do this alone. I race towards the car, waving my arms like I'm bringing a plane into land. It won't see us. It won't stop. She'll find us, she'll –

The cab pulls over by the side of the road. We've done it. I scream instructions at the driver to get us to a hospital and practically drag Nathan into the back seat, where we collapse on to each other. He says nothing but shows me the message he wrote:

Sorry Katja. It looks like you're not the only one who's good at faking their own death

He's even added a winking emoji.

"Oh my…" The laughter, loud and uncontrollable, takes over at the thought of our escape, of Katja being so baffled by our absence and reading Nathan's words. Nothing has seemed funnier. Seconds later, I'm hit with a mammoth rush of emotion, and I'm no longer laughing but sobbing.

We both are.

NATHAN

We did it. We're free. Elena tumbles into my lap, both of us shrieking with laughter at the note I sent Katja. Only then she's in floods – trying to say something to me, but crying so hard I can't make out a word. I pull her in close and break down too. Every bit of shame and guilt I've been holding back to get through this situation flies to the surface.

I can't imagine what the taxi driver makes of this. The pair of us hooting with mirth, then howling like idiots in the back of his car, clinging to each other as though we might break into pieces if we didn't. He goes on listening to Five Live, which has some boring late-night debate about railway sidings, as though none of it was happening. I guess as long as he gets paid he doesn't give a shit.

"I'm sorry…I'm so sorry!" I tell Elena over and over again, choking on tears that soak the sequins of her shoulder straps. Another thing I've damaged. They'll probably rust now.

This is what happens when you stay strong for too long. I've never felt more wretched.

She's going to leave me. I know she is. All the ugly crying in the world won't change that. She'll probably dump me at A&E and leave me to it. "He says it's just a scratch," she'll tell the nurses. "Probably be fine if you stick a wet paper towel on it," like I fell over in the playground at school.

I wouldn't blame her if she did.

Elena's calmed down by the time we reached the nearest hospital but I'm still in a state. The burst of adrenaline which got me through our escape has worn off, and my neck is throbbing.

Flashes of agony kick my emotions all over the place. All those years I thought the worst pain in the world was from that childhood incident when I stapled my fingers together for a dare.

That was nothing. Both of these pale in comparison with the thought of being dumped by Elena.

The car park is empty at this time of night, and a fresh wave of tears overtakes me when the taxi drops us outside.

"If – if you want to leave me here, it's fine…I understand," I tell her. "You deserve better than me after – after what I did…" It's no good. We're done.

She grabs my hands.

"It's OK, Nathan," she says. "It doesn't matter any more. All that business with Katja – you can't change what happened – it was wrong. But – but you saved my life tonight! That cancels everything else out. You could've walked away and left me to die – and you didn't. That's what I'm going to remember." She stands on tiptoe and pecks me on the lips. Now things don't seem quite so bleak.

"I love you to pieces, Nathan Flynn. I'm not going anywhere except with you. But no more fuck-ups, OK?"

Elena's fixing me with a look of pure devotion. She's in a pitiful state, shoes missing, dress destroyed, face full of tears and dirt, covered in my blood. And yet, she's never looked more beautiful to me than she is at this moment. She loves me. I'm forgiven. I fold her into a hug, relief flowing as she nestles into my shoulder – the good one.

"Thank you," I say to her in a subdued, shaky voice. "I swear – I'll never hurt you again."

"You'd better not," she says. It's OK, she's smiling. "You'll have Lindsey after you if you do," and the comment coaxes a laugh out of me despite everything. We walk arm-in-arm into A&E, and she sits with me, keeps me calm, and fetches me vending machine tea that tastes of tepid, sugary sludge. We're both too drained to talk more, even though there's a lot still left to say. For now, having Elena by my side is enough.

Thankfully the cut on my neck looks a lot worse than it is – a couple of stitches and a clean-up with some fucking painful antiseptic, and I'm good to go. Oh, and a tetanus jab. That was the worst bit. Thank you, Katja, for that. As a final favour to my ex, I told them I'd slipped at a party and caught myself on a piece of broken glass on the floor. I had the chance to get her banged up for attempted murder, but when it came to it, I couldn't do it. The thought of her becoming even more vengeful if I had her arrested didn't bear thinking about.

Besides, in a strange way, I'm mourning our break-up, as dead as my feelings for her may now be. We were together for a long time, and it can be hard to lose sight of the person you think will be your happy ever after. Even if they do turn out to be a massive psychopath who tries to kill you with a shoe.

Thank God I have Elena to help me move on from everything.

"No more secrets, ever," she says to me as we walk out of the hospital to start our lives together. And I know we won't have any.

From now on we'll treat each other as we deserve to be treated.

Four Weeks Later
ELENA

"You're not going to believe this!"

Lindsey's face fills my laptop screen as I launch into our latest FaceTime conversation. Nathan's parents are away for the summer at their timeshare villa in France, leaving us to our own devices in their huge, sprawling house – and we're certainly making the most of it. I'm still shaken by what happened. We both are. But as long as we have each other, we'll cope with whatever life throws at us.

I haven't forgotten about my best friend back home though, and today I've got some news that has left me buzzing with excitement.

"Go on…" Lindsey breaks off a slab of Dairy Milk and sips her wine. Some things never change.

"I've been offered a new job!"

"Oh wow…that's amazing news! Her face falls, and she drinks more. "I guess that means you're staying in Dublin, then?"

Poor Lindsey. She must be missing me so much. She must have realised I can't come back to London, at least not yet. Even so, she will hate what I'm about to tell her because the job isn't here. It's in Australia. Visas permitting, we're heading Down Under, where I get to work at a local equivalent of Spark, earning a lot more money. Nathan gets to work on his novel.

And, fingers crossed, we're free from the spectre of Katja Lake.

It's as I expected. She's stunned. "Elena…I don't know what to say."

"I know! You'll visit, right? Might even be a job for you there once I'm settled."

I'd love Lindsey to come and work with me. She looks sad at being left behind, and I know she's outgrowing Gleam.

I also know this is the right thing to do. I want to leave behind all the harm Katja caused and make a fresh start where nobody knows about my past. Where she'll find it very hard to track us down. This time, I promise to be a model employee. Super-friendly to everyone I work with.

Even those who irritate the living shit out of me.

THE PRESENT

Lindsey feels conflicted as she drains the rest of her wine. On the one hand, she's thrilled for her best friend. On the other, she knows it could be a very long time before she sees her again. What an exciting few weeks it's been though, with Elena and Nathan's daring escape – and the part she played in it. All those years being little more than Elena's sweet, ditzy sidekick has been leading to this moment.

She had to help because she felt terrible about everything that happened. Seven years on Laura Lucas' story had been reduced to a distant, cautionary tale for young writers starting their journey up the journalistic ladder. It never occurred to anyone that her sister might come looking for answers, assuming that Elena killed Laura. What a ludicrous thought. Elena might not suffer fools gladly, but she could never harm another human being. Lindsey reflects on this as she pours more Chardonnay. She's well aware that Elena has no idea what happened that fateful day.

She, on the other hand, knows every last detail.

Lindsey might have spent her time at Gleam in Elena's shadow, but it didn't stop the pair forming an unshakeable bond. She was easily influenced by her witty, attractive colleague, despite lacking Elena's privileged upbringing, stable family background, and popularity. Lindsey had been an awkward loner at school, seeking solace from her parents' divorce and her lack of friends in pop music and celebrity culture. All she'd ever wanted was to get a job writing about it.

Elena's friendship at Gleam had been a dream come true – united by their dislike for Laura Lucas, the over-confident newcomer who failed to fit in. Elena didn't hesitate to tell their editor how she had behaved at that awful Tyler Bard launch party, knowing her job could be in jeopardy for not keeping a better eye on her. After she exaggerated the truth, Lindsey seized the opportunity to bring Laura down a few more pegs. She played pranks on Laura, interfering with her work, her computer, anything to make it look as though she couldn't do her job properly – all desperate to win Elena's approval, although Elena had no idea she was doing it. She even smashed Laura's precious family photo, the one she kept on her desk, knowing nobody would suspect a thing. And Laura accused Elena, who swore blind that it was nothing to do with her.

Lindsey felt bad the finger of blame was pointed at her friend, but she knew she wouldn't get in trouble – their editor adored Elena, while Laura's reputation was tarnished beyond repair. Besides, she knew Elena wanted her gone and was sure she would be grateful to Lindsey for speeding the process along. Lindsey would do anything to make Elena happy. Their boss wasn't the only one who adored her. Laura on the other hand, hated them both – and would have done anything to be rid of them.

Everybody had been looking forward to the big Gleam concert for weeks – but the night before, Elena started to feel unwell. She'd been out for a birthday lunch at a tapas restaurant that day, going heavy on garlic prawns, and by midnight, she had her head down the toilet every hour, throwing up until there was nothing left in her stomach but bile. Eventually, she crawled back to bed, groaning and shattered, every muscle in her body aching as though she'd birthed a fifteen-pound baby without an epidural – and realised she would be unable to make the event.

Gutted as she was, she could barely stand up, let alone chaperone pop stars around a crowded venue for several hours. After calling in sick, she crashed out and didn't wake up again until late afternoon.

Lindsey was disappointed that her partner in crime was missing. They had grand plans to celebrate in style at the after-show party. But she was delighted when her editor gave her the task of looking after some of the acts that had been assigned to Elena – including her partner Tyler Bard. He was charming and flirty; she knew she shouldn't get too close. She also knew if Elena were there, she would have been flirting right back – and when Elena was around, with her golden hair and her dazzling smile, who ever noticed someone as unremarkable as Lindsey? No, this was her time to shine.

So, when Tyler came off stage, parched and sweaty, and asked Lindsey for water, she was only too happy to lead him to the upstairs storeroom where the bottles were kept – knowing what would happen when they got there. A few more smutty jokes, a couple of lines of coke from Tyler's wallet – and one thing led to another.

Until stupid, troublemaking, Laura walked in and caught them at it. Lindsey panicked, even in her drugged-up state, realising that she had handed Laura the opportunity to call her out over her behaviour. Elena could be relied upon to talk her way out of anything – and had her family to support her when she couldn't – but Lindsey's job was all she had going for her. She knew if she lost it, she wouldn't get another one.

So, she fought back.

She hadn't meant for Laura to fall out the window when she pushed her. She hadn't realised it was broken. But when she tumbled out and was pierced by the railings, she saw the solution to all her problems staring up at her, begging for help.

Instead, she shut the window and walked away, leaving Laura to die – and erasing the evidence of her infidelities from existence. If only she had known how easy it was to get rid of her, she'd have done it sooner.

The police came to investigate, and for a while, Lindsey was worried. But nobody witnessed what had happened – even Tyler kept quiet for the sake of his relationship and his career, not to mention the fact he'd been so off his tits he barely remembered Laura anyway.

With no evidence of foul play, it was ruled as a misadventure. She'd got away with it.

Until Katja showed up.

Lindsey doesn't mind admitting it's affected things for her. She's been stuck at Gleam ever since, scared to move on in case her secret is discovered. Elena had long since concluded she had no ambition – but nothing could be further from the truth. With her experience, Lindsey could have been editor ten times over anywhere she wanted. But there was safety in staying put, where the staff had been replaced by new people who knew nothing about Laura and her death.

If there is one thing Lindsey has become good at though, it's keeping her head down and getting on with her work.

Because nobody suspects the dependable, quiet people of wrongdoing, do they?

Lindsey contemplates the events of recent weeks as she drains her wine. For the first time since Laura died she weighs up her options. Elena's plans have emboldened her. It's been confirmed that Katja doesn't have any evidence that Laura was murdered, so it's unlikely the police will reopen the investigation.

Maybe it's time for her to emerge from her shell and take a few risks. Not to mention dispense that bitch Katja Lake with some payback for the way she treated her beloved Elena.

Perhaps she could torment her and then push her out of a window.

After all, she has already got away with it once. Her phone bleeps. A message from Elena:

Forgot to mention, I thought you might find this interesting

Lindsey reads the attachment and smiles. She knows now that this is her time to move into the spotlight.

She opens her laptop and begins to type.

Another Four Weeks Later
KATJA

"Katja! Are you going to be in there all day?"

Alexandra bangs on the bathroom door. Apparently, I'm taking too long. Tough shit. I turn back to the mirror, pulling kissy faces at myself as I paint my lips bloody crimson.

"Katja? I'm going to be so late if you don't get a move on…"

Why is she such a fucking weirdo? I'm starting to regret the decision to let her move in.

I'm not letting a flatmate from the seventh layer of hell spoil today for me. Not the day Paula's due to announce her replacement at work. I can't prolong it for ever, and after spritzing some Calvin Klein Eternity on my wrists, I emerge from the bathroom. Alexandra glares at me through a sludge-coloured face mask, her red hair a chaotic halo around her head. She looks like a troll doll who's fallen into a vat of Play-Doh.

"About time!" she tells me. "The alarm didn't go off again, I'm in such a rush…"

"Don't stress so much!" I snap, "It's not my problem if you can't get up in time!" I smile to myself as I slip back into my room, slip quickly into my favourite black leather mini-skirt and straighten the bed. The one in which I now sleep alone.

Not that I'm bitter.

Well, actually, I am. I'm furious.

My phone buzzes as I leave for work. I glance down and see a message from Daniel:

Just letting you know the offer of a drink still stands

That's the fourth WhatsApp this week. Does he never give up? I want to grind whoever gave him my number into a paste.

All this is the fault of my two-timing bastard ex-boyfriend, of course. If only Nathan hadn't grown a fucking conscience when he did, acting like a typical spineless male, Elena would be dead. But she escaped, all because of his betrayal. Where are they now? How the hell should I know? They've obviously blocked me on their social media and phones. They could be anywhere.

It's not as if I had the chance to look for them, either. Nathan's message confirmed to me that he was still alive, and I kicked myself for falling for the old death- faking trick. Particularly as I was taken in by his shit acting. I thought about showing the message to Bonnie, to properly drop them in it, except I wasn't that keen on having to confess I'd done the same thing. There is such a thing as wasting police time, after all. The whole 'attempted murder with a shoe' might not have gone down too well either had Nathan mentioned it. He still could. He'd better not.

As it was, I kept quiet, muttered something about drinking too many tequila slammers, and nodding off on the side of the dance floor. Poor me, such a lightweight. I kept protesting that I was quite all right and that I'd like to go home, but Bonnie was so worried she wouldn't let me.

She even called my therapist on my behalf and tried to get me an emergency appointment. With every passing minute, I knew Elena and Nathan were slipping from my grasp and that there was nothing

I could do about it. I mean, you can't tell a police officer you have to leave in order to kill your mortal enemy, can you?

In the end, she only let me go after my counsellor – who sounded pissed off at being woken up – had agreed to see me the next day. Bonnie insisted I stay with a colleague, so I wasn't alone, and James was only too happy to let me sleep on his sofa in spite of my protestations.

By the time I went home, it was almost nine, and I discovered Nathan's side of the wardrobe empty, and all his things gone. He must have grabbed it all and fled before I could return and cut him into pieces small enough to put through the blender. I knew then I'd lost him for good. I did love him once. But the thought of him sticking his dick in Elena makes me a little bit sick in my mouth. Paula announced at work the following Monday that both of them had been in touch, confirming they would not be returning to Spark. That sealed the deal.

She is welcome to him. Nathan is dead to me. Or at least he will be if I ever bump into him again.

As for Elena? I haven't given up hope that little Madam will turn up one day. She and I have unfinished business. She cannot hide from me forever. It makes me even madder when I think about how close I got to achieving my aims. The thought of Elena's agonising death kept me going through every day at work, every bit of James' pointless prattle, every order Paula barked at me. All those pub socials, smiling until my cheeks ached while listening to the crap spouted by that bunch of losers. The same bunch of losers I'm stuck with, because things didn't go the way I was expecting.

I should look on the bright side. They didn't believe a word she said about me. I've become more popular than ever since she left. Now it's my turn to be Queen Bee. All Paula has to do is confirm it.

I walk into Spark with my head held high. James and Molly are having a loud, in-depth conversation about crispy pancakes. Just do some bloody work already you idle Squawkers. He claps his eyes on my outfit. I only wanted him to do that to make Elena feel bad, but he won't stop. I'm pretty bored with it now.

"Morning!" he shouts. "Love those boots – you've outdone yourself today, darling!"

Better play along. "Thanks," I coo in my sweetest voice, dropping my bag on my desk. "I had to make the effort – big day today, after all."

"Oh yes of course!" James is excited. "I'm sure that job is yours! Paula's making the announcement later. I am keeping everything crossed."

He shouldn't. Because once I'm in charge, his shitty little YouTube show will be the first thing to go. Viewing figures have fallen off a cliff. Blame management. I nod a good morning to Molly, who is stuffing her guts with a cholesterol-filled Danish, perch on my office chair and fire up my computer, just in time for new boy Jake to walk in, seven minutes late.

I cannot think for one minute who Jake reminds me of. Dishevelled hair. Well-toned. The sort of person I'd have to stand on a stepladder to kiss. It didn't take them long to replace Nathan. Maybe it's time I did too. My lip curls at the sight of his muscular forearms, at the black tattoo peeking out of the sleeve of his T-shirt. I could do a lot worse.

"Morning, Jake!" I shout. "Good weekend?"

"Yeah," he says in his soft Scottish accent, as he flings his jacket across the desk and sinks into his chair. "What's on the agenda today, then?"

"Well," I tell him, "We've got a team meeting at nine-thirty. Paula is announcing the new acting editor – who, I believe, is going to be me."

Jake gives me a strange look. "Are you quite sure about that?"

"Of course, why wouldn't I be?" What's he talking about?

"Maybe you'd better take a look at your rota." Without explanation, Jake flicks on his computer and slumps back into silence.

Thanks for nothing, Jake. Surely, he doesn't mean…I log in as fast as I can, my anxiety levels rising. I open up my rota tab and scroll down to the showbiz section. There, to my absolute horror, as I scan the Editor's column, I see what Jake was talking about.

WHO ON *EARTH* IS LINDSEY GRANT??

Acknowledgments

When I first embarked on this whole writing lark, I told myself that I would hear the word 'no' from a lot of people I submitted *Trouble-maker* to, but I'd only ever need to hear the word 'yes' once. On that basis, I can't express how grateful I am to Vulpine Press for being the people who said yes.

Specifically, thanks to my editor, Mark Husbands, for taking that chance on me, for his amazing work in helping *Troublemaker* live its best life, and for dealing with my many questions, my 1 a.m. overthinking, and my yellow highlighter obsession with such grace and good humour.

To my husband Leslie Bunder and daughter Emily: Thank you both for being so incredible throughout this process, even when faced with the words 'NOT NOW I'M WORKING' for about the 952nd time in a row. I love you both to pieces, as Elena might say.

Thanks to my mum, Helen, for saying everything I write is brilliant even when it isn't, to my brothers Ian and Hugh Westbrook, and every other family member I haven't mentioned.

Thanks to authors Kerry Birds, Anna Britton, and Nicky Shearsby for their ongoing support; Lindz McLeod for invaluable query letter help; Jenn Taylor for the legal eagle stuff; and Natasha Pszenicki for the awesome author photos. Also, I thank Roy D. Hacksaw, Paul

Lynch, Gwennan Thomas, Karen Hewis, and Mark Hewis for their help and advice and for being generally awesome humans throughout.

A special huge thanks to everyone at *metro.co.uk* – especially its incomparable editor Deborah Arthurs for her encouragement, feedback, and so graciously allowing me to take the piss out of everything she holds dear.

And last but not least, an enormous debt of thanks to my former *Empire* editor Philip Thomas, one of my biggest journalistic mentors, to Lesley O'Toole for my first ever break at *TV HITS*, and anybody else who's ever given me an opportunity, or ignored me. Because if it weren't for all you lovely people, this book probably wouldn't exist.

C.R. Westbrook is a writer with a CV that includes *Metro, Empire,* and *BBC News Online,* among others, writing about showbiz, film, and TV.

Troublemaker is her first fiction novel, coming twenty-five years after her first literary endeavour, writing biographies of Brad Pitt and Leonardo DiCaprio, which were translated into Japanese, Spanish, German, and even English.

She lives in West London with her husband, Leslie Bunder, and teenage daughter, Emily. When she's not writing, she is a dedicated Eurovision fan, an enthusiastic film quizzer and a distinctly average badminton player.

You can find her on X at @c_r_westbrook and Instagram at @cazza_writes, and on email: hello@crwestbrook.com